NATIONAL *Singles* DAY

3Aussies Press

To say thank you for joining me on this journey, I would like to give you a gift, a free copy of my first contemporary mm romance novella, My Accidental First Date.
Visit https://dl.bookfunnel.com/foxhchxb5r to tell me where to send it.

Chapter One

Flying Solo

Jack

THREE ARMED GUARDS STEPPED forward to join the man standing at a wooden podium; their eight eyes locked onto me. Hundreds of weary, wait-angry passengers turned to stare.

The pre-check line was twenty deep, and the main boarding line snaked back and forth so many times the wait had to be at least an hour.

Yes, I was in uniform. Yes, I was running and dragging a rolling suitcase and clinging desperately to the laptop bag dangling off my shoulder. But none of those things mattered. Streaking headlong toward a TSA checkpoint, even for a crew member, always garnered attention. I might've received fewer stares if I'd actually been streaking through the airport, my junk flopping in the breeze. At least those gazes would've been mostly amused.

I skidded to a stop before the podium and reached for the badge dangling at my chest. The moment my hand left my laptop strap, the darn thing slipped and fell. I reached to grab it, but lost my balance and kicked the rolling bag, sending it toward the waiting pre-check passengers.

At least I managed to grab my laptop before it struck the ground.

"Running a little late this morning, Jack?" the agent I saw nearly every morning said, an amused smirk twisting his lips.

"Jerry, help. I'm *so* late." I didn't have to pretend to be desperate. My voice came out as one extended, miserable plea.

Jerry grunted, which was the closest he ever came to laughing.

"Chuck, grab that bag, would you?" he said to one of the guards who'd suddenly lost interest in my rapid approach. "Badge." He pointed, no longer showing any sign of amusement or humor.

I straightened the strap on my shoulder, then held my badge out to be scanned.

"Have a good flight," he said, as if I hadn't nearly blown through his checkpoint.

"Thanks." I took my bag from Chuck and broke into another run. "I'm laaaaaate!" I called behind me, earning another grunt from Jerry and a few chuckles from the others.

The Plane Train took forever and was so crammed with passengers, I could smell the Irish Spring on the skin of the man beside me. Don't get me wrong, that's a nice enough scent, but we hadn't even met. I didn't need to know what soap he used. By the time we arrived at my terminal, I knew which spots on his body he'd missed.

As I stepped off the train, a familiar sign greeted me, and my heart sank.

This was the point where I'd normally stop at Starbucks for a massive cup of coffee. Well, not exactly coffee. A skinny mocha latte with extra no-fat whip, a half pump of hazelnut, one squirt of caramel, a sprinkle of chocolate shavings, four Splenda packets, and extra room in case I wanted to add more milk. They didn't have a name for what I ordered, which bordered on offensive. It was a fantastic drink and deserved recognition.

Unfortunately, there would be no skinny Jacky frappy flappy for me that morning. I would have to settle for the brutal brew we served on the plane.

Great.

By the time I reached the gate, the last of the passengers had boarded and the gate crew was closing the door.

"Wait!" I yelled, throwing the last of my breath into extra speed. "Please!"

The woman in the red coat turned, a sour twist to her lips matching the bitterness in the bun on her head. Yes, her bun was bitter.

"Jack Sutton?" Her face looked like my name tasted of gasoline mixed with dog poop.

"Yes, that's me." I skidded to a halt a step from her—and the door that nearly barred my way to work.

"Only thing left is a jump seat in back, and you might have to check that roller." She glanced down, her nose somehow resisting the rest of her head and turning upward.

"Thank you so much," I said. "I'm never late. Really."

She rolled her eyes and stepped aside. "Badge and punch in your code. You've held us long enough."

I swiped my badge and entered the digits as quickly as possible, then raced down the jet bridge.

Thankfully, there were still passengers standing in the aisles, searching for empty bins. No one paid any attention to the flight attendant breathing heavily as he struggled to keep from smacking people with his laptop.

"Hey, handsome," a familiar voice called from a seat about halfway toward the back.

I followed the sound to find Emma, my perpetually perky partner, seated comfortably by a window. Her chestnut hair was parted slightly to one side and pulled back in a tight knot. The ruby of her lipstick was almost electric.

"Hey, Em. Love the lips."

She grinned as a few passengers turned to see the lips I'd complimented so publicly.

"Love the hair," she said, referring to my black mop that refused to lie down. I'd long since given up on styling it, allowing it to roam freely like some unruly buffalo. Ironically, it was also the feature that got me the most attention, aside from my eyes. Having eyes almost White Walker blue made my eye game pretty strong.

"Thanks." I grinned at our usual complimentary greeting.

I eyed the overweight man in the center seat beside her, then the kid who couldn't have been older than twelve by the aisle, realizing there was no hope of sitting together. "I'm headed to the back. They've got me sitting on the toilet this flight. See you in Miami."

She waved her fingers like she was playing an invisible trumpet and blew me a kiss.

My heart sank as the working attendants sent the first bag forward, indicating a full flight with no more luggage space. I turned, ready to surrender my bag, to receive my first pleasant surprise of the day.

"I'll put your bag in the crew closet up front. We've got just enough room for one more." A twenty-something guy with high cheekbones and pink mascara nearly made me jump. He batted his eyes and scanned me like he was a copier and I was a piece of paper.

"Uh, great, thanks," I said, trying to draw his eyes back above my belt.

He stepped so close I thought he might try to kiss me, then whispered, "Sure thing, honey. I'm Mikey. I thought I knew all the hotties in uniform, but you're fresh meat. What's your name, shugah?"

His accent screamed Deep South—or maybe just screamed, I wasn't sure.

"Hi, Mikey. I'm Jack. Just Jack."

He giggled and covered his mouth. "Just Jack. Like on *Will and Grace*? That's priceless. I like this one." He shoved his index finger into my chest like he was testing the doneness of a steak. "Call me if you need anything, *just* Jack. We have the best nuts you've ever put in your mouth on this plane."

My face must've turned beet red because he burst into girlish giggles then twirled and sashayed to the front with my bag. Passengers within ten rows turned and watched as I ducked my head and fled to the safety of the plane's rear,

THE FINAL DING SOUNDED and passengers rose to deplane. The flight attendants working the back of the plane popped up and began gathering their belongings. I figured we had another ten minutes before all the slow-moving folks in front of us gathered their luggage and exited, so I remained firmly planted in my jump seat and continued to read a dog-eared copy of *Heir*

of Magic by J.D. Ruffin. Nothing passed the time like a good tale of magic and intrigue.

"You still reading that stuff?" one of the attendants said, her head practically resting on my shoulder from behind.

"That stuff?"

"That's one of your Dungeons and Dragons books, isn't it?"

I chuckled. "No. This is more like *Game of Thrones* or *Lord of the Rings*. But I do love my D&D."

She tsked in my ear, then straightened. "How can a man as pretty as you be such a nerd?"

I closed the paperback, careful to keep my thumb in place, then craned to look back at her with a lopsided grin. "Aww, you think I'm pretty."

She reached down and flicked a lock of hair off my forehead. It promptly rebelled and fell back over my eye.

She shook her head. "You know you're pretty, baby. You own a mirror. My people mourn the fact you're on the other team."

"Your people? Are you the female Moses? Leading women everywhere out of the land of the gays?"

"Something like that." She snorted. "Where are you headed, anyway? It's weird, you two connecting out of Miami."

"Long haul to Barcelona."

"Ooh, fancy international boy," she said, one brow raised appreciatively.

I shrugged. "Not sure how fancy being cooped up in a metal tube for ten hours is, but I like it well enough. Passengers on the long flights are always in a good mood."

"Huh. That would be nice. You should've seen some of the guys on this bird. Almost made me want to jump out the back."

I nodded in sympathy. Any flight attendant with more than two days of service had experienced wild children, drunk or otherwise unruly passengers, and any number of other uncomfortable situations. It was a good gig most of the time, but there were days …

"I turn around in an hour, then I'm done for the week," she said, drawing me out of my memories of horrific passengers of the past. "Have fun in Spain."

I shoved a bookmark into the pages and stuffed the book in my laptop bag, then smiled up at her. "Thanks for the commute. See you next time."

"Okay, dungeon boy." She winked and made her way down the aisle.

I stood and tossed the laptop bag strap over my shoulder, then headed toward the front of the plane, surprised to find Emma still sitting patiently in her seat.

"Hey, you," I said.

She smiled and stood. "Escort me to my gate?"

I extended my arm, like the gentleman I was. "Of course, m'lady."

She grinned and slapped my arm playfully. "Grab my bag above your head, would you?"

"Anything m'lady desires." I handed the roller down, then followed her off the plane.

We marched down the center of the airport toward our departure gate. Passengers milled about on either side. The occasional beeping of a golf cart ferrying workers or passengers needing assistance punctuated the constant hum of conversation. It was a typical day at the office for us, the beginning of a very long back and forth across the pond.

"You ready for this one?" Emma asked.

"Oh yeah. I've only done Barcelona once before, and we didn't have much time between flights. We get a whole day to sightsee this trip."

"Your second time on this route and they put you in front?" A hint of jealousy threaded her question.

"Don't be jelly. I've been doing long hauls for years. I just haven't done this route much."

She nodded like she understood but didn't look up, so I decided we needed a subject change.

"Coffee before we board? I was too late to grab Starbucks in Atlanta."

Her face brightened back to its normal brilliance. "Absolutely."

Twenty minutes later, armed with serious caffeine, chocolate, and sugar—not necessarily in that order—we reached our gate and stepped onto the massive Airbus A350-900, the largest bird in Delta's fleet.

"Holy shit, this is a big plane," I said, more to myself than to Emma.

She chuckled. "Thought the same thing myself the first time I stepped on. It's nice having extra room, but more room means more passengers. Put your big boy pants on. You're going to need them."

"Maybe I'll have a low-maintenance group," I said as she headed toward the back of the plane, while I turned left toward the forward cabin.

"Famous last words," she called over her shoulder without looking back.

Our crew leader, a woman with a tight gray bun and sharp jaw, stepped up, clipboard in hand. "You Sutton?"

"Uh, yes. I'm Jack."

She eyed my face, then scanned my uniform, as if searching for dog hair or lint. "Neat, well presented, handsome. The hair's a mess but should work. You'll do." She nodded like she'd just ticked every box on some mental list, then returned her gaze to her clipboard. "Delta One has been bought out. Your entire cabin is one group. Headquarters wants them happy. Got it?"

Delta One was our premier cabin service offered on long-haul and a few priority flights. The food and service afforded to customers who could handle the price tag made flying first class look like a discount service. We poured endless champagne, prepped fresh, exotic meals, and catered to our customers in what Disney called "the wow experience." I enjoyed working Delta One, mostly because the fliers were relaxed and easygoing, but also to see the surprised looks as we rolled out each wave of food and drink. Even the most seasoned passengers were stunned by the red carpet treatment of Delta One.

The greeting I'd received from my flight leader was almost as startling as the service I'd soon deliver to passengers. I'd never had a scolding *before* a flight. I almost felt like slinking to the back with Emma and giving another attendant the privilege of sucking up to VIPs, but I'd never abandon my duties.

"Got it. Yes, ma'am. I'll do my best."

"No." She shook her head, her eyes narrowing. "You'll do better than that."

And just like that, Hurricane Grandma blew down the aisle toward my poor, unsuspecting friend.

"She likes you." A soft voice behind turned my head. "She normally ignores new members of her crew until there's something to criticize."

The petite twenty-something in a neat purple blazer adorned with glittering, bedazzled flight wings grinned and batted her overly round eyes.

"Oh, uh, great. Good to know." I extended a hand. "I'm Jack."

She glanced at my hand, smirked, then took it, her slender fingers just teasing my skin. "Mallory." She did that copier scanning thing that made me really uncomfortable. "It's very good to meet you, Jack. We'll be doing Delta One together."

"Great," I said, painting on my brightest smile. "This should be fun. Know anything about our group? Sergeant Grandma said somebody bought out the entire section."

Her eyes somehow widened further. "Really?" She looked around, counting the fancy tubes whose seats fully extended into beds. "That would cost over a hundred thousand dollars."

I nodded. "That's what I was thinking. Bet we have a bunch of cranky old rich guys. You'll have to charm them."

She looked up like I'd slapped her. "And what if they're more into athletic guys with flyaway hair and piercing eyes? You gonna take over the flirt brigade?"

"Ma'am, yes, ma'am." I flashed her more teeth, straightened my back, and saluted. "The gays are my people."

"Well, that's disappointing." She shook her head. "Why don't you take greeting, and I'll prep round one."

There were ten rounds of food service over the course of the flight. By the time we were done with them, the Delta One passengers would either be loosening their belts or be so full they'd wave off the last courses. We wouldn't hear a single complaint about "airline food."

"You got it," I said, grabbing a tray and loading it with champagne flutes. "How much time do we have?"

A ding beat her to the punch, indicating the boarding process had begun at the gate.

"Ooh, guess I need to hustle."

I filled the flutes and dropped a strawberry in each, then placed a stack of cocktail napkins on the corner where passengers could easily grab them. A moment later, I waited near the boarding door at the entrance to the coveted Delta One section. Steel Bun stood across the entryway, in position to greet each passenger and direct them toward their seat. She glowered at me, then eyed the champagne, and the tiniest hint of a smile tickled her lips. Instead of making her appear more pleasant, she looked like she'd tasted something sour. No sooner than the almost-smile appeared, it vanished.

"Welcome aboard," she said, turning from me and allowing her frown to ease as the first passenger stepped up. He was an elderly man using a walker, which she quickly took from him and walked him up the aisle toward the Comfort Plus section. Seven more pre-boards arrived, each headed to the back of the plane.

Still I stood, flutes in hand, fizzing away.

Then a thirty-something man with buzzed hair and a thick five o'clock shadow stepped aboard. His T-shirt was so tight I could tell he was freezing—or, at least, his nipples were. And then there were his arms, bulging against threadbare sleeves. He glanced at his ticket, then held it to Steel Bun. Her lips pursed as she raised an open palm in my direction.

The scruffy man turned toward me and I nearly swooned. He was stunning.

"Welcome aboard. Champagne, sir?"

He froze, stared at the flutes, looked up at me, then back at the flutes. Then he turned toward a man I hadn't seen board, a much taller, much broader man whose smile extended nearly to his ears.

"Champagne? What the fuck has Cooper done now?" the scruffy man asked the giant.

In answer, the hulk reached over his shoulder and snatched a flute from my tray, raising it in salute. "Whatever he's done, I love it. Now, get moving. There's people behind us."

The first man took a glass and napkin, gave me a sheepish grin, then scooted past. I had to step out of the aisle to let the larger man pass. His shoulders were nearly as wide as the walkway. *Jesus*.

By the time I'd straightened and turned back toward the boarding door, another member of their party had arrived. Locks of blond hair fell nearly to the shoulders of a tanned, sharply featured man whose steely blue eyes nearly knocked me backward. His shirt wasn't as tight as those on the first two guys, but there was no missing the defined chest that held his T-shirt aloft.

I sucked in a breath and held out my tray. "Hi. Drink. I mean … I'm … uh … champagne. No, *I'm* not champagne. I'm Jack. Yeah, Jack. I mean, welcome. Champagne?"

The guy cocked his head and smiled. My chest swelled.

He reached forward and took a flute, sipped, then grinned wider. "Thanks, Jack. Guess I'll see you around?"

My nod was like a stutter. "Yeah, guess so."

"Awesomeness. I'm Steph."

He raised his glass one last time, and I nearly dropped my tray when he rubbed against me as he passed toward his seat in the front row.

Chapter Two

Amuse Bouche

Steph

Getting crushed by a gazillion tons of water didn't scare me. In fact, the idea of being chased by a massive funnel got my heart racing in ways few things could.

But staring into another dude's eyes for longer than a brotherly *'sup?* was terrifying.

Jack didn't seem to have that problem.

His crystal blues were deeper and brighter than any water I'd ever surfed, and the way he stared … God, he was intense. It didn't hurt that he was hot as fuck, and when he smiled with those perfect pearly whites, my insides curled into a ball.

I got past him with as little contact as the tight aisle would allow, stowed my rolling bag, and flopped into my seat. There was a complimentary kit filled with an eye mask, toiletries, and a few other goodies. Rummaging through it allowed me a moment to catch my breath and *not* wish I was still trapped in his gaze.

"Hey, Rookie." I turned to find Sam's chin resting on my seat back, a shit-eating grin plastered across his face. "You wanna join the Mile High Club or what?"

I nearly spat champagne. I'd only known Sam and Miguel since the start of our vacation, which, technically, had only just begun. From everything I'd been told, they were a committed, loving couple with no desire to fool around.

What the hell?

"Uh, Mile High Club?" I stammered.

Miguel, Sam's cop husband who smiled more than should be legally allowed, appeared beside him. All I could see was his nose and eyes, but it was obvious his shoulders were shoved against Sam's as they peered down at me.

"It's where you get laid while the plane's in the air. You know, a mile in … "

I rolled my eyes. "I know what it means."

"So? You wanna go for it?" Sam nudged.

"I … uh … you two are hot and all, but … really …"

Sam cracked up. "Not with us, dummy. With our resident sky mattress." He motioned toward Jack with his head. "He's fucking hot. Did you see those eyes?"

"I wanted to squeeze his arms. And check out his ass in those tight pants," Miguel added.

I knew better than to follow their gaze. No good would come from encouraging them, but I'm a guy and … fuck it.

"Pretty damn hot, right?" Sam whispered.

I nodded slowly, unable to steal my eyes from the smile Jack gave the latest passenger to arrive. Something brightened in the guy's face every time he smiled, like a happy switch flipping and sending ripples of warmth to everyone around.

What the actual fuck, dude? I chided myself.

The champagne must be going to my head. That had to be it. Granted, I'd only taken a sip or two so far, but it *had* to be the booze.

I grew up around the hottest guys on the planet, and they were rarely clothed in more than a napkin's worth of cloth. We'd high-five, shove, hug, sometimes even wrestle on the sand. Sure, they were handsome and athletic. And surfing planted smiles on all of our faces: usually wide, out-of-breath, endorphin-laced, cartoon-Goofy smiles. I never wanted to stare longingly into any of their eyes. I certainly never wanted to touch …

"Bet he's a good kisser. Look at those lips," Sam growled.

"Look at Rookie," Miguel said, drawing Sam's scrutiny back toward me. "He's whipped … or I bet he'd like to be. You think he's into the rough stuff? Likes getting tied up, maybe having his balls wrapped up tight like—"

"Miguel!" I hissed.

Sam laughed, sounding more like a motorcycle engine revving than an amused man.

"Guys, are you torturing Steph?" Nate, my teammate on the Memphis Mangoes baseball team, finally appeared. As he stowed his carry-on, he purposefully bumped Sam with his hip. "Leave the poor boy alone. It took a lot of effort to convince him you two were harmless."

Sam's eyes widened. Miguel laughed, his joy an infectious tenor to Sam's bass.

"Harmless? You lie to your friends? Nate Stringer, I raised you better than that." Miguel's mock scolding sounded just like my mom had when I was little, though the twist to his lips made it clear there was nothing serious in his words.

"Yes, Dad," Nate said, surprising me by caving. He never submitted to anyone. "Still, be nice to Steph, at least until we're on the cruise and he can't run away."

"Hey!" I squeaked, but all three were laughing too hard to hear.

"Are the big bad men being mean to you, little one?"

All four of our heads turned to find our flight attendant, Jack, standing in the aisle behind Nate with an empty tray tucked under his arm and one brow cocked nearly to his lustrously floppy hairline.

"I'll have you know, this is a harassment-free flight." He stepped past Nate and leaned down to whisper loudly, "I'll protect you, baby. Just call Jack if they're too much for you to handle."

What happened to the scared little rabbit who'd nearly dropped his tray when I'd first boarded? Jack had seemed so thrown off, so unsure, almost shy. Now, he appeared larger than life and was chucking serious fuel on Sam and Miguel's fire.

And looking like an Italian god while doing it.

Damn.

I could practically taste his lips as he licked them, his tongue teasing slowly over the supple cherry skin.

I was mesmerized.

Transfixed.

Dickmatized.

The howls and catcalls that followed flooded my face with crimson far brighter than Jack's lips and nearly sent me crawling under my seat. I reached back, grabbed the handle, and yanked, closing the sleeping tube over my entire seat.

I might've been hidden, but the sounds of the guys' laughter and banter cut through loud and clear. Jack's hand patted the glass section that let me see out—and him see in.

"Oh no, Steph. No hiding during takeoff. Hood up and tits out."

Sam howled and repeated the phrase; tears ran down Miguel's cheeks.

This was going to be the longest flight ever.

Chapter Three

Call Me, Maybe?

Jack

Over the next ten hours, I served the boys in Delta One course after course of food paired with four different wines. As the cabin lights dimmed for the dead-of-night sleeping hours, I stepped down the aisle with the final dessert, a cherries jubilee minus the flaming liquor. Even Delta One had its limits.

"Dear God, no. No more food." Sam waved a meaty paw in the air.

"Give that to me," Miguel chirped, reaching across his husband to grab two plates of cherry goodness.

Sam looked up, his face tinted a light green. "I don't know where he puts it. I'm a big boy, but seriously."

I chuckled and patted him on the shoulder, then stepped toward the aisle where the next couple sat.

It was unusual to have an entire section filled with one group, but this had been one of the most fun trips I'd worked. The guys were funny, silly, utterly irreverent, and unmerciful in their banter and teasing. It also didn't hurt that my section looked more like a model convention than a tourist flight. Every one of them was cover-ready.

And then there was Steph.

"Somebody's got a flight crush," Emma singsonged in a whisper as she stepped into the forward galley. Her section was a mile away in the back, but she always came to visit once the passengers passed out for the night.

"What are you talking about?" I feigned ignorance.

Her elbow jabbed into my ribs. "Don't play coy with me, mister. The whole crew is talking about you and the surfer. Even Mount St. Helen thinks it's cute."

"Helen?" I was shocked our crew leader thought anything was cute, ever. "Seriously, Em, there's nothing to tell. The entire group's hotter than hell, but they're all partnered up. Besides, in a few hours, I'll never see them again. What difference would it make if—"

"You *do* have a crush!" she whisper-squealed and clapped her hands together. "I knew it. So, tell me all about him."

I rolled my eyes. "I don't know anything really. We haven't had two minutes alone without one of the other guys popping over the seat to eavesdrop."

She giggled again. "That means you've tried. Eeee!"

I blew out a frustrated breath. "Okay, fine. I tried. He seems nice."

"Nice? Have you seen those arms? And his eyes ..."

"Yes, yes, he has pretty eyes."

"So?"

"I ..." What was it about this guy that made my insides curl? "I'm not sure. Every time I walk by, he looks up and a wave of four-year-old-waiting-for-Christmas-morning tickles my belly."

She hugged herself tightly and grinned. "Go on."

"His dimples are possibly the cutest thing I've ever seen on a guy's face, and his eyes ... sweet Jesus, his eyes could melt icecaps."

"I can see all that. What do you know about him?"

I thought a moment. "Well, he plays baseball for some team in Memphis I've never heard of."

"Baseball? Like, professional baseball?"

I shrugged. "Maybe. He called them the Memphis Mangoes."

She covered her mouth and hopped up and down. "No. Freakin'. Way."

"What?" I tilted my head.

"The Memphis Mangoes are the best. My little brother worships them. They're like the Harlem Globetrotters of minor league baseball, doing all sorts of crazy stunts and stuff. It's as if baseball and the circus had a baby. It's *so* much fun."

"Huh. He's a circus performer?"

"No, silly." She slapped my arm. "He's a real baseball player. He probably played in the minor leagues but didn't make it into the majors. He's got to have talent to play with the Mangoes, and he's also got to be really funny too. This is so amazing!"

When I didn't say anything, she asked, "So, when are you going to see him?"

"What? What are you talking about?"

"Jack Sutton, you are not letting that hottie Mango off this plane without making plans."

I laid my head back against the metal bulkhead. "Em, he lives in Memphis and I live in Atlanta. Even if—"

"And you're a flight attendant with *free* flights anywhere, anytime."

She had me there. "Still—"

"Still nothing."

A ding sounded above, indicating Helen wanted me to answer the phone. I grabbed the receiver, acknowledged her instruction, then hung up.

"What now?" Emma asked.

"Your presence is required in the back, by order of Her Majesty."

"Ugh. She's *such* a pain," she whispered, then stuck her finger in my face. "When I come back, you'd better have his phone number and email address. Hell, get his social security number. We can check his credit."

"Em!"

I watched her shimmy up the aisle, gripping one headrest after the next for balance. She was an incredible friend but could be downright pushy when she wanted to be. The whole idea was ridiculous.

An odd motion caught my eye, and I craned my head around to peek into the cabin.

The lights were dim. All the Delta One boys had their sleep hoods covering their bodies. Even Miguel had given up eating and was resting peacefully.

I glanced down at the first row where Steph lay prone. All I could see were his legs and feet. He'd shed his shoes. The hint of a few toes poked through threadbare white athletic socks.

And that's when I noticed his twitching. Like a golden retriever dreaming of chasing a cat, Steph ran in his sleep.

A wide grin parted my lips as I stared, and I almost laughed out loud.

What was he dreaming of? Was he a boy again, chasing a baseball or playing tag with friends? Was he a Mango, rounding the bases after a line drive? Was he running from some sharp barb tossed by Sam or Miguel?

That made me chuckle.

Whatever dream drove his twitching, the childlike motions were almost as cute as his dimples.

"LADIES AND GENTLEMEN, THAT chime indicates that we have begun our final descent. Please take a moment to check your area and ensure you have sunglasses, headphones, iPhones, iPads, children you prefer to keep, desktops, car batteries, refrigerators, and anything else you brought on board."

A wave of anxious chuckles traveled through the cabin as passengers stretched and began preparing for landing. Steel Bun might've been a hard ass, but she was a cheeky one. Passengers always loved her closing act.

As I stepped to the back of my section, Emma caught my eye. "Get his number," she mouthed, then winked and turned away.

"Hoods and trays up, please," I said to the salt-and-pepper member of the Mango crew sitting in the back row between his partner and Ethan, the precocious youngster who would've been my favorite of the bunch had it not been for a certain surfing baseball player in the front row.

With each row, a different set of men, each as hot as the last, smiled up and thanked me for taking care of them. I'd seen plenty of passengers blown away by the Delta One experience, but never before had I felt such gratitude and warmth from an entire section. The bond, not just between the couples but across the group, was clear. It felt more like a family reunion of close brothers than a group of friends going on a vacation.

And then there was Steph.

He was the new guy, apparently. Sam and Miguel were relentless in their teasing and attention, but the others, while friendly, didn't interact with him much, but I expected that would change as they spent more time together. Steph seemed like a great guy.

"Hey, Jack." Sam's rumble jarred me out of my thoughts. He motioned for me to lean in, like a spy imparting a secret mission. Miguel leaned across the center console to listen in. "You should give Steph your number."

"Totally," Miguel added. "He's hot. Have you seen his ass?"

I nearly dropped my tray of dirty glasses.

"No, he's been sitting the whole time," I said through a tight smile. "And guys, he's right there." I motioned with my head to the seat in front of Sam, only inches from where we whispered.

"My ass is fabulous," Steph called over the seat.

My face flushed.

Sam and Miguel burst out laughing.

I straightened, secured my tray, and bolted toward the galley. A hand reached up before I could escape and grabbed my wrist.

Any flight attendant would tell you that *that* act by a passenger sounded alarms louder than any found in the cockpit. Passengers *never* touched flight attendants—at least, they shouldn't. Gripping us, holding us in place, keeping us from running away while blushing, was *strictly* forbidden, punishable by ... well ... it was just punishable.

Startled, I looked down, ready to unload on whoever was holding me in place.

And every word I'd ever spoken caught in my throat when I saw Steph's smile and bright eyes. My gaze fell to his hand holding my wrist. He followed, staring down. His thumb stroked my skin, and a shiver ran up my spine.

Still, he didn't let go. And I didn't pull away.

"I have a request of my flight attendant," he said, his voice as measured as any passenger asking for a refill of coffee.

"Uh, okay, sure," I said, still struggling with my native language.

His smile widened at my discomfort. "I'd really like that number. You know, the one Emma and Sam told you to give me."

A glass finally fell off my tray and rolled down the aisle. Sam caught it under his boot, a snarky smirk crawling across his face as he took in my petrified features.

It's important to note at this point, I was a confident guy. I rarely got flustered. I dealt with the public every day, and was fine handling weird, awkward, or uncomfortable situations.

And I dated, dammit.

I was *not* scared of men. I was *not* shy. I was *not* afraid of conversation or flirting or, hell, making out in the corner of a bar.

But Steph ...

Fuck me running. What was it about this surfer-turned-baseballer that had my insides flipping like some third grader's bad tissue-paper origami?

"Number? You want ... I mean, you're talking about my ... like, my phone? You want my phone number?"

Steph's thumb traced a circle on my arm, and fire bloomed beneath my skin.

I fucking shivered right there in the aisle.

"Yes, your phone number. And your last name … and your email address … and your Insta handle … and any other way you'd let me contact you."

I blinked.

Steph had seemed so awkward, so afraid to say, well, anything. Where had he found basketball-sized balls? Damn, they were swinging and smacking me in the face in that moment.

"Uh, okay."

"Okay?" His grip released and doubt crept into his eyes. "Okay, you want to give me your number? Or, okay, can this flight land so I can get away from this creepy passenger?"

I was blowing it. He was starting to doubt …

"Just … wait right there," I said.

He grinned. "I kind of have to. You made me buckle up."

"Right. Just … " I flushed again. "I'll be right back."

I ducked into the galley. It was only a few feet from where Steph sat, but the faux wall between us felt like a comfort blanket. I set my tray down and breathed, then looked at the wall pocket where my iPhone glared back accusingly, as though Siri might suddenly scream, "Go get the hottie's number, you idiot."

Without thinking, I filled a fresh glass with water, grabbed a napkin, scrawled my name, number, and email, then stepped from behind the wall. Steph's gaze was fixed, like a dog who'd just watched his human go into a store. It was so fucking cute.

"Here's your water, Steph." I set the napkin on his tray table, then dropped the glass on top of it, like I would when serving any other passenger. My writing wobbled up through glass and liquid.

Steph's smile brightened to impossible proportions.

And something in my chest swelled, testing the strength of my ribs to hold it in.

Dammit.

He lifted the glass, downed the water, then raised it toward me. "You told us we had to give you all our glasses already."

The playful grin curling the corners of his eyes was too much.

When I reached for the glass, our hands overlapped, and I couldn't take it anymore. I leaned down and kissed him.

Right there, on my plane, in front of Steel Bun, Emma, Sam, Miguel, and every other Mango that ever fell off the tree, I kissed Steph.

His hand found the back of my head and he held our lips together.

A cheer erupted across Delta One.

Chapter Four

Day Off

Jack

Emma stood near the boarding door, rolling suitcase behind her, one foot tapping impatiently. "Hurry your ass up. The cleaning crew can do the rest."

I knew she was right, but it was a point of pride for me to leave my station in better condition than when I found it. Delta One was a special experience for passengers, one most could never afford. I wanted whoever sprawled beneath the sleeping tubes next to enjoy a perfect experience, starting with a sparkling clean seating area.

"I'm almost done. Barcelona will still be there in ten minutes."

She crossed her arms, like some pedantic teenager forced to wait on a parent.

"You're *so* obsessive." Her valley girl accent made me chuckle—and think of Steph. He didn't exactly ooze *90210*, but he definitely slipped into surfer mode when he had a drink or two in him or was especially relaxed.

"What are you grinning at?" she snarked, her raptor-like gaze never leaving me.

I shrugged and tried to hide the blush I knew was creeping up my neck.

"You're thinking about *him*, aren't you?" Her arms un-crossed as she leaned against the bulkhead. "One kiss and you're whipped. Look at you. Is your skin hot just remembering his lips? Did you reach down and feel his firm chest, squeeze his biceps? Did you reach lower and—"

"Em!"

"Emma Louise Alcott!" That wasn't her full name, but Steel Bun was the ultimate mother—or grandmother—when she was correcting us. She liked to make up middle names just for the scolding effect. "This young man is already in enough hot water. He crossed a *serious* line—in front of other passengers, no less. Don't encourage him."

"A kiss might do *you* some good, maybe get laid," Emma muttered, a tad too loudly.

I nearly spat holding back a laugh.

Steel Bun's glare was a spearpoint stabbing and rending Emma's chest, over and over, until there was nothing left but bits of pulp and purple uniform ... and perhaps the golden, bedazzled wings she always wore.

"Okay, I'm done," I said, desperate to save us both from the wrath of one of Olympus's last remaining Titans.

"Try not to embarrass the airline ... again," Steel Bun admon-ished before brushing past Emma and vanishing down the jet bridge, turning back one last time to yell, "And at least call him."

"She really does need to get laid," Emma laughed.

"I heard that," her voice echoed from the distance.

We doubled over like kids caught looking at nudie pics, then stepped off the plane, bumping shoulders and giggling.

"What do you want to do today? We have a whole day and night here. That *never* happens."

She hooked her arm around mine. "I need a nap before we do anything, then I want food—good, authentic Spanish food—somewhere we can sit, watch people, and have sangria brought to us in giant buckets."

"I'm up for all that."

"And then I want to go shopping." Her grip on my arm tightened. "Have you ever been down to the Passeig de Gràcia or the *Bàrri Gòtic* streets?"

I shook my head. "I don't even know what a *Bàrri Gòtic* is."

She giggled again. "It's the Gothic Quarter. A walking area with the best shops in the city. You're gonna love it. Trust me."

I didn't love the idea of shopping all afternoon, but Emma was my bestie and whatever we did would be an adventure. "Sounds great. Let's get checked in, knock out some Zs, then hit the streets."

"You make it sound like I'm selling my pretty putty."

I nearly missed a step. "I never mentioned your putty. And I'm sure it's pretty, but I've never seen it."

"We could fix that—"

"Ew, Em. My team does not peek at putties. We do not touch putties. We do not let putties paw at us or claw or bite ... or whatever it is putties do."

Her laughter grew with each mention of the word "putty." By the time I'd finished, I worried she might need an oxygen mask ... or somewhere to relieve her putty.

"I bet you'd like to see that surfer's putty."

I did trip over my own feet at that. "A man putty is very different from a woman putty."

She stopped walking, released my arm, planted balled fists on her hips, and cocked her head like a perky cheerleader. "How? Please enlighten me.""How what?""How is a man putty different from my pretty kitty?"

My eyes darted around the airport, horrified someone might be watching her display—or worse, listening.

"Go on." She waved a hand like a queen commanded a servant. "I really want to hear this."

I pinched the bridge of my nose and closed my eyes. "Dear God, what have I done? I promise, I've been a good boy."

She slapped my arm. "Stop praying and answer."

We turned and resumed our walk toward the airport exit. "First," I said, unsure quite how to avoid sinking deeper in the pile of the quicksand-poop-muck-salad I found myself in. "A boy doesn't have a putty. We don't call it that or think of it like that."

"Yes, you do."

"What?"

"You put tab A into slot B. That makes slot B a putty, by definition. It's just math."

"Math?"

Her head cocked again. "Gay math. Trust me, it adds up. There's a guy on TikTok who teaches gay math. Look it up. It's science and shit."

It didn't happen often, but I was speechless.

"So," she went on, unperturbed by the brilliant shade of my cheeks, "if you and surfer boy hook up, one of you will get your putty petted and popped."

"Emma!"

Her brows shot up. "Are you denying you want to pop his putty?"

"Yes!" I gaped. She stopped walking again. "I mean, no. Of course not. But yes. I do, I mean . . . I would. Dammit. Can we please stop talking about putties?"

She laughed. "You're really cute when you're flustered."

"I hate you. Deep in my soul, where it's dark and lonely, there is a well of hatred reserved just for you."

She hooked my arm again and squeezed tightly, pressing her cheek to my shoulder. "I know. I hate you too."

I'D NEVER BEEN SO glad to step into a cheap hotel room as I was that day. Em had been right. Ten hours on an overnight overseas flight was a killer, especially when my body clock was still set to Daylight Saving Time back home. I shoved my suitcase into the corner, stripped off my uniform, and fell onto the bed without even pulling the covers back.

Then my phone buzzed. *Dammit.*

I was going to ignore it, but the tiny voice in my head that was controlled by endorphins, or whatever magic sauce got me excited every time my phone chirped, was determined I would check the screen. I groaned and reached toward the nightstand.

I stared. Normally, I would ignore random texts from unknown numbers, but this texter knew my name. That got my attention.

The question mark was intentional, my way of asking, "Who the fuck are you, and why didn't you declare yourself in your first text?" It also could simply mean, "I don't know this number," but I wasn't feeling that generous toward someone who stood between me and a nap.

> **UNKNOWN NUMBER:** OH, SORRY. THIS IS STEPH. YOU GAVE ME YOUR NUMBER, BUT I DIDN'T RETURN THE FAVOR. I FORGOT.

I bolted upright. All thoughts of sleep or napping fled. Putties suddenly popped into my head. Lots of them. They were pretty too.

Dammit, Emma!

I couldn't let Steph be an unknown, unnamed caller. That would've been rude. It would pain me every time I saw him type, and that simply wouldn't do.

But what to name him?

I strained my memory for all the things he'd told me about himself, all the conversations we'd had in our nine glorious hours together, all the things I'd heard Sam and Miguel …

I had it.

Surfer Poo.

I created a new contact and punched in the name as fast as my thumbs would allow.

> **ME:** OH, HEY! HOW ARE YOU? WHERE ARE YOU?

My heart raced faster than a cat high on catnip. I barely knew this guy, but the entire room spun just thinking about him. When had I reverted to a twelve-year-old who'd just had his first kiss? I was glad he couldn't see me.

Well, fucking fuckety fuck.

Oh ... my ... gawd. He was flirting like a champ!

Then my phone rang, the weird whirring Apple deemed worthy of a FaceTime incoming call. I nearly dropped my iPhone while straightening my hair, which was always a lost cause but seemed like the thing to do when a hot surfer-baseball-muscle boy was calling.

I pressed the answer button, and his face appeared. The background was a mirror image of mine: a hotel room with a decidedly Spanish flair.

"Hey, dude." A brilliant smile revealing perfectly white teeth exploded across my screen.

I grinned. "Did you just 'dude' me? Really? I thought we were more than that already."

He chuckled. "One kiss and you think you're past 'dude' status? *So* presumptuous."

"A boy can dream, can't he?"

His eyes crinkled. I wanted to reach out and touch them on the screen.

"Steph, move it!" a familiar voice boomed in the background as a pounding sounded against his door. He reflexively looked back, then turned toward me with a disappointed pout.

"Sorry. When Sam and Miguel set their minds on something, there's no putting them off."

"No worries. I needed this nap anyway. It's really good seeing your face again."

"Yours too." His smile returned. "I don't know how much reception I'll have for the next two weeks, but I'll text, if that's okay."

"You'd better."

He started to say something, then caught himself. A second passed, then he said, "That was a great kiss. Took forever for the hard-on to go down so I could leave the plane."

I nearly dropped my phone again.

"Text ya soon," he said quickly, then the screen went blank.

I fell back on the pillow and stared at the ceiling.

Chapter Five

Eli

Jack

If my body clock had been scrambled in Barcelona, it was utterly dazed and confused when I stepped back into my apartment in Atlanta a day and a half later. Eli, my best friend, had left all the lights turned off with the shades and curtains closed, casting my living space into the dead of night, despite it being ten o'clock in the morning.

"Apartment, I feel ya. I barely know what time it is either," I said into the blackness.

A tiny yawl preceded purring, sounding like a NASCAR race revving at the start.

"Rufus?" I called, and was immediately rewarded with an injection of love as needles dug into my leg and my overly affectionate cat climbed his way up.

"Ow, shit." I danced back, as if *anything* could shake him loose. His purring grew louder as he climbed faster, a mountaineer slamming steel spikes into the ice on his ascent.

I shoved my rolling bag away and reached down, gripping the mangy beast in both hands. He was barely large enough to need one palm, but he liked to be cupped.

"Let go, buddy," I tried to soothe, desperate to release the clamps I was sure had already drawn blood. "Daddy's home."

He yawled again. It was a pitiful sound, something one might expect if he'd been caught beneath a boulder or trapped in the mouth of a Doberman.

He wasn't hurt. It's just how he sounded.

I'd found Rufus two years earlier under the stairs of my apartment. His mama had birthed her litter and moved on, apparently not realizing little Ruf hadn't followed. He'd been no bigger than my fist at the time, all ears, eyes, and grossly patchy fur. I'd assumed his head would grow, his ears and eyes would become proportionate, and his fur would fill in. Alas, the gods of ugly creatures had visited him a time too many. His body grew, but only a little. His ears exploded and his eyes bulged. The only fur to fill in was a thumb-sized patch of white on his chest. The hairless patches, which looked like I'd taken a bikini wax kit to his whole body, remained as unsightly as ever.

Eli teased us relentlessly, mocking Ruf's scraggly do while making movie star references to my own lustrous mane that sprouted in all directions.

I had good hair. He wasn't wrong.

But Rufus, well, he redefined cute. And I couldn't love the little fur ball anymore.

He squirmed out of my hands and hopped onto my chest, digging his nails into my skin so he could bound onto a shoulder.

"God, kid, stop that with the nails or I'm gonna make you wear those rubber tips."

His motor roared in my ears as he slammed his waifish body against the side of my head. A wet nose then left a trail of something disgusting from my collarbone to my chin.

"Eww. I love you too, I think."

It was as if he knew he was the runt—the rejected one—and loved me more for loving him. We were quite the pair.

"You want to take a nap with Daddy? I'm really wiped out."

Yawl.

I scratched his knobby head. "Alright, let's do this."

With my passenger onboard, I walked through the den to the hallway, past the bathroom, and into my bedroom at the end. Thankfully, Eli hadn't tinkered with the thermostat, and the apartment was frosty, just how I liked it. Nothing said "great sleep" like a freezing apartment and massive fluffy, heavy blankets.

I stripped down to my undies, crawled under the sheets, and lifted them to allow my shadow to join. Rufus curled under the covers and wedged into my right armpit, where he slept most nights. His rumble rattled my chest.

In less than a heartbeat, we'd drifted off.

The clouds surround me in pillowy comfort.

In the distance, I see a break and can barely make out the land below. Smears on the canvas reveal

*whole towns divided by a patchwork of brown, yel-
low, and green.*

Farms.

*I check the instruments and guess I'm somewhere
over Europe—maybe Germany or France.*

Why am I flying over Europe?

*The thought repeats itself again and again, but
the rolling farmland that unfolds below when the
clouds vanish is mesmerizing.*

God, I love flying.

*"Jack," a voice calls out in the distance. Is there
someone sitting on a nearby cloud? How is that
even possible?*

"Where's my Jack-o-Lantern?" the voice, now chipper and annoying, persists.

The sky shatters.

The farms dissolve.

Fire blooms in my ribs.

"FUCK, RUFUS!" I GROANED, as my constant companion made biscuits in my side. Clearly, he was done napping.

"Jackisha. Where are you, honey bear?" A light somewhere in the apartment flicked on and I realized Eli was back—and I was no longer peacefully unconscious. "Please tell me you're naked. Mama needs a show."

I loved Eli like a brother—a painfully annoying, flamboyantly ridiculous younger brother who never knew how to blend into the background. Hell, he didn't know the background existed. All of which was hilarious when one realized Eli was a bespeck-led nerd with scruffy brown hair that curled so tightly on his head it looked like pubes ... or a Chia Pet ... that was probably a kinder description. None of that mattered. Eli strutted his stuff like he was the king of the runway. Okay, that would be *queen* of the runway, definitely queen. He looked like an accountant, his flame burned brightly, and he was impossible not to love.

Like? That came and went. Love, that belonged to Eli.

"Has anyone told you to fuck off lately?" I rubbed my eyes and grumbled. "What time is it?"

"Seven thirty, sweetie pie."

Seven thirty? Had I slept all day and all night? Was it really the next morning?

"Oh, crap. I'm late. I'm supposed to be at the field at eight-thirty."

The silhouette of Eli's head appeared in my doorway. "Seven thirty at night, silly. Didn't think you slept for, what, eighteen hours? That would be crazy, even for you. Although, from what I've seen, you could use the beauty rest."

He had to duck as my pillow slammed into the space he'd just occupied.

"Why are you here?"

"Because"—his silhouette straightened and leaned against the doorframe, arms crossed—"you promised me a dinner for watching that throw pillow you call a cat."

Yawl.

"Hey, not nice. Rufus is adorable."

Eli laughed. "In the same way roadkill is adorable to a vulture."

"Remind me why we're friends."

"*Best* friends." His voice brooked no argument. "Because I'm fabulous and you desperately need light in your life."

With that statement, he flicked on the bedroom light. Rufus ducked back under the covers. I squinted and shielded my eyes.

"Ooh, look, man titties."

I yanked the covers up to my neck.

Eli laughed. "Like I haven't seen those and everything else you wag around town. Jesus, Jack, you act like an old woman in winter."

I didn't fully get that but was afraid to ask for an explanation. Sometimes, it was better not to know.

"Fine, give me a minute. I need to wash up and dress."

He clapped his hands like I'd just won an Oscar. "Yay. Bestie date."

Yawl.

"Oh, shut it, dustbin."

I cradled Ruf under my chin and scratched his ear, the one that looked like chewed-up leather. "You really should be nicer to Rufus. He's sensitive."

He twirled about, then vanished. "I'm waiting. Don't make me go through your things out of boredom."

I grunted and rose, setting Rufus back on the bed. He stretched his tiny paws and yawned up at me.

"Like there's anything to go through," I called. "All I do is fly."

"And work out," he added. "Those boobs don't grow themselves. Unless you're pregnant and haven't told me. Are you lactating? Seriously, you can't keep secrets like that from your best—"

"Leave a message at the beep," I yelled back, then turned on the shower, drowning out whatever retort he lobbed back.

Thirty minutes later, we sat at a center table at Roasters, my favorite comfort food dive in the heart of Atlanta. The place wasn't fancy, all wooden tables and worn booths, but the rotisserie chicken and fresh veggies were to die for. And, unlike most places in town, most of the dishes at Roasters were healthy. Hence, the post-workout crowd packed the place, most still wearing their tiny shorts and stringy tank tops, which meant there was usually a lot of meat on offer—and not just on the plates.

Damn, I loved Roasters.

"The peacocks are out tonight," Eli said as he sipped tea that was so sweet I was surprised the sugar made it through the plastic tube and into his mouth.

I glanced around, earning a few nods and appreciative grins. "Yeah, it's pretty in here tonight."

We chatted about everything and nothing, a pair of Golden Girls who'd been reunited after only two days but had a lifetime's worth of stories to tell. That's how it was with Eli, a perpetual family reunion that made even the crustiest old gay smile.

Midway through a bit of chicken, my phone chimed.

Eli's brow shot up.

"What?"

He pointed with his fork. "You have a text message."

"And?"

"No one *ever* texts you. Except me." He held up his phone. "And I didn't do it. I'm right here. See?"

I shook my head. "Yes, dear, I see you. A satellite could spot your flame."

He plopped his phone down and huffed. "My brilliance is clear, but that doesn't get you out of this. Who's texting?"

I shrugged and touched the screen.

SurferPoo has sent a text message.

"Surfer Poo?" Eli nearly fell out of his chair. "First, who names themselves something like that? Second, do you have a man you haven't told me about? Jackson Luicious Eloise Sutton, you'd better start talking."

"Luicious? Eloise?"

He crossed his arms. "They're fine names, especially when you piss me off. Now talk."

I tried not to roll my eyes but failed. "Fine. There was this guy on the flight to Barcelona—"

"A *passenger*?" His jaw dropped. "Jack, no. Really. Just no."

Eli was a flight attendant for a competitor, but airlines were all the same. Rules were rules, and all flight attendants lived by them. You *never* got involved with passengers. Ever. Not even a little. No matter how hot or cute or smart or … whatever. You just didn't. Nothing good came from mixing business and pleasure.

"We just talked. It's a long flight." My defense was about as thin as the hair on the bald guy sitting behind us.

Eli crossed his arms and glared. "Details. Now."

I laughed and stared at my plate. "His name is Stephan, but he goes by Steph."

"You gave him a nickname already? I mean, other than the brilliant one in your phone?"

I shook my head. "No, that's what Sam and Miguel called him."

He cocked his head. "Sam and Miguel?"

"His friends. They're kind of the ring leaders of the group that rented out Delta One for the flight."

His eyes widened. "*All* of Delta One? They bought the whole thing?"

I nodded.

He whistled. "Wait, you know this guy's friends' names? Were you sitting in his lap the whole time? What the hell, Jack?"

The waiter stopped by and refilled our glasses. He looked to be in his early twenties, maybe in college, with burgeoning shoulders and a baby chest trying to peek out of a too-tight shirt. His dimples were like little divots of joy when he smiled.

"You need saving, hon?"

I grinned up at the puppy. "No, thanks. He's harmless, like a chihuahua. He'll yip a lot, maybe pee on your shoe, but that's about it."

The puppy laughed, patted my shoulder, let his hand linger a moment too long, then stepped away.

"See!" Eli pointed at my shoulder. "You could nab any guy you wanted. With your face and hair and that damn body of death, all you have to do is bat your eyes and men line up. Why are you sticking your dick in the airline passenger pool?"

I held up my hands in surrender. "No dick has been dipped in the making of this story. Promise. We just talked … and there was a kiss."

"You kissed him?" His voice rose enough to draw eyes from other tables. The suggestion of kissing had a few leaning in to listen. My cheeks reddened.

"*One* kiss. Right before deplaning. He just—"

"Dear God. I'm going to the restroom. I can't with you right now. You are going to flight attendant hell. There's no saving you. While I'm gone, I want you to think about what you've done."

"Yes, Mama E."

He rose, flicked his non-existent long hair back, then sashayed toward the restroom at the back of the restaurant. A few guys at nearby tables waited, their eyes locked to see what I would do.

Then I remembered the text. I hadn't even looked at it. I scooped up my phone and flicked the screen.

ME: Aww. He's worried about me.

SurferPoo: Don't be ridiculous. You have flight privileges. You go down, so does my chance for freebies.

ME: Ha ha. You sure know how to sweet talk a guy.

SurferPoo: Dude. I'm smooth as a newborn's shit. When I sweet talk you, you'll swoon.

ME: You Duded me again.

SurferPoo: It's a beachy term of endearment. We only dude those we like.

I really didn't know where the conversation was going, but every message stretched my smile a bit wider. I could feel it in my cheeks. This guy wasn't just pretty, he was sharp, and that turned me on even more than his eyes—and they were world class.

ME: So, how's the trip?

SurferPoo: Dude, you wouldn't believe this ship. This Cooper guy blew so much money putting us up in the fancy cabins. Like seriously, it's crazy.

ME: LIKE, TOTALLY.

SURFERPOO: RIGHT!

ME: WHERE ARE YOU NOW?

SURFERPOO: WE SPENT THE DAY IN CANNES. BLAH, BLAH, MOVIES, SHOPPING, BLAH. NOT REALLY MY THING, BUT IT WAS PRETTY, AND HANGING OUT WITH SAM AND MIGUEL WAS A BLAST.

ME: THEY SEEM LIKE GOOD GUYS. THEY WERE SURE ALL OVER YOU ON THE PLANE.

The dots danced, then stilled. Then danced again. Still, nothing came through. Finally ...

SURFERPOO: THEY'RE HARD TO EXPLAIN. IT'S LIKE, THEY'RE THE MOM AND DAD OF THE GROUP. THE GUYS EVEN CALL THEM MOM AND DAD.

ME: THAT'S EITHER CUTE, WEIRD, OR KINKY. I'M NOT SURE WHICH.

SURFERPOO: HA. I DON'T THINK IT'S KINKY, NOT WITH THESE GUYS. THEY'RE THE MOST COMMITTED COUPLE I'VE EVER SEEN. SERIOUSLY.

ME: SO, NO HANKY PANKY WITH MOMMY AND DADDY?

I was just teasing, carrying on the conversation, but the dots stilled again. They remained frozen so long Eli returned before Steph finally replied.

SurferPoo: Nah. They're amazing and totally hot. I mean, damn, fucking hot, but I doubt they'd do a Steph sandwich.

Huh. That was an interesting answer. He doubted it, but he didn't say it was something he wouldn't want—or *do*—if given the opportunity.

Before I had time to consider too deeply, Eli reached across and snatched my phone.

"Hey!"

He looked up, like a professor glaring out the top of his glasses, and waggled his index finger like Ru Paul after a bad runway walk. "Oh, little one, you must submit to inspection. You've been a very bad boy." He began to scroll. "Oh. Oh my. Oh, holy mother of Zeus and Jason Statham." He looked up. "Is he a player? Man meat? A gigogay?"

"Gigogay?"

"You know, a gigolo but gay."

I put my head in my hands. "No, he's not a gigogay."

"Why all this flirting with the couple, then? I don't like it. Not one bit. Mama does not approve."

"There's nothing to approve. We met, talked, I flew home. He lives in Memphis. What could possibly happen between us?"

Eli set my phone down with two fingers like its filth might rub off. "Nothing, if you know what's good for you. Mama will be watching."

I picked up my phone and stared a moment, then pecked a quick message.

Me: Gotta jet. Have fun with the boys.

Chapter Six

Dreams and Lessons

Jack

Steph didn't text again that night. I caught myself lying in bed, staring at my phone on the nightstand, wondering if it would vibrate.

Unfortunately, the only vibrating in that bed was Rufus. For such a scraggly little guy, he purred like a Harley with a bad muffler.

I reached up and killed the lamp, consigning us to blessed darkness.

Steph might not have revisited my phone, but he soon haunted my dreams.

Sam and Miguel ... and Steph?

Naked.

Covered in whipped cream while wrestling in a kiddie pool of Jell-O.

Sam and Miguel kiss. Then Sam grabs Steph roughly and pulls him in so all three men's lips meet. Tongues blur as mouths press and squeeze.

Three hard cocks smack together, and Sam grinds against them both.

Miguel grabs Steph's chest, squeezing and pulling, then he grips the back of Sam's head and slams their mouths together.

There's nothing gentle in his touch. He's all desire, possession, and passion.

Steph and Sam are his.

Steph moans.

Sam groans.

Miguel grips Steph's hair, pulling his head back to expose his neck, then Sam and Miguel attack, teeth and tongues devouring Steph like vampires feeding on a kill.

The dream shifts and Sam has Steph bent over a counter, pounding into him.

Steph cries out. His fingers grip the edges of the marble.

Miguel, standing in front of him, lifts his head and shoves his fat dick into Steph's mouth.

"Suck it," he commands. "Eat my cock."

Steph opens wider, takes Miguel down his throat, relaxing against a gag.

Sam grips his hips and pulls Miguel forward, harder.

Skin slaps. Lips smack. Steph gags but cranes forward, devouring as much of Miguel as he can fit in his mouth.

Drool dribbles around Miguel's cock, out of Steph's mouth.

Steph tries to cry out, but his mouth is full.

Both men shove themselves inside him.

Sam's body is a rock covered in stubble. Miguel is Adonis, a mountain of muscle. Steph is the corded rope stretched in between.

The dream shifts as I turn onto my side, my erection twitching when the sheets brush against it.

Now Steph stands in a hot tub with steam billowing. Miguel is behind him, inside him, arms wrapped around and kneading his chest. Sam is in front, standing on the pool's edge where Steph ...

Steph's face is buried in Sam's ass. He works back and forth, wedging his tongue deeper, spreading Sam's cheeks with his hands.

Sam presses his palms against the wall, leaning over, his cock dribbling in long, thin strands. He moans, then yells in a primal roar.

Steph comes up for air and grabs Sam about his waist, pulling him down into the water. He grabs Sam's head and bends it back, licking and kissing and biting his neck.

Steph guides himself inside Sam.

"Fuck me, dammit," Sam barks. "Fuck me as hard as you can."

Miguel reaches around Steph and pulls Sam into him, deeper, harder.

I can barely see where one man ends and the others begin. They move as one. Sliding in and out like a ballet of erotic perfection.

Miguel's hands reach past Steph to grip Sam. Sam's head lolls back to rest on Steph's shoulder. Steph slides deeper inside Sam.

Sam rages, all guttural and gruff. I can almost feel Sam's ass tighten as Steph strains to hold back.

Everyone's abs clench. Their chests heave. The muscles of their arms grow taut.

Sweat pours off Miguel, glistening from a light that cuts through the steam.

He shoves harder.

Thrusts faster.

My heart races through the dream. My sheets soak with sweat.

Steph reaches up through reality and grips my shoulder. His eyes pierce me. His hands seize me. His nails dig into my skin.

He leans down and bites. He burns for me. He devours me.

When his head lifts, his eyes never leaving mine, he thrusts into Sam as Miguel drives even deeper into him.

My breath quickens. My cock throbs.

"Feel me, Jack. Feel me deep inside you," Steph demands, one world speaking to another.

Miguel howls as he rocks both Steph and Sam, bending them both over the side of the pool.

Steph yells, "Fuck!" then reaches forward to grab Sam's cock, milking him like his survival depends on it.

Sam's body rocks, then he bellows, "Fuck him, Miguel! Harder! Dammit, fuck me, Steph! Don't stop!"

Cum explodes, painting everything around it.

Sam is a geyser erupting more times than any man should, even in a dream. Wave after wave.

*Still, Miguel thrusts, forcing Steph deeper into
Sam.*

*Sam arches back, grabbing Steph's head, turning
it so their lips meet.*

They're a blur of teeth and tongues and lips.

Sam gasps.

Steph screams.

Miguel cries out.

I woke in a pool of sweat and stickiness, with a bleeding
shoulder from Rufus's claws.

"Fuck, Rufus, what was that for?"

Yawl.

"I need serious help." I threw my head back against the pillow,
my chest heaving, cock still twitching.

Yawl.

"Not you too. Eli's already on my ass."

That thought made the dream return ... how Sam and Miguel *and Steph* ...

"I really need to get laid or take a shower. Maybe both."

"You look like shit," the man beside me said.I glanced in the mirror and winced at the bags staring back. "Didn't get much sleep last night."

Collum flicked a few switches on the control panel and grinned sideways at me. "That good? Did you at least get a name?"

I groaned.

Collum was a good guy and a great flight instructor, but his awareness of people ended with the recognition that a passenger existed. Raised on a farm in South Georgia, he might not even pick up on *Eli* being gay, even if he slapped him in the face with a feather boa.

"Nope. No names. In fact, there was no getting laid."

"Aw, shit. Sorry. Good-lookin' dude like you, I figured you fuck every night of the week."

I was only a third of the way through the in-plane portion of my training, but had already spent enough time cooped up with Collum to get his humor. He was gruff, vulgar, and completely harmless.

"Thanks, C. Even a champ has to sleep, right?"

He nodded thoughtfully. "Yeah, guess so. Rest up so you can conquer the field again."

"Something like that." I chuckled. If only he knew that my field involved penises.

"Alright." His voice flipped into teacher mode. "Time to take her up. This time, you have the stick. I'm just an observer. I won't touch anything unless you fuck up my plane."

I chuckled again. "I'll do my best not to fuck anything up."

"Right. Off we go," he said, pointing to the speaker an inch from my lips, reminding me to call to the tower as the next step.

Permission received, the Cirrus SR20 shifted from purr to whirr and lurched forward. A few anxious moments later, our wheels left the ground and Atlanta grew smaller beneath us.

"Does that ever go away?"

Collum's head turned. "What?"

"The rush. It's amazing."

He nodded. "Sure is. And no, it never goes away. Just look around. We're in the fucking clouds."

I laughed. It was an old joke, a worn-out conversation, but it was also the truth. How could anyone fly among the clouds and not smile or laugh or feel like their heart was going to leap out of their chest?

There wasn't a feeling like it in all the world. The freedom of soaring high above the ground was a drug unlike any other.

And I could never get enough of it.

That's why I'd been so determined to get my pilot's license. The idea of being in the cabin for the rest of my life was sickening. I wanted to *fly* the bird, not ride in back.

"Alright, circle around, call the tower, and take us down," Collum ordered.

"Already?" I was a five-year-old who didn't want to leave the playground.

"Flying is the easy part. Landing is where shit splatters. You need practice. Once we're down, we'll go back up so you can do it over again."

That made me feel better. It wasn't a quickie flight with an hour of classroom. We'd take off almost as quickly as we landed.

I gave him a thumbs-up. "Calling it in."

Chapter Seven

Homeward Bound

Steph

"You ready to get home?" A meaty hand landed on my shoulder.

I nearly jumped overboard. "Holy fucking mother of fuckery."

Sam's laugh was a gear against metal.

"He's still a scared little rabbit," Miguel said from behind. I could *hear* his grin.

"You okay?" Sam stepped up to the railing, eyeing me sideways. "You have that look on your face."

Miguel appeared on my other side. I felt his presence before I saw him. His annoyingly muscular arm flopped across my shoulders so his hand could twiddle Sam's buzzed hair.

"I'm okay. Guess I'm just a little sad to see the trip end."

Miguel's arm flexed, an approximation of a supportive hug. "It has been pretty amazing, hasn't it? How many cities did we visit? And that whole *Game of Thrones* thing? How cool was that?"

I nodded, my eyes still fixed on ripples in the water. "Yeah, all that."

"But?" Sam said, his Spidey sense obviously tingling in its supernatural way.

I turned to eye Sam. "It'll sound dumb."

Sam's eyes narrowed. "Steph, what's going on? Talk to us."

My head lowered, and I fidgeted with a smudge on the railing, pretending to clean it but only smearing it across the metal.

"I don't have a lot of family," I said. "I guess ... I don't know. You guys have just been so ... Shit. Sorry, I'm an idiot. Just ignore me, okay?"

Miguel surprised me, reaching up with his other hand, gripping both my shoulders, and spinning me to face him. When he spoke, it was the tone I suspected he used when in uniform and dealing with a troublesome kid in the neighborhood.

"Look at me, Steph, and hear what I'm about to say. You're one of us now, plain and simple. If you give us the chance to prove it, off this ship and in the real world, you'll find we're a pretty amazing family ourselves. I shouldn't talk for the other guys, but I know their hearts. You'd be welcome in any of our homes, anytime, no matter what. You don't even have to ask. Just show up. That's how family works. It's sure as hell how this one works."

I stared into Miguel's eyes, unsure I'd ever seen such sincerity in anyone's gaze. My whole body lodged in my throat, making it impossible to reply, and the urge to throw myself against his chest and bawl like a baby was almost too much to resist.

And I was a grown-ass man.

What the actual fuck?

I turned away, not trusting myself under his scrutiny. Ships moving about the port in the distance caught my eye. It felt strange, watching our crawl toward Barcelona. It wasn't that I hadn't known we'd return. It was a two-week cruise; of course it had to end when we completed our Mediterranean route. It was just odd realizing the group of men—and Annie—who'd been strangers to me less than a month ago would soon scatter to their respective homes. Annie, Sam and Miguel, Joe and David, and Ty, Gabe, and their new baby, Mila, would all return to Nashville. André, Nick, and their rascal, Ethan, would fly home to Columbus. Which left Cooper, Nate, and me making our way back to Memphis.

A couple of weeks ago, I'd been worried about spending two weeks with such a tight-knit group, insecure that I would be the odd man out, the stranger crashing their family reunion. Those fears died the moment I met Sam and Miguel. It also became clear as a summer sunrise why that pair was the star around which all the others orbited.

Sam and Miguel were a force of nature. Individually, they were smokin' hot men who could've sold magazines just by gracing their covers. Together, they were love personified. I'd met couples who were in love. Most were young, but there were a few who'd been together forty or more years who could put the Disney love story department to shame.

But Sam and Miguel—they were a story unto themselves.

I'd never known two men so deeply entwined, yet so free to accept and embrace those around them. There was a palpable bond linking them that was so natural I couldn't conceive there had ever been a time when they weren't together. It didn't seem possible. Surely, they were conjoined, identical twins or halves of one soul who'd been separated at birth only to fall madly in love with each other the moment their eyes opened.

Okay, maybe that was a little dramatic.

But they were insanely connected, umbilically or not.

For the first few days of the trip, they'd flirted incessantly, dropping not-so-subtle hints about wanting a Steph spread on their meaty sandwich. Loafy sandwich? Meaty loaf?

None of that made sense.

They wanted me in the middle. But they *didn't*.

Flirting was their way to show acceptance, to make me feel wanted and part of the group. Despite wanting me to feel more comfortable, the whole notion of squeezing between them made me more skittish than a cat walking a tightrope over a foaming bath.

Don't get me wrong, I might've busted a sleeping nut or two dreaming about it. Fuck, it would've been hot. But it also felt dirty and wrong.

I might lose my gay card if anyone back home found out I felt that way, but screw them.

Sam and Miguel were an ideal, not some tawdry pair to be ravaged up against a wall … or over the kitchen table … or in the …

Dude, stop! I chided myself.

About halfway through the trip, they'd made it clear I was one of them, a part of the pack, a member of their family. Sam and Miguel also reaffirmed that their commitment was between the two of them and that adding a third wasn't in the cards.

I was oddly relieved. And disappointed. Which made me feel guilty … which also felt odd.

It was a whole circle of life thing in a sexual, emotional form.

And it wasn't just Sam and Miguel. I already knew Nate pretty well. We were teammates. We practiced or played together every day during the season. In the off-season, I spent more time at his and Coop's house than I did in my apartment. Going back to Memphis with them would be fine; great, even.

But the others ...

Nick and André were another pair of amazing guys, and their little boy, Ethan, might've been the cutest thing ever created. He'd taken to calling me Uncle Steph, and I couldn't wipe the smile off my face whenever he was around.

Annie was a walking Broadway show. I didn't think it was possible to be near her and be sad. Between her effervescent smile and the tunes that teased her lips, she fit in with the group as well as any of the men.

I didn't have much time to get to know the others well, but they seemed like great couples too. Even the congressman, David, was as likable and humble as the rest, not at all the arrogant prick I assumed a politician would be.

Leaving, seeing others go in their own directions, felt like losing a part of myself, something special I hadn't known was missing and had only just found.

Goodbyes sucked.

I stared over the railing as the city resolved into view. Smears became dots, then outlines, then a skyline. Cars appeared, then people. Finally, the harbor rose before us.

"Thanks, guys," I finally managed, still unable to turn and face either of them.

Miguel's arm found my shoulders again. Then Sam's fell atop his.

"Why don't we plan a visit soon?" Miguel said. "You come to Nashville with Coop and Nate? We'll return the favor once the season starts. I haven't seen Mango ball in a while. Might be nice to be a kid for a day."

A grin finally found my lips. Nothing made me happier than the giggles of the little ones at our games. There was something in the laughter of a child that filled my soul.

"I'd really like that," I said.

"Good," Sam said. "I'll tell Cooper to start planning. Knowing him, you'll take the Concord and the flight will last thirty seconds."

Miguel and I chuckled at the absurdity, knowing Coop would do it if he could.

"What happened with that sky mattress? He still texting?" Miguel's sudden change of subject jarred me out of my sentimentality.

I shook my head. "He's a flight attendant, thank you very much, and his name is Jack."

"Ooh, he knows his name. That's more than you could say for your hookups back in the day," Miguel said, shoving Sam playfully.

Sam puffed up. "I knew their names. They just didn't know mine. They kept calling me, 'Oh God,' or something like it. I found it endearing and entirely appropriate."

Miguel groaned. "Fuck, I walked into that, didn't I?"

I couldn't help but laugh. Those two just made me feel good.

"So?" Miguel said. "When's the last time you talked to Jacky Poo?"

I rolled my eyes. "He texted about an hour ago."

Sam whistled. "Have you been texting this whole time? And you haven't told us? Or let us see?"

I felt the sudden urge to protect the phone in my back pocket, but dared not move lest they find out where it was.

"Well, there wasn't much to report. We've just been texting, talking about nothing, that sort of thing."

Sam and Miguel exchanged a meaningful look.

"What?"

"That's how it starts. Trust me. Miguel stalked me by text until I gave in and married him."

Miguel laughed. "Stalked you? You practically begged me on your knees."

"Babe, that wasn't what I was doing on my knees and you know it."

"Whoa." I stepped back from the railing. "TMI, Mom and Dad. No one needs to hear about their parents doing ... whatever that was."

"Oh, come now, little one. Don't tell me you haven't dreamed of being the Steph-o-naise in a Sam and Miguel sandwich." Sam cocked a brow.

Miguel crossed his arms.

I turned four ... no, eight shades of red.

"I knew it!" Sam punched Miguel's shoulder. "He *has* dreamed about us. You owe me ten bucks."

I gaped.

Miguel laughed, reached into his wallet, and handed Sam a ten.

"You bet on—"

Sam wiggled his brows, grabbed Miguel's arm, and strode away.

I resumed staring into the water, unable to wipe the goofy grin off my face, still somewhat horrified by the exchange of currency I'd just witnessed.

My phone buzzed, and, magically, my grin widened as the screen lit up. It was Jack.

> **DeltaOne:** You in Barcelona yet?

> **Me:** I'm staring at the harbor now. Should dock soon.

> **DeltaOne:** When's your flight home?

> **Me:** Pretty soon. We don't even stay here overnight. I think we board around eight.

> **DeltaOne:** Cool.

> The dots danced for an eternity before words appeared.

> **DeltaOne:** So … pretend we were in the same city and could meet up. What would you want to do?

Just like that, I was fifteen and passing notes in class. The same butterflies I imagined assaulting every awkward teen suddenly battered away at my ribcage. Despite the unseasonably cool air and constant breeze off the sea, sweat beaded across my forehead. Our chat suddenly felt like that prepubescent conversation where your first date asked what kind of tree you would be if you were a tree.

Sweet Jesus, please don't ask me that. How the hell do I answer without looking like an idiot or whatever?

ME: I DON'T KNOW. I'M PRETTY SIMPLE.
DRINKS AND DINNER?

DELTAONE: WHAT WOULD YOU HAVE TO
DRINK?

This is the weirdest text conversation ever, and it's about to get worse. I can feel it.

ME: YOU'RE GONNA LAUGH AT ME.

DELTAONE: NO, I WON'T (MUCH).

ME: SEE! YOU WILL.

DELTAONE: COME ON, HUMOR ME.

ME: A GINGER SNAP.

I stared at the blank screen, willing the dots to dance, but nothing happened. Like, forever.

Seriously, dude, fucking respond. It's just a drink.

Why am I so freaked out?

Why are my palms sweating?

The dots finally wiggled, and I breathed again.

DELTAONE: I SWEAR I DIDN'T LAUGH
(MUCH), BUT I DID CHANGE YOUR NAME IN
MY PHONE FROM SURFER POO TO GINGER
SNAP.

ME: I TAKE BACK ALL THE NICE THINGS I EVER SAID TO YOU. I EVEN DEFENDED YOU TO SAM AND MIGUEL. THEY CALLED YOU A SKY MATTRESS!

DeltaOne: THAT ONE'S TOO OLD TO BE EFFECTIVE. NO POINTS. NOT EVEN FROM THE RUSSIAN JUDGE.

ME: FINE, BIG BOY, WHAT WOULD YOU DRINK?

DeltaOne: FIRST, YOU HAVEN'T SEEN JUST HOW BIG I AM YET, SO YOU MIGHT WANT TO SAVE THAT DESCRIPTION. SECOND, I WOULD HAVE A DELICATE GLASS OF PINOT NOIR TO START THE MEAL, THEN SWITCH TO CABERNET SAUVIGNON WITH THE MAIN COURSE.

ME: I DON'T KNOW WHICH HAS ME MORE SPEECHLESS: THE SIZE TEASE OR THE HOITY-TOITYNESS OF YOUR DRINKING HABITS.

DeltaOne: I PREFER THE WORD "REFINED." I CAN'T HELP THAT YOU'RE A BARBARIAN. WELL, A FRUITY BARBARIAN.

ME: NO, NO, NO. YOU WILL NOT NICKNAME ME OR CALL ME A FRUITY BARBARIAN. THAT IS FORBIDDEN. I USE MY TRUMP CARD.

DELTAONE: NO ONE GAVE YOU ANY CARDS, CONAN THE COCONUT SPLITTER.

ME: GOD, I HATE YOU. THAT'S TERRIBLE!

DELTAONE: YOU DON'T HATE ME, BUT YES, THAT IS TERRIBLE. I'LL WORK ON IT.

ME: REALLY UNNECESSARY.

DELTAONE: OH, BUT IT IS.

DELTAONE: GOTTA RUN. EMMA'S CALLING AND I KNOW BETTER THAN TO KEEP HER WAITING. HAVE A FUN LAST DAY IN BARCELONA.

My cheeks hurt from grinning at the screen. Sam and Miguel could *never* see any of that.

Chapter Eight

Return Flight

Steph

THE GANG SPENT THE hours between deboarding and our flight home sitting on the patio of a local restaurant, eating, drinking, and laughing together. We consciously ignored the ticking clock that would soon send us on our separate journeys.

Annie regaled us with song after song, reveling in the applause that followed, both from our group and from diners at tables scattered around us. David told stories from his time in the SEALs and answered a relentless stream of questions about his experiences in Congress. Oddly, the two sounded like similar battlefields, complete with their own fired shots and exploded bombs. Cooper was in rare form, his word vomit scattering to the farthest corners of the city.

I couldn't remember laughing so much in so few hours.

Little Ethan hovered over baby Mila, letting her grip his thumb in her chubby fingers. I wasn't sure which of them cooed more. Clearly, Nick and André would need to trade visits with Ty and Gabe on a regular basis, lest they each face tiny, child-sized pitchforks and torches.

Through it all, Sam and Miguel sat hand in hand, smiling and scanning the room, proud parents who couldn't take their eyes off the family they'd created. When they did occasionally break eye contact with the rest of us to enjoy a private moment, it seemed the world stopped spinning in their gaze. I'd never been so transfixed by a couple, and, from the dreamy sighs I heard around me, neither had the others.

It's funny. I'd never been surrounded by so much love and acceptance, so many families whose bonds were knitted together, forming a quilt of support stronger than folded steel. And yet, in the middle of it all, I'd never felt so alone. I wasn't the only single person there—Annie was my compadre in eschewing couple-dom—but I was the only guy. And, let's face it, being single at twenty-five was different from being single in one's seventies. At least, that's what I told myself when I watched Annie.

Miguel's fingers traced the roadmap of Sam's hand, and I couldn't stop my mind from drifting back to before my parents fell out of love. That's what divorce was, right? It's how I'd seen it back then, as a seventeen-year-old. My heart ached to see them hold each other the way these guys did, but I knew that was a wasted dream. My hope now was that one day, I might find a man who looked at me with a fraction of the affection in their eyes.

I sipped sangria and tried to smile at Annie's hilarity.

I tried not to think about happier times when my mom rode the waves and Dad cheered her on, his hand on my shoulder and my brother still with us.

I tried to live in the present.

But the past was a looming mist, undeterred by mortal interest. It crept and plodded, covering and consuming, enveloping all who stood too near.

My loneliness was an impenetrable shroud, a curtain through which no light could escape, no hope could live.

How could one from a broken home find hope? How could one who felt so broken be hopeful?

"You okay?"

I hadn't noticed Sam release Miguel's hand and stand. I'd missed him walk around the table. When his hands gripped my shoulders and he whispered in my ear, I nearly tossed sangria across the patio.

"Oh, yeah, sure. I'm good. Shit, you scared me."

His chuckle was a tiger's purr, low and deep. "Liar," he whispered. "But we'll let you get away with it this time. Just know you can talk to us, okay?"

I hated Sam and Miguel. They were hot and sexy and muscular and loving and kind and sweet and affectionate and considerate and amazing friends. Fuck them. Assholes.

Who got to be so perfect? It just wasn't right.

And yet, I don't think I'd ever felt as close to them as I did in that moment. They *saw* me. They got me.

That was special, right?

"Thanks, Sam," I choked out. "I'm okay. Just got a little lost in the past."

He squeezed my shoulders, then kissed the side of my head like a mother might. "You're a great guy, Steph. We love you."

Fucking Sam.

I lost it right there. Tears dove out of my eyes like tiny, wet Cirque du Soleil acrobats, spinning and falling. They tickled as they danced, and I swatted them away, irritated by their presence. Sam's arms were around me faster than I could react, his head nuzzled into the side of my neck. The musky scent of a man who'd just flown in the same clothes for nearly a day assailed my nose, granting an odd comfort in my moment of distress.

I probably should've excused myself, fled to the restroom to gather my wits, but Sam was a strong-ass man. I don't think I could've moved if I'd wanted to. So I did the only thing I could: I surrendered to his embrace and let the tears fall.

The others *had* to notice, but I glanced through watery windows to find their conversation unabated. Annie still sang. Neighboring tables still clapped.

"They know I've got you," Sam whispered, reading my thoughts. "I've got you, Steph."

And I knew, without a moment's doubt, he did.

For the first time in years, I no longer felt so alone.

THE SECURITY LINES WERE a piece of cake. The Delta One logo on our tickets probably helped, but from what I saw, the Spanish were masters of moving people. We slipped through check-in, customs, and security faster than the one security checkpoint had moved back in Miami.

The others headed toward the gate, while I stepped away for one last pit stop. By the time I boarded the plane, everyone in our group was settled into their seats and rummaging through the goodie bags waiting for us.

"Welcome aboard, sir," a young woman with pulled-back blonde hair and a sassy smile said. She eyed me like a butcher might a slab of beef right before he whacked it with his cleaver.

"Uh, thanks." I glanced at my ticket. "I'm 3B."

She pointed with an open palm. "I know, Steph. You're that way."

I tried not to gape. Then I realized she'd called me "Steph," the shortened form of my name used by friends. I started to ask how she knew me, but she winked and fled to the back of the plane before I could finish.

Dazed, I turned left toward our section. When I got to my seat, two things stopped me in the aisle.

First, there was a drink waiting, and it wasn't the champagne everyone else was enjoying. A squat crystal tumbler was filled with a single ball of ice and golden liquid. Several pieces of assorted fruit lounged on a toothpick beneath a colorful paper umbrella.

The second show stopper was even more strange: a single piece of ginger root stared up at me from my seat.

I glanced around the cabin. There were no attendants visible.

That was odd too. Delta One was *never* abandoned. Delta One was where toes were sucked ... metaphorically, of course.

But there was no one attending to our people. No toes were being sucked.

Sam and Miguel peered up, again seated in the row behind me. Each of them wore the same shit-eating grin I'd come to fear. They knew something, but there was no chance they were going to speak.

So much for Sam "having my back."

Unsure what else to do, I turned and stowed my rolling bag in the bin above Nate's window seat, then picked up the ginger and sat. The tiny television was already on, an old episode of *Baywatch* playing. I didn't even know *Baywatch* was a thing on planes.

Without thinking, I grabbed the drink and took a sip.

"Like it?" A voice I hadn't heard in weeks tickled my ears as bubbles tickled my tongue. I looked up to find Jack, inky hair flopping in all directions, crystal eyes sparkling in the cabin lights, standing by my seat with one hand resting on the seat back in front of me.

"It's a ginger snap. If I recall, that's your drink of choice," he said, a playful grin teasing his lips.

"Jack? What are you doing here?"

He laughed, and I swear I heard Sam howl behind me. "I work here, remember?"

I stared, openmouthed, unable to think.

"You told me when you were going home, so I requested to work the flight. I know how much you missed me, and thought this would give you another chance to watch my ass as I walk by a hundred times."

Miguel coughed through a fit of laughter behind me. Ass-holes.

Jack leaned down and a sweet hint of cologne spun my gears. "You *are* happy to see me, aren't you, Ginger Snap?"

God, his lips were so full and wet … and close. His breath was warm and—

"Uh, yeah, of course. I mean, sure. Right. Dude, definitely."

The entire cabin erupted, and echoes of "dude" bounded off the cabin walls as the conversation was repeated from one row to the next.

Apparently, Sam and Miguel hadn't been the only ones eavesdropping.

Crimson spread from my neck to my ears to my forehead.

Jack, heedless of any steel buns who might be nearby, whispered, "Good," then leaned down and kissed me ... right on the lips.

Yeah ... all that ... before takeoff.

Chapter Nine

Home Sweet Home

Jack

The flight home felt like a nine-hour date mixed with waiting tables. Still, seeing Steph again reminded me why I'd been so excited to take that leg. He was even cuter than I'd remembered, with his square jaw, brackish hair, and lopsided grin. He hadn't had a haircut in the weeks preceding his vacation, and the extra ten days had made it a complete mess. It was all I could do to keep my fingers out of it.

The fact he flitted between confident and skittish made him even more adorable. It also made teasing him irresistible. I'd never known anyone who blushed as easily as Stephan Breeden—and his rosy cheeks consumed my thoughts from the moment the plane landed and we said goodbye.

Fortunately, there was no time to pine over a boy when I returned, as Eli was lounging on my couch, watching a rerun of *The Great British Baking Show* with Rufus curled up against his chest inside his zip-up hoodie.

"Honey, I'm home," I said in my best imitation of Lucy's husband.

"Get your ass in here. They're about to do the technical challenge and it sounds brutal. Paul is such an asshole to these poor bakers."

The Great British Baking Show was a television competition featuring amateur bakers from across Britain. Most of the contestants were pretty good, but none were professional. The technical challenge was the second of three challenges featured in each episode, but unlike the first and last of the bakes where practice was allowed, the technical was a surprise to the participants—and it usually involved cryptic instructions such as "make the batter," and a finished product none of the bakers had ever seen. It was a morbid combination of gladiatorial spectator sport where we hoped for a face-plant and a culinary competition where a few shocked everyone by rising to the challenge.

What gay wouldn't enjoy a show that combined an opportunity to judge and snark while recognizing true talent in the kitchen?

I left my roller by the door and threw myself onto the couch. Eli promptly scooched so close we were practically in each other's laps, then hooked his arm around mine like he was about to walk me down the aisle.

It was pretty much how we watched TV together. God, I loved Eli.

"So, how's Ginger Snap?" I'd made the horrible mistake of telling him about that nickname.

"Jack," I emphasized, "was great. I mean, we were on a plane, and I was working. He was as great as he could be while I had to shuffle around serving endless food and drinks."

He nudged me with his elbow. "Come on, details. Did you take him to the galley and clean his kitchen?"

"Eli!"

"What about check his dipstick? That's a plane thing, isn't it?"

"You're terrible."

"So that's not a no to the dipstick checking?"

"No!"

"To which? Dipstick or kitchen? You don't have man-floss caught in your teeth, do you?"

I threw my head back, a combination of exasperation and amusement. "No, there was no flossing or lubing or dipsticking. I kissed him at the beginning of the flight and that was all he got."

"How disappointing."

I wanted to argue, but he was right. I'd dreamed up a dozen ways to get him naked on that flight, but never had the courage to suggest one. Truth be told, I wasn't sure I wanted to do that with Steph. He was a good guy, not some hookup. Whatever was sparking between us deserved better than an uncomfortable blow job in a cramped airplane restroom barely large enough for one person.

"Not really. We talked a lot."

He sat up and turned to face me. "Jackson Pollock Anderson Cooper Sutton, you talked a lot?"

I tried not to laugh, but that was a good one.

"Yeah, it was easy. I mean, you know how it is with some guys, like forcing a conversation, like they can't hold down their end or don't have enough going on in their heads to make things interesting? Steph wasn't like that, not even for a minute. It just flowed, easy and free."

"Honey, that was not the kind of easy and free flowing I had in mind for you and a hot surfer." He slapped the back of his hand against his forehead, a Southern belle about to faint. "I have so much to teach."

I shoved him playfully, earning a muffled yawl from Rufus within his jacket.

"I think … I think I like this guy, E. I don't know when we'll see each other again, but I know we will. I'm pretty sure he likes me too."

"Oh shit. Danger, Will Robinson. The sky mattress has feelings."

"Sky mattress?" I said in mock offense. "That would be *you*, not me. I don't know anyone who can stretch their legs over their head in the polyester shit we wear like you. You put the love in Luv Jet."

He pretended to flick his hair. "Nobody gives service in the sky like Eli."

"That should be the airline's slogan."

"With a big ole picture of my smiling mug on the plane. Damn straight."

I laughed. "Nothing straight about it."

"Mmm kay."

Paul and Pru had reemerged to perform the judging of the technical challenge, so all talk of airplanes and boys paused. I could try, but wrenching Eli's attention from this part of the show was pointless.

Nothing stood in the way of a good baking disaster.

Chapter Ten

Memphis Blues

Steph

It felt strange walking back into my apartment. My roommate, Alden, was at home in Wisconsin for the off-season, not scheduled to return until right before spring training. Nate was one of four Mangoes who lived in Memphis year-round. The other two were married with small children. Even in the off-season, when there were no games or practices, the families of those men consumed their every waking moment. It was as if they tried to make up for the endless hours away from their wives and kids when baseball slept.

I guess I got it. It made sense. Still, it left me floating in my own ocean, an island with nothing but chilly sea bashing about.

My apartment—the one that hadn't been disturbed or dusted during the weeks we were at sea—was a monochrome reminder of just how alone I was.

I tossed my keys in the bowl by the door, then struggled with my oversized luggage down the short hallway to my bedroom.

Most of my clothes were in desperate need of laundering, but my heart wasn't in housework. I scooted the bags against the far wall, flopped onto the bed, and stared up at the popcorn pimples of my ceiling.

Who thought of putting popcorn on a ceiling? I wondered. *Was a smooth ceiling just too boring? Were they alone, staring up, and decided to paint pregnancy on the surface?*

Yeah, I had weird thoughts when I was bored.

Ding.

I practically leaped at the familiar sound of an incoming text message. Science attributed a quick blast of dopamine to text message tones, delivering a burst of euphoria and excitement upon their arrival. I wasn't sure what the "in like" chemical was, but I was pretty sure a text from Jack triggered a cocktail of the two.

And I loved a good cocktail.

I ran back into the kitchen where I'd left my phone, sliding toward the counter in socked feet on hardwoods, and flicked it to life. The dopamine made a Pac-Man dying sound in my brain when I saw the text wasn't from my favorite flight attendant.

NATESTRINGEROFFICIAL: DUDE.

ME: DID YOU JUST DUDE A SURFER? ARE YOU TRYING TO SWEET TALK ME?

NateStringerOfficial: Of course. You know I've wanted to get in your pants since you became our catcher. The way you squat behind the plate like you're dropping a turd. That's so hot.

Me: Ha. Nothing screams "do me" like dropping a deuce.

NateStringerOfficial: You're a sick man, Steph Breeden. Very sick.

Me: I'm sick? You texted me. You invoked poop imagery, and not the kind involving a cute emoji. I may never be able to catch without needing to poop again. Thanks for that.

NateStringerOfficial: Great. I'm sure the umps will excuse you for a potty break anytime you like. You're not farting back there, are you?

Me: Like a demon. It keeps the batters off balance.

This conversation was going nowhere fast, but that defined most conversations with the guys. We were all basically twenty-something eight-year-olds who got paid to play our favorite childhood game. It was the perfect recipe for immature guy behavior—and we never missed a good opportunity.

NateStringerOfficial: Alright, Poop-o-Matic, I texted for a reason that had nothing to do with your disgusting bowel habits.

Me: There are other reasons for you to text?

NateStringerOfficial: Asshole. Come and have dinner. Coop is ordering from some new Greek place that's supposed to be the bomb. We can kill each other on the PlayStation while he talks.

Me: His stories do take a minute.

NateStringerOfficial: Minute? I'm married to him. They last a lifetime.

Me: And you love it. He's hot, sexy, and adorable. What more could you want? You're fucking lucky, dude.

There was a pause in the flow, then the dots wiggled.

NateStringerOfficial: I'm the luckiest guy alive. Cooper is beyond amazing.

ME: YEAH, HE MARRIED DOWN, THAT'S FOR SURE.

NateStringerOfficial: I THINK THE TERM IS "SETTLED."

ME: YES! THAT'S IT. COOPER TOTALLY SETTLED. YOU MARRIED UP, BUT HE FUCKING SETTLED.

NateStringerOfficial: YOU REALLY KNOW HOW TO BUILD A BROTHER UP.

ME: OH, DID PUDDIN' NEED SOME LOVIN'? I MISSED THE SIGNALS.

NateStringerOfficial: FUCK OFF. WE EAT AT SEVEN. GET YOUR ASS OVER HERE AS SOON AS YOU CAN SO I CAN BEAT YOU BACK INTO THE EIGHTH CENTURY.

ME: YAY. A SPANKING. I CAN HARDLY WAIT.

NateStringerOfficial: I'M HANGING UP NOW.

ME: THIS IS A TEXT. YOU DON'T ACTUALLY HANG UP. YOU JUST STOP RESPONDING.

Well, I hadn't received the orgasmic level of dopamine or endorphin or whatever the fuck hit I got when Jack texted, but it had been fun and gave me plans for the evening that didn't involve connecting the unborn babies on my bedroom ceiling.

I'd have to raise a glass to small blessings when I saw the guys.

It was a little after four when I walked into Coop and Nate's house. Nate was already warming up in front of the TV, his thumbs a blur on the game controller thing. He prided himself on being a master of video games, but he'd yet to beat me in a single combat. I grew up riding waves and crushing friends in the den. It didn't matter which game he chose, he'd have to rig it to beat me, and he knew it.

Still, we were eight-year-old boys in need of mindless competition.

"Where's Coop?" I asked as I fell onto the couch beside my bestie.

"Went to work out. I think he had something to check on at the dojang too."

"Gotta keep the little woman working."

Nate nearly dropped his controller. "Don't let him hear you. He's a fifth-degree black belt. He can kick your ass in four directions without breaking a sweat."

"Is he as good at *licking* your ass?" I winked.

This time Nate actually tossed the controller on the cushioned ottoman. "You're terrible. You know it's against the rules to ask—"

"About how good your hubby is in the sack?" My eyes widened. "Seriously, dude? Have you even been in our locker room? We're dudes *and* baseball players. It's not only recommended, it's required that we talk about cock and pussy."

Nate shook his head. "Not when it's my man's pussy."

"Oh, you like his pussy better than his cock?" I sat up on my knees and leaned in. "This is good. Keep talking. Is it all tight, or is he stretched out so you can pound him without popping off too fast?"

"Jesus, Steph!" Nate stood and stepped toward the kitchen. "I need a drink. You want anything? Not that you need alcohol for encouragement."

"Sex on the beach, please. Really, with you and Coop and his loose asshole."

"Steph!"

I laughed. I might be an easy mark for Sam and Miguel, but Nate was the ultimate wimp when it came to teasing. The guys were brutal and somehow managed to make the one dark-skinned man on the team blush. It wasn't red or pink, more like an odd purple, but there was no mistaking the mark of utter embarrassment. And we loved it.

"Fine. If you don't want to talk about his loose anus, let's talk about his rockin' cock or bangin' balls. Do they swing to and fro, or are they more snugglers? Snuggies? I never remember the right term.”

Nate appeared, two beers in hand, his face a hilarious mix of appalled and amused.

“Drink your fucking beer,” he said, holding a bottle toward me.

I held it up, as though examining it. “Is that about his size? You’ve told me he was impressive. I think you said something about a truck driving up your ass. That must mean *you’re* the one with the loose lips. Careful, those sink ships, you know.”

“God, I swear I haven’t forsaken you. Why do you call me to suffer?” he said, looking at the ceiling.

I punched his shoulder. “You love me, and you know it.”

“Like a heart attack.”

“Speaking of heart attacks,” I said. “What are you losing at tonight? Let’s get our game on.”

Nate took a long pull from his bottle, then set it on the end table. “How about Black Ops?”

“Cold War?”

“Done, comrade!” He saluted in the way I assumed he thought looked Soviet but was more like a contestant wiping their forehead on *Dancing with the Stars*.

“So, we’re Sovs?” I said.

“Damn straight. We’ve played the good guys long enough.”

I chuckled. “I think a few million people living on the other side of the world might take exception to you classifying us as the good guys.”

“Yeah, but they’re the bad guys. Of course they would say that.”

I shook my head. I loved Nate. He was one of a kind.

One disc load and a mind-bending number of clicks later, we were scooched forward and focused on the intense battle playing out on the screen.

"Hey, babe," Cooper's voice called as the front door squealed open in the distance.

Nate kept his eyes riveted to the screen. "Hey, hon. Steph's here, being an asshole and making me look bad. Can you come beat him up for me?"

The lithe, muscular form of Cooper Hawk, crowned in reddish blond hair that beamed almost as brightly as his lips, appeared around the corner. Sweat was soaking through his white T-shirt, leaving little of his insane definition to the imagination. In odd juxtaposition to his quirky, often amusing personality, Coop moved with the grace of a panther stalking his pray. I half expected him to duck a punch or throw a roundhouse kick at any moment, even in his own living room, just to prove he could.

"The kids say hi," Coop said to Nate before leaning down and kissing him on the top of his head.

He leaned over, bumping shoulders. "Coop might be the super ninja, but his students freak out over the baseball player when he visits."

Coop choked on his own laughter. "Super ninja? Ninjas are Japanese. Taekwondo originated in Korea, which is a totally different country on the mainland of the continent, not the islands of the Rising Sun, and ninjas are all about stealth and spying and assassination, while my chosen form is more about inner peace, balance, and the art of self-defense. Did you know the words *tae* and *kwon* mean foot and hand in English? *Do* means art. So it's literally the foot and hand art, nothing at all like the throwing stars and sneaking of the ninjas. You really should do your research before coming up with nicknames that make even less sense than whatever weak-ass strategy you're playing at in that game, because even I can see that you're about to get squashed like a bug by those three tanks and all those troops, and there's nothing even Steph, as good as he is, can do about it. He really should abandon your sorry butt and save himself."

As usual, Coop's rambling left the pair of us speechless, though I was unsure which part had truly stolen the moment: his comparison between ancient martial arts, his analysis of our game, or him calling out Nate's nickname game in front of me.

I laughed and tossed down my controller, reaching for my beer. "Have I told you how much I love Coop?"

"Dear God, don't encourage him."

"Technically"—Coop planted a fist on his hip—"a master of the fifth dan needs no encouragement. He is self-motivated and contains the self-control to handle whatever is thrown at him by whichever weak-ass, nickname-addled man attempts to box him in."

Nate turned to me and mouthed, "Help me."

I was too busy doubling over to lend a hand. Cooper Hawk was the only one of his kind.

"I'm going to clean up. Food should be here any minute." A second later, he called from down the hall, "Steph, you want to watch me shower? I saw you staring at my nipples. They are pretty hot."

Now it was Nate's turn to laugh as color flooded my face. "Is he—?"

"Of course not, idiot," Nate said, smacking me with a sofa cushion. "He's just baiting you. Don't let him. He'll start talking again."

"I heard that," Coop yelled from the bedroom. "Make yourselves useful and set the table."

"Yes, dear," Nate called back. He stood. "Come on. He's right. I was about to die anyway."

We grabbed our empty bottles and headed into the kitchen. Before our trip, I'd known Coop was rich. His grandmother had died and left him a fortune, but he and Nate lived a pretty modest life. Their house was in a nicer section of Memphis, but it didn't scream money. They were regular dudes living a comfortable life.

Now, with the perspective of the lavish vacation we'd just returned from, I knew Coop wasn't just rich, he was fucking loaded. He must've dropped a couple hundred grand on that vacation without batting an eye. In fact, at almost every turn, he sought more ways to spend money and spoil his little family. We were all dying to know just how big of a pot of gold he'd inherited, but none of us dared broach the topic.

Standing in their kitchen, surrounded by neat marble counters and the crisp lines of well-finished cabinets, I couldn't help but wonder at the decidedly middle-class life they lived. Even the plates Nate pulled from the cabinet were stamped IKEA on the bottom; and, while I had no issue with the place other than the fact I could never find my way out without assistance, it wasn't exactly known as a shopping haven for the wealthy.

I smiled at the glasses Nate pulled out of the upper cabinet. They were the same ones we had back home, when I was a boy growing up in the simple house of a surfer mom and an office dad. We weren't poor, but we struggled to meet national averages. Seeing those glasses, knowing Coop and Nate, somehow endeared them to me even more.

They were just good folk, plain and simple.

Ding.

I wasn't sure if my heart beat faster than my hand flew to my back pocket, but it was definitely a race.

"Ooh." Nate's eyes glittered. "Text from lover boy?"

"Fuck off," I said, flipping my thumb across the screen to wake it up.

> **DeltaOne:** What are you wearing?

Oh God. Did he want to have text sex? What was that even called? Stexing? Fuxting? Wait, it's sexting, right? It really didn't matter. I was standing in Nate's kitchen—no one was pulling out body parts and oiling them up. Besides, it wasn't something Jack and I had ever talked about. What the fuck was I thinking?

> **Me:** Um, jeans and a black T-shirt.

> **DeltaOne:** That's hot.

> **Me:** You think?

> **DeltaOne:** On you? Hell yeah. You could wear a grocery bag and make it hot.

> **Me:** Who is this and what have you done with Jack?

"Did he ask what you're wearing?" Nate asked.

I fumbled the phone. "No. He wouldn't ... I mean, didn't ... well, he did, but no, he wouldn't ... hasn't ever asked ... oh, fuck off."

Nate laughed as he set the last of the silverware on the table. "So he *did* ask what you're wearing. Are you about to iFuck?"

Dammit, that was good. Why hadn't I thought of that one?

"No, we're not iFucking—whatever that is. We've never even talked about sex. He's just teasing or being funny or whatever."

"Why so flustered, little one?" Cooper asked as he stepped into the kitchen.

Great. Two against one.

"I need to take this call ... I mean, text. I'll be right back."

I fled to the safety of the foyer. Several texts had come in since the dynamic duo's teasing had begun.

> **DELTAONE:** OH, IT'S ME. YOU'VE JUST NEVER SEEN ME WORKED UP.

> **DELTAONE:** AND THINKING ABOUT YOU GETS ME WORKED UP.

> **DELTAONE:** LIKE, REALLY WORKED UP. DO YOU KNOW HOW MANY THINGS I WANT TO DO TO YOU?

Oh God. Oh God. Oh God.

I wasn't a prude or anything. I'd slept with my share of guys, even though "my share" amounted to what I could count on one hand.

Fuck. Why did Jack fluster me so badly?

Crap, now he thinks I'm upset or scared or running or … fuck, fuck, fuck. What should I say to him? What should I type? I could make a joke about iSex or iFucking or whatever iDiddling we might do.

My thumbs hovered over the keyboard, shaking like a dog in the vet's waiting room. I was a grown-ass man. I was strong and brave. I was not scared of talking sex or whoopie or whatever this was, with anybody. Except maybe Jack. He scared me.

Why the fuck did he *scare* me?

ME: SORRY. GUESS YOU CAUGHT ME A LITTLE OFF GUARD.

DELTAONE: DID YOU LIKE IT?

ME: THE SEXY TALK OR THE BEING CAUGHT OFF GUARD?

DELTAONE: EITHER.

ME: WELL … YEAH. I GUESS. I MEAN, YES. FUCK, YOU TURN ME INSIDE OUT, JACK.

DELTAONE: AND THAT'S A GOOD THING?

ME: I'M STILL TRYING TO FIGURE THAT OUT, BUT I THINK SO.

DELTAONE: DOES THE IDEA OF GETTING NAKED WITH ME INTEREST YOU? EXCITE YOU?

ME: GOD, YES.

DELTAONE: WELL, THERE YOU HAVE IT.

ME: ANYWAY, HOW ARE YOU? WHAT DID YOU DO TODAY?

DELTAONE: HA HA. YOU THINK YOU CAN CHANGE THE SUBJECT LIKE THAT? YOU DON'T KNOW ME WELL YET.

Something about his use of the word "yet" sent a thrill through my chest. I liked the idea of getting to know him, of there being more than just a text buddy here.

> **ME:** YET? THAT SOUNDS LIKE YOU WANT MORE THAN A PEN PAL.

> **DELTAONE:** OH, I DO. SERIOUSLY, I DO.

> **ME:** ME TOO.

For the first time since the conversation began, there was a pause, as if Jack was the one with words stuck in his throat. By the time the dots danced again, Cooper and Nate had appeared and were looming over my shoulder.

"What's he saying?" Coop asked.

"I can't read the screen. He keeps turning away," Nate said, bumping my back as his chin rested on my shoulder.

"Guys!"

"You know you're going to have to tell us eventually, right?" There was no room for argument in Coop's voice. He sounded like I imagined his grandmother might when she was alive. From what he'd said, that woman was impossible to deny.

"Yes, Mother. Can I have a minute? I'll tell you both all about it."

Nate, already breathing heavily on my neck, reached up and bit my ear lobe.

"Ow!"

"That's for making us wait," he said, and the pair giggled their way back into the den.

When I looked down, there were more messages waiting.

DeltaOne: I want to see you.

DeltaOne: For real, not just on here or on FaceTime.

DeltaOne: I would come out there, but I have flight training and can't get away. You could come to Atlanta. I could show you the town.

DeltaOne: Please don't make me wait … or beg. I will beg. I'm not above it. Down on my knees and everything. Although, while I'm down there …

I actually snorted at that last one.

Me: Yes! Stop. No begging or knees. I want to see you too.

DeltaOne: Really? No knees? I'm good on my knees.

Me: You're impossible.

DeltaOne: Oh no, I'm quite possible. Get your ass over here and I'll show you.

Me: I walked into that, didn't I?

DeltaOne: Yep!

Me: When were you thinking? Spring training doesn't start until March. I need to get back into a good workout routine, but that's really all I have to do until then.

DeltaOne: I can do pretty much anytime, just need enough lead time to arrange your flight. My buddy pass is about to come in handy!

DeltaOne: Oh—Rufus is excited you're coming. He just crawled into my lap and pawed at the phone.

Me: Aww. How is little Ruf?

DeltaOne: Ugly as fuck and cute as ever.

Me: Can't wait to meet him.

DeltaOne: You realize we've been texting since the week before Christmas? It's halfway through January. That must be some kind of text dating record.

ME: I'm pretty sure others have done this longer. Is it weird we haven't actually talked on the phone? Or used FaceTime?

DeltaOne: Nah. Nothing we do is weird. Other people are irrelevant. We're amazing. And yes, it's a record for me too. By now, your legs would've already been stuck in your hoop earrings or …

ME: Ha. I see.

DeltaOne: I'm looking at the calendar. What about the first week in February?

ME: A whole week?

DeltaOne: Or a few days. Whatever. Wait, I have a long haul to Paris that week. What about the next week? I haven't scheduled that far yet.

ME: The week of National Singles Day? You really want to jinx us like that?

DeltaOne: ???

Me: It's an annual week of mourning where people wear black. Singles, that is, mourning the fact that love is dead, culminating in the holiday marking the St. Valentine's Day massacre.

DeltaOne: I'm pretty sure that's not what Valentine's Day is supposed to be about.

Me: That's news to me. I'll come, but we're wearing black and mourning like proper single gays. We can't let happy couples have their way with us on our holy week.

DeltaOne: If it gets your happy ass out here, I'll wear a black veil.

Me: Promise? That sounds hot. And my ass really is happy, btw, vertical smile and all.

DeltaOne: Gay Zeus, that was bad. Are you weird or what?

Me: Guess you'll find out soon enough.

ME: AND SPEAKING OF GAY ZEUS, GREEK JUST GOT HERE. GOTTA JET.

DeltaOne: YOU WHINE ABOUT ME ON MY KNEES BUT PUT OUT FOR SOME GREEK DUDE?

ME: HA. NO, GREEK FOOD. COOPER ORDERED AND IT JUST SHOWED UP.

DeltaOne: SOUNDS TASTY. THINK OF ME WHEN HONEY DRIBBLES DOWN YOUR CHIN.

ME: I DON'T EVEN KNOW HOW TO RESPOND.

DeltaOne: THEN DON'T. I HAVE A FLIGHT TO BOOK. SEE YOU SOON!

ME: SEE YOU SOON.

Chapter Eleven

On Guard!

Jack

THE REST OF THE week dragged like a tin can behind a newly-weds' car, all battered, bouncy, and noisy as hell. Everything I touched seemed to fall apart. I didn't have another flight until the next week, so my time was filled with logging flight hours with Collum, working out, and listening to Eli berate me for whatever had him worked up in the moment. The one positive that came with his rapid-fire ADHD was that no topic ever stuck in his mind long enough to involve a full beating. He'd move on quickly to some extra reason to whack me senseless. If nothing else, it kept things interesting.

"Sweetie." Eli propped his elbows on the restaurant table, laced his fingers, and nested his chin atop them. "Why are you playing footsie with this boy?"

"Footsie? What are you talking about?"

"First"—he sat upright and raised his index finger—"he lives halfway around the world. You and I both know long-distance relationships don't work. There are more than enough hotties in Atlanta to satisfy even your meager appetite. Just graze here at home and let the foreign cows be."

I sipped my coffee and resisted the urge to interrupt. Steph wasn't a cow. He was a hot surfer. He didn't deserve a bovine comparison.

Shit, I had it bad. I wanted to defend him.

"And second"—Eli's middle finger joined his index—"you two are being all third-grade passing notes in class with all this texting. You've known each other over a month. How many actual conversations have you had?"

I stuck my chin out. "We talk every day."

"Talk? You've never talked, except when you were in uniform and working." His index finger became a sword, stabbing toward me. "You either don't like this guy as much as you say you do, or you're chicken. I've known you for years. You've never been chicken of any boy. You crush them under your heel, bend them to your will, flick your hair until they swoon ... that sort of thing."

"You make me sound like Helen of Troy."

"Without the tits, yes. You totally are Helen, especially with that hair. I hate you for that, by the way."

"Thanks, I think."

"It was a rare compliment. Don't let it go to your head." He winked. "Back to the boy."

"Steph."

"Whatever." He crossed his arms. "You need to either up the stakes and actually talk to him or move on. I can't have a hottie best friend acting like a pussoi."

I nearly spat my coffee. "A what?"

"A pussoi. A French pussy. It's classier than the American one, and generally comes shaved with a thin mustache."

"You're a sick man."

He grinned. "*Merci, mon ami.*"

"I invited Steph to come to Atlanta. We're making all the arrangements now."

His eyes widened, and he clapped the tips of his fingers several times like some dastardly character in an old cartoon. "Okay, okay. That's good, little one. Tell Aunty Eli all about it."

"We're still working on dates. He's in the off-season, so he can come pretty much whenever, but I have flight training, then my Guard weekend, then two long hauls back-to-back. We're thinking the second week in February."

"Valentine's week?"

I shrugged. "Why not?"

"I might hurl. Give me a minute."

"Thanks a lot! You're the one pushing us to talk or meet or whatever. There you have it. We're meeting, for real."

"Fine, I'm impressed. Maybe you *are* learning."

I shook my head. "Learning? We did that *before* your little tirade."

"Don't be silly. This is just my latest rant. You knew Hurricane Eli was brewing and whipped out your parasol. Good man."

"Parasol? Aren't they used for sun? They would not remotely help in a hurricane."

"Pish. They are used for what I say they are used for ... and *nothing* helps with Hurricane Eli. Don't argue with my greatness."

I laughed. "Yes, Ghandi."

"I prefer Madonna."

"The Virgin Mother?"

"Of course not," he scoffed. "*The* Madonna, the singer, her early eighties iteration with the metal boobs. Don't you know anything?"

"Why do I listen to you? Seriously, why?"

"Because I'm fabulous and always right, and you know it." He spread his arms wide. "Anyway, I've made my point. The rest is up to you. I have a down and back to Tampa, and the Luv Jet waits for no man—not even Madonna."

"Yes, your holiness. Best you get a move on. It's my turn with the check. You go on."

"Thanks, sweetness," he said, hopping up and kissing me on both cheeks in an odd mix of European greeting and gay mugging. I was fairly certain the gesture wasn't supposed to include tongue.

I wiped my cheek with a napkin as he sauntered away, humming "Everybody" loudly and pantomiming gestures from a video I didn't recognize.

Eli was ... Eli.

I tossed cash on the table, but found it hard to stand. The Flying Biscuit was our favorite breakfast spot because it was too cramped to be cozy. Situated in the heart of Midtown, it was usually filled with gays getting their brunch on. Today was no different. There was more eye candy sitting around me than in Forrest Gump's box of chocolates.

A muscle head in a tight T-shirt two tables over said something to the twink sitting across from him. It caught my ear because his sentence ended with "dude." Something in my subconscious brain kicked in and all the men at all the tables vanished, and only Steph sat at a table in the corner, his blondish hair wiggling in the A/C blasting overhead, and a broad, toothy grin plastered across his lips.

My heart skipped a beat.

I blinked, then blinked again.

And all the men returned.

It had been some trick of my mind. Or had it been a tease of my heart?

God, I was turning into a Disney character. This was bad.

Without thinking, I grabbed my phone and stood. It rang.

No one ever called me. Who *called* anybody anyway? Didn't they know it was rude to call without texting first?

I glanced down to see the golden locks I'd just daydreamed about staring up at me.

Steph was *calling*.

On the phone.

To talk.

"Hon, you okay?" an older guy sitting behind me gripped my arm, concern creasing his already well-lined forehead.

"Uh, yeah, thanks. I'm good. Just didn't expect this call."

"Better answer. That's the fourth ring." He motioned with raised brows and a pointed gaze.

"Right," I said, raising the phone in salute without hitting the answer button. "Guess I should."

I wove my way through the tightly packed tables and lifted the phone, pressing the button as I reached the exit.

"Hey."

"Hey there. Bad time?" A heartbeat passed. "Sounds noisy."

I glanced back before stepping outside. "Eli and I were just having breakfast. I'm leaving now."

"Do you need to—?"

"No," I said quickly. "We're good. I mean, done. We're done, and he's already gone."

Why was I suddenly flustered? The entire time Steph and I had been chatting, I'd been the one to tease and rattle him. Now, with the sound of his voice, I was suddenly incapable of forming sentences. What the hell?

"Everything okay?" I asked, like an overprotective parent receiving a call from their kid.

"Yeah. Guess I just wanted to hear your voice."

I nearly melted right there on the sidewalk. Seriously, people would have to step over the puddle of Jack just to get by. It would've been horrifying.

"Really?"

"Yeah, really." He chuckled. "We've been texting so much, my thumbs have blisters. Besides, I'm driving, and you gave me shit last time we texted while I was in the car."

"Aww, you listen to me."

"I do now ... and I really like your voice."

Fuck, fuck, fuck. Do not melt. Stop it. No swooning or melting or anything remotely romantic and uncontrolled!

"I like yours too."

That sounded so third grade. Should I trade lunches with him now? Offer him my apple? God help me!

"You know, the more I think about coming to Atlanta, the more excited I'm getting. It's almost been a month since we saw each other. I kinda want to see your eyes again."

"Just my eyes?"

That was good. Stay snarky. Go on the offense.

"Hell no. I want to unwrap my present, see what I missed on that plane. And I want more of those kisses. Your lips are ridiculous."

I need a bench. I have to sit. Where the fuck is a bench?

"Uh, yeah, same. I mean, you have lips too. Nice ones. Nice lips."

"Oh, did I mention you have a hot ass? I was watching you walk back and forth to the little kitchen on the plane and, damn, your ass is round. Bet you could bounce a quarter off it."

"Galley."

"What?"

"It's called a galley."

"Your ass is called a galley? Isn't that suggestive?"

"No. The kitchen thing ... on the plane ... the kitchen is a galley ... not my ass."

"I'm confused." The giggle in his voice said he wasn't confused at all, just very amused.

"Never mind. Can we get back on my ass?"

He barked a laugh through the phone so sudden I had to pull it away from my ear.

"Already offering to bottom? Aren't you planning just a bit much?"

"I ... uh ... that's not what I ... Shit."

His laugh was full-throated now. "So you don't want to bottom? Are you all top? With that hair? And you think I'll believe that?"

"What? Wait, my hair ... it's not bottom hair. It's perfectly good top hair, thank you very much." I didn't mean to sound defensive, but my inner offended Girl-Scout-whose-customer-just-insulted-samosas leapt free.

"You just flicked your hair, didn't you? I could hear it through the phone."

"Did not," I said, flicking my hair.

"Just did it again. I heard it. That was a total bottom flick. Not even vers hair. Your hair only gets fucked, probably hard against the wall, all spread out, without even a hint of hair gel to make things easier."

"Are you still talking about my hair?"

"If the slipper fits, Dorothy." The smile in his voice was so bright I couldn't stop myself from grinning.

"This is a terrible first phone conversation. Shouldn't we be talking about the weather or what we'll do in Atlanta?"

"Spreading your hair seems like a nice agenda item."

I had no idea how to respond to that. This wasn't the shy, awkward, almost uncomfortable Steph I'd come to know in our texts. Where had this force of nature come from? I was utterly on my heels ... and I loved it.

"You haven't duded me once," I said, struggling to regain the upper hand.

"Huh?"

"By this point in our chats, you would've normally duded me at least three times."

"Maybe I don't dude guys I dream about."

My words stuck. "You ... you *dream* about me?"

"Sticky sheets and all."

The old guy who'd asked if I was okay inside the Biscuit tottered by, his arm hooked around an even older man's arm. "Sticky sheets are good!" he said, grinning from ear to ear and giving me a thumbs-up with his unencumbered hand. His laugh lingered long after he'd rounded the corner.

I switched the phone off speaker, realizing the whole of Midtown had likely just heard Steph threatening to split me—and my hair—wide open.

"What are you doing this weekend?" he asked suddenly.

My head spun. Where was he going? We weren't supposed to meet for weeks.

"I only ask because I have all this time off and … shit, waiting is driving me crazy. Jack, I want to see you. I want to get to know you for real, see if this … whatever it is … is real or if I'm just attracted to your decidedly anal hair."

I spat a laugh. "My hair is not anal. It would be far curlier and coated in—"

"Stop! Thou shalt keep clean. It's the first rule of bottoms. Have you not read the Gay Handbook?"

I had to cover my mouth, I was laughing so hard. "No, I'm afraid my handbook never arrived."

"We clearly need to remedy that." He huffed like he was annoyed with a willful child. "Now, back to me missing you, or wanting to see you, or whatever the fuck this feeling is. What are you doing this weekend?"

My heart sank. "I have Guard duty."

There was a long pause. "Guard duty? What is that?"

"I'm in the Georgia Air National Guard. This is my weekend for duty."

"Like the military? Uniform and everything?"

I chuckled. "Yes, uniform and everything."

"Fuck, you just got hotter. How is that possible?"

Again, he had me speechless.

"What do you do in the Guard? Why are you even in it?"

I got that question a lot. "The second question is easy. I want to be a pilot, always have. The ANG has a great pilot training program, and serving can rack up a ton of flight miles, which I'll need if I ever hope to get hired to fly commercial."

"Jack, that's *so* cool. I know you said you had flight lessons, but didn't realize this is what you meant."

"Oh, those are just one step in a really long process. I have to get my private license first, before I can even apply to the Guard program. It's an entire path and there's no guarantee they'll even accept me. It's pretty competitive."

"I really am impressed. We give each other shit, but you're awesome, you know that?"

There was something in his voice; not quite awe, but definitely bordering on it. I suddenly felt like crawling under the bench I'd found to sit on. Doing the Guard thing made me an oddity within the Atlanta gay community, but I was proud of my service. That it might help me earn my commercial wings one day was an added bonus. Steph's reaction, though, cast it into a whole new light.

"Thanks," was all I could think to say.

"Bet you look hot in uniform."

"What?" I hadn't seen that turn.

"Your ass in a uniform, I bet it's ridiculous. Will you wear it for me? Call it a fantasy. We could film it and call it military porn. Then I could take it off you, one piece at a time, really slowly."

My ears burned, and I knew my face must've been brighter than the signs at the stadium. He'd run past flirting, through sexy talk, and straight into ... what? Filming our own porn?

"I'm teasing, Jack. You know that, right?" he said, reading my mind.

"Oh, yeah, of course. Dude, seriously. Sure."

He laughed. "Did you just dude the surfer? Maybe I should talk about peeling your pants off your ass more often."

"Maybe next time I'll fight back."

He grunted. "Who said anything about fighting? Unless you're talking about sword fighting. Nothing revs my engine like a little fencing."

Jesus, was nothing sacred?

"I'm teasing again," he said quickly. "I like that we laugh so much."

My chest warmed. "Yeah, me too. You make me smile more than I have in a really long time."

"You have a great smile," he said, without hesitation.

The warmth blazed, and my cheeks hurt from the grin. "I can't wait to see you."

"Me too. Really. I know it's only a few weeks away, but it feels like forever."

"I hadn't thought of it like that until you said it. Thanks for that."

"I'm here to serve, m'lord." He chuckled. "So, I'm pulling into the gym. Let me get this workout done. I have a totally hot boyf—" He caught himself. "*Date* I need to look good for."

"I'm sure you already look good," I said, trying not to turn into a puddle of mush. My logical brain knew I should run from anyone who used the B word so soon. Hell, we'd never even had a proper date. But I couldn't run from Steph. All I wanted to do was run toward him, into his arms, to wrap myself in his scent and—

"Hope you say that soon. Talk to you later?"

"Absolutely."

I stared, grinning like a goofball, as his picture vanished and the screen went dark.

Chapter Twelve

Pacing the Benches

Steph

I HADN'T BEEN ALL that motivated to hit the gym in advance of spring training. The months of eating whatever I wanted and not killing myself on a padded bench had been a wonderful break. I hadn't exactly let myself go like Nate—his belt had to be let out a notch or two—but I'd allowed myself to enjoy a few extra beers and foods I'd normally avoid, like pizza and lasagna.

Then Jack came along, with our cozy text courtship morphing into face-to-face whatever, and I didn't know of anything that motivated an athlete to kick into beast mode more than the threat of wearing a banana hammock on a beach.

It would be February in Atlanta. There weren't any beaches nearby, and it would be too cold to display any of my greater goods in the open air. Still, we'd see each other, and, being men, there was a better than zero chance that one or all articles of clothing might hit the floor. I couldn't have him "pinching an inch," as the old commercial said.

"Shit, Steph, you tryin' to make me look bad here?" Nate slumped against the incline bench, one hand wiping the sweat from his forehead.

I let the bar fall onto the rack with a satisfying clank that echoed throughout the empty weight room. I'd only been working out regularly for a few weeks and was already back up to my old bench-press weight.

"Nah. You don't need me for that. Your flabby abs do a fine job without me."

"Asshole." He flicked me a bird, despite a grin forming on his lips. "It's my winter layer. I needed it to keep the Memphis chill at bay."

"Isn't that why you married Coop?"

That earned me another bird. "What's with all the working out? You've been pulling two a day for weeks, and camp isn't starting for another month. I mean, shit, look at you. You're more ripped now than last season, and a few pounds bulkier."

"Four pounds so far. Like it?" I flexed a bicep, proud of how the skin pulled taut over the hardened muscle.

He nodded appreciatively. "Walking gun show. Love it."

I stretched out, readying myself for the next set, but Nate spoke up again. "You doing all this for that guy? The flight attendant?"

I sat back up and turned toward him, unsure how much I was willing to admit—to him or to myself. I ran a hand through my hair and stared at the bench.

"That answers that," he said with a chuckle. "You really like this one, don't ya?"

I looked up. There wasn't anything mocking in his eyes, just the gaze of a concerned friend.

"Yeah, guess I do."

"When do you leave for Atlanta?"

"Today's Wednesday? Day after tomorrow," I said.

"Huh."

I stood, the next set forgotten. "What?"

"Nothing."

"Nathaniel Stringer, you don't 'huh' somebody and walk away. That's like screwing somebody standing up without the courtesy of a reach around."

Nate coughed through a laugh. "Is it really? Are those the same, really?"

"Yeah, totally," I pouted. "So, out with it."

He blew out a breath. "What do you like so much about this guy? What's got you so pumped—pun intended?"

I paced between the benches, lost in my own head. "Well, he's funny. And super smart. I mean, shit, he's *really* smart. Did you know he wants to be a pilot? I mean, he doesn't just want it, he's taking lessons and should have his private pilot license soon. That's hard, Nate. You think just anybody could do that?"

Nate watched me wearing a line in the carpet without saying a word.

"And he's really nice. I mean, he's a total smart ass, which fits in with all of us great, but underneath it all, he's a genuinely nice guy."

Nate's mouth opened, but I cut off whatever he was about to say.

"Did I mention how funny he is?"

Again, Nate's mouth opened, then closed.

"We talk every day, twice most days, sometimes more, and I can't remember a single conversation when I wasn't about to pee myself laughing. And Nate, we *never* run out of things to talk about. You know me. I'm not a talker. I mean, I like to talk, but not really, not with most people. People suck. Most people suck, anyway. But not Jack. He doesn't suck. He's funny."

Nate's lips shifted from a tart line into a toothy grin. "What?"

"You said Jack doesn't suck. Are you planning to prove that theory or do you hope you're wrong?"

I gaped. Here I was, baring my soul, and he was diving into the nearest gutter.

"Easy, tiger. I'm teasing." He chuckled, then held up a palm. "Wow, you really do have it bad to get all huffy over a little blow job humor. You're usually the one cracking the dirty jokes."

"Yeah, but that's about you and Cooper, and we both know you two are hung like fucking horses—not even regular horses, race horses, the ones whose dicks leave a trail on the track as they round the turn."

Nate was doubled over.

"We're not talking about you two. This is my Jack we're talking about."

Nate stopped laughing, and his brows nearly hit his hairline. "*Your* Jack?"

Shit, did I actually say that?

"You know what I mean," I said, entering fourth-grader defense mode. "Just Jack."

Nate spat another laugh. "Okay, Karen."

"Fuck off."

"Nope, that's *your Jack's* job."

I snatched a nasty, sweaty towel off a nearby bench and hurled it at him.

"So sensitive," Nate teased. "So, you flying down Friday?"

"Yeah."

"When do you come home?"

I hesitated. This was where the Nate train might gather steam. "Wednesday."

"What?" he nearly shouted. "You're staying *five days* on your first visit?"

I nodded, but couldn't meet his eyes.

"Steph, buddy, you know I love ya. I want you to be happy and all, but dude—"

"You can't dude—"

"A surfer. I know. And yes, I can. I'm your best friend. It's my job." He crossed his arms, and I knew it was about to get rough. "I just want you to be realistic. You don't know this guy, not really, and you're going to be stuck with him in his apartment for five days. Have you really thought this through?"

I knew he had a point, but I didn't want to hear it. My heart said five days wasn't a bad thing. In fact, it wasn't nearly enough.

"Are you sure you know what you're doing?" he asked.

"No, of course not. Fuck, Nate, I haven't known what I was doing from the moment I met the guy. He's had my head so twisted out of shape. How am I supposed to know what to think?" I gripped the back of a bench and rested my head on it. "All I know is how he makes me feel, and I've never felt anything like this before. I don't even know what *this* is, dude."

I hadn't meant to sound so frustrated or fish-out-of-water, but that's exactly how I felt. I'd never been a control freak. Hell, the idea of making a plan made me itch. Following one, at least one that didn't involve baseball plays, made my skin crawl. Just thinking about dating or getting to know a guy or whatever the fuck we were doing turned my whole world upside down.

Still, when my eyes closed and I saw Jack smile, I *knew*. What did I know? Shit, I knew I wanted to get to know Jack. Everything else was so far out of my experience that my head hurt trying to think about it.

"Nate, I know it all sounds nuts, but something in my gut just knows Jack is … something. I think he's different, maybe special, or has the potential to be special." I beat my forehead against the bench. "Man, I don't know what I'm saying. I'm so fucked. I'm not picking out curtains or anything, but I'm not worried about spending a few days together either. The only thing I know for sure is that I have to try. I just have to."

Nate stared so long I thought my heart might beat out of my chest.

"Please say something."

He stared a moment longer, then nodded once and stood. "Alright then. Do you need a ride to the airport?"

It always amazed me how quickly teammates stepped up to have each other's backs. And Nate was so much more than just a teammate; he was family. I respected him, trusted him. His voice mattered—even when my heart was set on a path.

"Thanks, man," was all I trusted myself to say.

Chapter Thirteen

Friday Night Lights

Steph

My flight touched down at Hartsfield-Jackson airport two minutes after six in the evening. The captain clearly misjudged the distance as we slammed into the concrete, sending every passenger lurching forward.

I barely felt a thing. My heart was rattling far more than the wheels against the runway.

I'd flown across the southeast for what? A date? A boy? Was I completely insane?

Every time I blinked, Jack's face filled the darkness. Black curls with minds of their own, rich, electric eyes the color of a cloudless sky, one perfectly formed dimple at the center of his chin ... it all made me a bit woozy.

Or was that the flight? I'd never struggled with air sickness before, but it could've been the flight.

Yeah, it had to be the flight.

The wave of rising passengers finally crested at my row. As I stood, bony fingers clamped about my forearm, and I glanced back at the bent old woman who'd kept me company.

"You have fun with Jack." Her gap-toothed grin was as warm as the glow in her eyes. "I'd give anything to have another date with my Robert."

I hadn't meant to tell her about my reason for visiting Atlanta, but when she'd spent half the flight talking about Robert, her husband of fifty-four years whom she'd lost only months earlier, my heart couldn't hold my mouth in check. I apologized again and again for raising happy hopes in the face of her tragic tale, but she gripped my arm and urged me to continue.

"Honey," she said. "Make me smile. I've been sad enough lately for a lifetime. Tell me about your Jack."

There it was again. *My* Jack.

It was insane. I barely knew the guy.

Still, the sound of it stirred something in me, something foreign I didn't recognize but—

"I hope you find what you're looking for," she said, squeezing my arm with surprising strength.

I turned toward her, reached down to help her stand, then wrapped her in the tightest hug I could manage in the awkward confines beneath the seat's luggage compartment. She was short enough not to notice, but I had to bend at an almost painful angle.

She patted my back as my mother once did, and I felt a lump form deep within.

"I have a good feeling about you two. This is a good trip, Stephan. I just know it," she whispered.

When we pulled apart, I had to fight back whatever blasted emotion tried to leap out of my eyes. Dammit.

I nodded, gave her one last arm squeeze, then turned and followed the other lemmings off the plane. I would love to say the old woman's kindness had bolstered my confidence, but my nerves only rattled louder in my head.

This was it. I was here. There was no turning back.

"How do you look that good after a flight?"

I tripped over my rolling bag and face-planted right in front of the gate desk.

Several passengers turned and bent to help me up, but all I saw was Jack, leaning against the desk, a lanyard with his ID around his neck and a smirk on his lips.

"Did you forget I have a secret decoder ring that lets me greet you at the gate?" He wiggled his ID in the air. "Being crew has its privileges."

I had forgotten, anticipating at least a few more minutes of roaming the corridors and riding the Plane Train before I had to face my nemesis ... I mean, date.

Yet, here he stood.

Fuck, he looked good. The almost silky shirt clung to his chest and arms in just the right way. Its rich navy made his eyes practically leap out of their sockets. I felt a little dizzy trying to stand and had to brace myself on the desk.

"You hit your head?" He was by my side gripping my arm in a flash, concern replacing sarcasm so fast I thought someone else had stepped forward to assist. "Easy, don't rush."

"I'm okay, just a klutz." I smiled weakly, trying not to stare into his vampiric eyes.

His grip softened but didn't release; his hand sent warmth all the way to my toes. "Sure you're okay? We can sit if you need a minute."

"I'm good," I said, straightening and gripping my roller handle. "Lead the way, *mon capitan*."

He squeezed my arm, much as the old woman had. "Hungry?"

"Starving."

"Great. We have reservations in thirty minutes, just enough time to get there. Come on."

I was more of a beer and burger kind of guy. The idea of reservations made my stomach flip even faster than it had before. Was I going to totally embarrass myself by using the wrong fork? What if he took me to some French restaurant with words I couldn't pronounce? I could see him and the waiter laughing as I struggled with the menu. Would he want me to pick from a wine list? I didn't know a red from a blue, unless it was on a uniform or printed on the bottom of a surfboard.

Shit, this was getting more complicated by the minute.

Maybe Nate had been right. Maybe I was out of my depth and this entire trip was a bad idea. What did I really know about Jack, anyway? Why did I think we could work—or whatever it was guys did when they liked each other enough to not run away? What had Nate and Coop done that was so magical? I'd watched them for more than a year and still couldn't understand their secret sauce.

Was I going to be one suggestion away from throwing up on my shoes for five straight days? The thought nearly made me hurl right there in the airport.

"I'm so glad you're here," he said, snapping me out of my mind-numbing thoughts. "But I need to admit something."

I dared a glance. His eyes were fixed on the floor ahead.

"What's up?" I said, like we were bros catching up at the gym.

"I've been really nervous all day."

I nearly tripped over my roller again. "Really?"

He nodded and looked up. "Shit, Steph, you really do look great."

My heart did one of those Simone Biles things, sticking the landing and earning a ten, even from the bitchy Russian. Why was she always such a—

"I went to the gym twice today. I mean, you're a professional athlete. You probably have abs on your toes and don't even have to work for them. Not that I assumed we'd take our shirts off or anything, but if we did— and I kind of hoped we might—I didn't want to be so far out of your league that you ran out the door and never wanted to talk to me again. Not that you're so shallow that you'd only care about looks or bodies or anything like that. I don't think you are. Fuck, I'm screwing all this up. I'm sorry. I'll stop talking now."

I'd stopped walking about halfway through whatever that had been. I could feel that my mouth was hanging open but I couldn't figure out how to close it. There definitely were no words, at least none I could think of, to respond to … that.

"You're staring. Shit. You're just staring. Have I scared you off already? Say something. Shoot me and put me out of my misery."

How could such a confident, model-perfect guy turn into such an insecure puddle of mush in the middle of an airport? What had I said? It was like watching a slug after a kid had tossed salt on it, which was gross and cruel and absolutely not something I did when I was a boy … more than once … or three times.

"You're still just staring." He shrank further.

Passengers flowed around us as a river rushed about a boulder. A few cast annoyed glances our way, but most simply ignored the boys standing awkwardly in the middle of their path.

I don't know where my own confidence came from. A moment earlier, I'd been worried about soiling my breeches. And yet, listening to Jack struggle, seeing him wrestle with the same demons I'd been battling, somehow gave me strength. Or maybe my protective instincts kicked in and I had to do something to restore his faith. I'm not sure.

I reached up, grabbed his face in both hands, and kissed him like we'd been lovers for a century. The passengers around us vanished. The dull roar of a thousand conversations stilled. Even the hum of the planes outside ebbed to a gentle whisper.

Jack startled and nearly pulled back, but in less than a heartbeat I felt him lean into my touch and accept the lifeline I offered.

Applause from a group of teenage girls in basketball uniforms sitting at a nearby gate pulled us apart, goofy grins lighting each of our faces.

"Well, alrighty then," he said, the dimple I'd missed so badly appearing prominently in his chin.

"Take me to dinner or lose me forever," I said.

"That isn't how that quote goes," he cocked a brow.

My grin widened. "I know, but you haven't earned the correct quote. Let's see how dinner goes first."

His laugh and lowered head reminded me of a teen on his first date who'd just been embarrassed by something sweet. I could barely contain my heart in that moment.

"Come on. We don't want to be late to this place. It's amazing."

Then he did the last thing I expected: he hooked his arm around mine and led me down the corridor.

Chapter Fourteen

Rufus

Jack

MAGIC IS A FUNNY thing. Unlike in books and movies, it can't be called or controlled. It just happens in its own time and on its own terms.

I'd been a wreck all day. Steph was coming. He was about to be more than just a text or voice over the phone. Making this a long visit had been my idea, and it had sounded amazing when I'd first thought about it, but, standing in the airport waiting for Steph's plane to taxi to the gate, I'd begun to wonder what insanity had taken over my brain that day.

Who had a five-day-long first date?

First dates were awkward affairs where two people who barely knew each other tried not to offend or get food stuck in their teeth. It was a test of all the hopes and dreams drummed up in the pre-date across-the-room gazing stage before you learned the other person snored or picked their nose or farted at the dinner table. In that idyllic, dreamlike place between meeting and a first date, the other person was perfection personified.

And then the first date swung in like a valentine-shaped wrecking ball to shatter any illusion that dating that person was a good idea. In fact, most first dates ended with a hope of never having to wave at that person across the grocery store cucumber aisle again.

Yes, cucumber aisles were fantastic gay pickup spots, especially in Midtown, Atlanta. Just trust me on this.

Jack stepped into the terminal and promptly kissed the carpet.

I would've laughed if I hadn't been so terrified he'd bloodied his lip or banged his head before we'd even realized we weren't a match.

Then he looked up and his eyes met mine.

All those doubts and fears shattered into a million tiny stars, winking in a magical night sky where everything was beautiful and perfect and baby rabbits sang Disney songs out of their cute furry asses.

Okay, maybe I'd been the one to hit his head. I was nervous. Sue me.

Then Steph kissed me.

Right in the middle of the busiest airport in the country, Steph grabbed my head in his sumptuous, meaty, perfectly calloused hands and planted a whopper on my lips.

He tasted of Coke and ginger snap cookies, like the ones we passed out on the plane. It was familiar and oddly comforting.

There was no tongue. The French remained in their cottages. There were only lips and hands and the slightest moan that said he wanted me so badly he would rip off his clothes and take me against the automatic trash can if I asked him to.

I might've been projecting there.

Still, the moment lingered and was perfect, and I felt my-self drifting at his touch. I could've died right then and my life would've been complete. The baby rabbits farted in perfect harmony, a cappella, which was really hard with furry asses, especially ones topped with fluffy tails.

That's when the magic thing happened.

A fairy or angel—or flatulent rabbit with wings—floated down from the dingy ceiling with one flickering light and whis-pered in my ear, "Take this man to dinner before he bites you."

It seemed like an odd thing for a smelly, furry angel-thing to say but I went with it, hooking my arm around his like we'd been together for half a century and leading him out of the airport.

"DINNER WAS AMAZING," STEPH said as we stepped from my car onto the sidewalk that led to my apartment. "I'm usually more of a pub and beer kind of guy, but that restaurant was sick."

I'd taken him to The Consulate, a posh James Beard grant winner voted one of ZAGAT's Sexiest New Restaurants and Bars that featured a rotating global menu whose items were both comforting and exotic.

It was Papua New Guinea night, which had both of us staring at the menu like kids seeing the lion exhibit at the zoo for the first time. Unsure how to proceed, we agreed to surrender to the will of the culinary gods and our server, Adele (yes, like the singer), asking her to simply surprise us with whatever she thought was the tastiest morsel from each section.

She did not disappoint.

The first appetizer, *saksak*, which I was afraid to pronounce, were oversized dumplings filled with seasonal mushrooms and kale. A second small bowl of *kaukau* arrived. This sweet potato, mashed with ginger, garlic, coconut milk, OJ, and smoke papri-ka, was to be scooped up with house-made taro chips.

Adele rightly guessed her athletic patrons would prefer a healthy main course and selected a pineapple curry pot filled with chicken, taro root, sweet potatoes, pineapple, okra, green beans, shallots, coconut milk, and a host of seasoning that gave the dish the most mouthwatering steam to ever waft from a bowl. We didn't even bother with the side of sticky rice, just devoured the curry sauce thing on its own.

But that wasn't enough.

She then laid a Kokoda snapper ceviche before us. The chilled fish was so fresh and dripping with lime juice that I almost thought we'd been transported to a beach somewhere in the Southwestern Pacific.

It wasn't a meal; it was a journey.

I grinned. "'Sick' is a good thing in surfer land, right?"

He chuckled. "It's almost as good as 'rad.'"

"Whoa, that good? Awesomeness."

He frowned. "Don't ever say that again. That was terrible."

He looked offended. My heart thudded. Then he winked, and I realized he was teasing.

"You're an ass, you know that?"

He bumped shoulders. "And you love it."

Dinner had been so much better than I'd hoped. From the minute we sat in the car at the airport, the conversation flowed, just like it had every time we'd texted in the month or so since we'd met. We talked of nothing and everything, laughing and teasing, smiles only leaving our lips long enough to sip or bite or chew.

At one point, Adele asked how long we'd been together and if we were celebrating a special day. A jolt shot through me as I looked to Steph, wondering if he'd be embarrassed by the question and its implications; but he reached across the table and grasped my hand, smiled as he stared into my eyes, and said, "It's a very special night, thanks, Adele."

For the second time in only a handful of hours, I thought I could die happy.

Who the fuck said things like that? Especially about me?

I was trying to play it cool, to not drool or dribble, but I was starting to really like this guy—probably way too much for the infinitesimally short time we'd known each other.

But Magic has a mind of her own.

"I need to warn you about Rufus," I said as we stood at my door.

"Oh?"

"He's really sweet and adorable, but ... he kinda looks like roadkill."

Steph nearly doubled over. "Did you just say your cat looks like roadkill?"

My cheeks flushed. "Uh, yeah. Just wait. He's really the sweetest cat in the world but, I mean, bless his heart."

"Oh no." Steph straightened but struggled to speak through snorts. "You didn't just 'bless his heart,' did you?"

I nodded. "He needs a lot more than that. Brace yourself."

I unlocked the door and motioned for Steph to enter before me, then followed and flicked on the lights.

Yawl! came from the couch where His Majesty had been sleeping peacefully.

"I hear a putty tat," Steph said in a cartoon singsong that made my insides bubble.

Two massive ears popped above the couch back a second before a pair of saucer-sized eyes.

Blink.

Blink.

"Holy shit, where's the rest of his fur? Did he survive Chernobyl or what?"

I swept past and scooped up Rufus, cradling him as he nuzzled my chin with his head. His Harley-like purr reverberated throughout the apartment.

"Don't be mean," I said. "He's very sensitive, and he can't help it if he's beautiful."

Steph reached up and scratched behind his ear. The purr grew louder.

Rufus reached up and pawed Steph's hand then wriggled out of my grip and leapt onto his chest.

"Oh, crap." Steph stepped back, startled, then reached up and secured the cat clinging to his shirt by deadly sharp claws. "Hey, little guy. Did you want to check out the new guy Daddy brought home? You need to make sure I'm okay?"

"Wow, he likes you," I said, my eyes wide. "He doesn't like *anybody* but Eli and me, and he really only tolerates Eli because he feeds him."

Rufus was doing the head nuzzle thing under Steph's chin, and his motor had revved into high gear. Perhaps cutest of all, his raggedy tail had curled completely around Steph's wrist.

"Do you two need a room? Should I make up the couch and sleep out here?" I teased.

Steph's eyes flared. "Oh, um, I guess we haven't even talked about ... that."

He stepped around and sat on the couch, careful not to disturb his purring cargo. Rufus was dutifully making biscuits out of Steph's chest. I wondered how many bloody tracks would be left in Ruf's wake.

"Do you want me to make up the couch?" I asked, desperate to keep disappointment out of my voice.

"No ... " He looked up as I sat on the far end. "No, of course not. It's just ... Jack, I don't know how to say this. Hell, I barely know what I'm doing. I don't date; not much, anyway. Baseball takes up all of my time, and Memphis isn't exactly the gay mecca, and I know I seem all confident and sure of myself, but ... I don't know."

It was so strange to watch him struggle with his words. I'd babbled incoherently at the airport and he'd seemed so calm. Now, he was blithering and all I could do was watch.

"I want to hold you, more than anything. I've dreamed about holding you all night, smelling your skin, feeling you next to me. If I'm honest, I've dreamed about a lot more too."

"Oh really?" I wanted to hear this.

"But I don't want you to think ... I mean, I do want ... fuck. Jack, you're the hottest guy I've ever been out with—by a mile. I don't want you to think I'm just here to hook up with a hottie." He ran a hand over his head and rubbed a cheek across Rufus. "I'm a pro baller. I know what it's like to wonder if somebody's there because they're interested in what I do rather than who I am. You're already so much more than that. I mean ... we just met ... I don't mean we're more—"

I had to put him out of his misery. I reached over and rested my hand on his leg. His eyes snapped to my hand like it was a snake that had just crawled into his lap.

"How about this? We sleep in the same bed, you hold me and I hold you, but that's it for tonight? We can see what tomorrow brings when the sun rises."

He blew out a breath like I'd just saved him from dying of thirst or drowning. "That sounds great."

"Good, because I suspect Rufus will curl his furry ass in between us no matter how we sleep."

He laughed and scratched Ruf's ear. "I think you're right. And that's perfect too."

Chapter Fifteen

Morning Wood

Steph

Jack surprised me, suggesting we change into house clothes, pour a nightcap, and curl up with Rufus on the couch to watch a movie.

"All that sounds great, but I'm not sure I'll make it long enough for a whole movie. This day's kinda wiped me out."

He grinned up from the couch as I strode into the room wearing a maroon Mango T-shirt and silky gray shorts.

"If you keep flopping around in those shorts, I'm going to have a very hard time making it through a night of platonic cuddling."

I could feel my cheeks burning as I glanced down at the shorts that revealed more than they hid.

"Shit, sorry. I didn't even think—"

He laughed and hopped up from the couch, pressing a finger to my lips. "What do you want to drink? I have cab, merlot, pinot … no white wine. White's for pussies. If you want something stronger, I can whip something up. The bar's pretty well stocked. Eli insists on that."

I offered a sheepish grin. "Beer?"

He stared and blinked as though I'd just answered in Chinese.

"Or scotch. I could do a scotch on the rocks."

Someone hit "play" and he blurred into action. "One scotch, coming right up. The remote's on the couch. See if there's anything on you like. We can always try Netflix or Prime if there's nothing on regular TV."

The moment I settled into the soft cushions, Rufus climbed aboard. His purr preceded the habitual biscuit thing, this time in my lap.

"Ow, little guy. Stop that. My shorts aren't thick enough for your claws." I pried him loose, holding him close to my chest. He nuzzled against me, probably comforted by the closeness to my heart.

Jack appeared a moment later, one hand cradling a long-stemmed glass filled with red wine, while the other held a fancy crystal tumbler filled with ice and golden liquid. He set the tumbler on a coaster on the coffee table then plopped down, this time beside me rather than on the opposite end. My arm couldn't get around his shoulders fast enough. Before I could blink, both fur ball and fur boy were snug against me.

"*Press Your Luck*?" he asked in an amused tone.

"I kind of got stuck."

Jack's hand found my leg, his warmth leaching into my skin.

"I actually love this show," he said. "I didn't care for Elizabeth Banks at first, but she's grown on me. She's really good with the contestants."

I could hardly believe it. Jack liked *Press Your Luck* too?

"I can't believe you like this show," he said, reading my mind again. "You're such a jock."

His head rose against my chest as I chuckled. "Jocks can't like game shows?"

He lifted his head to face me. "Aren't you guys into ESPN twenty-four seven? Or macho car racing? Or Steven Segal blow-shit-up movies?"

I shook my head. "I'm a baseball player. You're thinking of football guys. And even those guys aren't balls-to-the-wall like people think. You'd be surprised how many play music or sing or like opera."

"Opera? Seriously?" He rested his head back on my chest.

"Okay, I made that up, but there are a lot of guys who like things you might not expect. Take Henry Cavill."

"Where am I taking Henry Cavill? Do tell. I'd drive him anywhere, anytime. I might even take him somewhere in my car too."

I thumped the back of his head.

"Henry is this massive muscular dude, a real man's man, but he's also the biggest nerd on the planet. He loves video games and fantasy books. He's nothing like the meathead people make him out to be."

"He's an actor, not a pro sports jock."

"True, but still. When you meet the team, you'll see."

His hand stopped rubbing my leg.

"What?"

"You want me to meet your team?"

Shit, had I said that? I mentally slapped myself. Fuck, fuck, fuck.

"Uh, well, sure, if you want. I mean, most people think it's cool, meeting pro players and all. I just … thought you might … I don't know."

His hand left my leg and pressed against my chest next to Rufus. "I think it's sweet. I'd love to meet your team someday."

My heart resumed its normal beating pattern.

"Oh, look. Whammy!"

"That sucks. Poor girl. That's her third," he said.

"She gone," he said as she hit yet another whammy.

"That would stink, getting all the way to the bonus round and getting knocked out and going home with nothing."

I grunted agreement. "At least she won thirty grand in the main game."

"Right."

"What's next? I picked that mess. It's your turn," I said.

Jack grabbed the remote and began scrolling through the menu.

Rufus yawned. His tiny legs stretched, and his claws poked out as far as they would go, then retracted. If I hadn't seen it, I wouldn't have believed the little guy could open his mouth that wide. The sound that came out might've been the cutest little thing I'd ever heard.

It made me yawn.

"Sounds like somebody's ready for bed," Jack said, tossing the remote onto the coffee table.

"Sorry."

"Don't be," he said, pushing himself upright. "You've had a long day, and you flew. Travel always saps the energy."

"Even for you? You fly all the time."

He nodded. "Especially for us. Come on. Let's hit the sack. You don't snore, do you?"

I grinned. That was going to be my line. "Nope. Barely make a peep."

"We'll see about that."

I DIDN'T REMEMBER FALLING asleep. Rufus had curled up on the pillow above my head. Actually, he had molded his tiny body onto my head, like he was Saran Wrap and I was a dish to be kept fresh. I didn't have the heart to move him and was somewhat afraid he might claw my face if I tried, so I simply wrapped my arms around Jack, who lay in front of me, kissed the back of his head, and drifted off.

None of us moved or rolled over or anything—not even once—all night. God, that was a peaceful sleep.

And Jack ... fuck, he felt good.

We'd agreed to just hold each other, but we hadn't said anything about wearing T-shirts and shorts. I usually slept naked, preferring the feel of silky sheets against my skin, but Jack had climbed into bed fully clad in protective armor, and I wasn't about to do any different. Still, I could feel his strength beneath the fabric. He might not be a pro sportsman, but he clearly worked his body. I wanted to explore so badly, to feel down his stomach to his abs, to trace their outline and see if a happy trail led to—

"Good morning," he muttered without turning. Then, in the most unfair move ever made in the history of sports, he scooted his butt back and wiggled it against my morning-hardened cock. It twitched; blood raced from all corners of my body to flood the zone. "Somebody's happy this morning."

"You're cheating."

He rolled over to face me and our cocks pressed against each other, pulsing and throbbing.

"Now I'm cheating."

Rufus, annoyed by the sudden movement, sprang off the bed and skittered out of the room.

"Alone at last," Jack said, one hand reaching up so his fingers could trace my cheek.

His black hair lay in perfect curls against the white pillowcase. Dim light from the rising sun peered through the drapes, framing his face and lighting his eyes. I sucked in a breath, taken by how ridiculously beautiful he was.

"We promised to hold each other all night, and we did. Now it's morning."

It was a statement, but also a question. I was afraid to answer.

"Can I kiss you?" he asked.

I nodded, but didn't speak.

He scooted forward so our torsos met. Now the length of us, every inch, pressed together. He smoothed my hair and stared into my eyes.

I had to gulp back my nerves.

"I really like you, Steph. More than I thought I would, and I was pretty sure I'd like you a lot."

"Me too," I breathed more than spoke.

Then his lips pressed into me and words were meaningless.

His hand cupped my face and his tongue slipped free, grazing mine. I wrapped my arm around his body and pulled him even closer.

He ground himself against me and the suddenness of his erection pulsing next to mine made me shiver. He pressed in again. This time, I pressed back.

Our kisses deepened, still gentle, still probing, but the tension in our bodies was building, and I wondered how long we should—how long we *could*—hold out.

I wanted him; to feel him, to touch him. I wanted the clothes between us to fall away so friction and heat could ignite whatever this was between us. This flame. This blaze. God, this inferno I knew would rage as long as this man was in my presence.

We'd known each other for a blink, and I hungered for him like some ancient Greek in a story of myth and legend. How was it possible?

His hands gripped my arms, then trailed to my back. When he squeezed my butt and shoved us together, I moaned out loud.

"Can we take off these clothes?" he asked.

Without speaking, I grabbed the bottom of his shirt and pulled upward until he lifted his arms. I stared down at his chest, its rise and fall, the perfect lines, the pink of his nipples.

"You're amazing," slipped out.

He kissed me, then forced my arms up so he could return the favor.

Bare chests melted together as we embraced and kissed. I rolled him onto his back and lay on top, pressing my weight into him, then he flipped us over and pressed himself down on me.

I traced the muscles of his back, played with each divot, trailed his spine. When I reached the elastic of his waistband, my fingers slipped beneath, and he wiggled his cock against mine, begging me to go lower.

So I did.

My hands gripped his hairless butt, squeezing and kneading, pressing us together.

"Get me out of these fucking pants," he ordered.

"Yes, sir," I said through a grin.

A moment later, we lay naked, the covers tossed off the bed, each on our side facing the other.

"This is what a pro baseball player looks like? Damn," he said, his hand roaming my stomach.

"You like?"

He grinned up. "I want."

"What do you want?"

His eyes widened slightly. "You really asking?"

I nodded.

"I want it all."

"Is it too soon? Should we—?"

"I'm not going to lose interest, Steph. Fuck, you're all I think about. I actually dreamed about us naked, like this."

"Really?" My voice quivered. "Me too, but ..."

He cocked his head. "But?"

I hesitated, then looked away, then looked back at him. "I really, *really* have to pee."

Chapter Sixteen

BRUNCH

JACK

"YOU HAVE TWO OPTIONS this morning," I called through the bathroom door. It struck me as cute that he closed the door to pee. We'd just been naked in bed, about to do naughty things with the body parts he now shied from showing, but I guess it made sense. We had just met, sort of, and peeing was personal … sort of.

It really didn't make sense, but it was cute.

"Okay," he said tentatively, probably thinking I was about to ask if he was a top or bottom.

"I can cook or we can go somewhere to brunch."

"Oh, right, breakfast," he said, relief flowing through the door in more ways than one.

"If you choose option A, you'll have to watch me scramble, literally, which isn't always a pretty sight. The end result is tasty, but the process kicks up a lot of dust. If you choose option B, there's a one hundred percent chance we'll be surrounded by the Midtown flock of gays. We might even run into people I know, which could feel a little like a family reunion followed by a police interrogation. And you, my friend, would definitely be the suspect."

Water flowed, then stopped, then the towel rack I'd needed to tighten since moving in rattled. The door opened, and Steph nearly ran into me leaning against the door frame.

"Shit, you scared me," he said, jumping back a step. Then he looked my naked body up and down. "On second thought, you can scare me whenever you like. Damn, you're even hotter in the light."

There's a certain amount of narcissism that comes with working out as hard as I did just for the looks of it, and I was a confident guy. Still, Steph's sudden praise had me blushing and examining my feet. I was beginning to think this guy would always turn me inside out with only a few words ... and that thought made me smile.

He closed the gap between us, wrapped his arms around me, and pulled our bodies together. He was already stiffening again—and this time, peeing had nothing to do with it.

"Or"—his voice was a husky whisper as he nibbled my ear—"Option C involves the protein-packed liquid breakfast of champions."

I felt his grin as he clamped down on my lobe. My whole body shook with pleasure.

"Option C sounds amazing," I whimpered. "But I know you're hungry—like, for real hungry. You're an athlete and you need your nutrition and shit."

My legs were going weak as he grabbed my ass, squeezing and tugging, then bit harder.

"Nutrition and shit," he chuckled, sending warm, moist breath down my neck. I shivered again. "I'll definitely have to take that back to the team dietitian. She'll love it."

I found an ounce of self-control, pressed my palms into his chest, and pushed him back. He was freakin' strong and barely budged, but I managed an inch. "Are you making fun of me?"

His head raised so our eyes could meet. "Absolutely."

First, I was taken by his boldness. Then the humor glimmering in his smart-ass eyes had me grinning. When his dick twitched, scraping against mine, I remembered how naked and worked up he was, and that nearly won the morning.

But I held firm ... so to speak.

"Brunch, then."

He blew out a breath that bordered on disappointment.

A jolt of pride bounced around inside me. This amazing man wanted me, and I was fairly certain it wasn't all about the sex—though that dish was also clearly on the menu. If I was honest with myself, I wanted to feel him naked against me all day and never worry about stupid things like food or getting dressed or leaving the bed, but I also really liked him and wanted to do this right. I wanted him to know I cared about more than his body, and the only way I could think to do that was to resist the overwhelming urge to drop to my knees and take him in my mouth—and go to fucking brunch.

I'd always loved brunch. How had it turned into *fucking* brunch all of a sudden?

"Okay, fine. Brunch it is. But it will cost you."

I cocked a brow. "Oh? What's the price?"

"A kiss."

Without waiting, he pulled us together again and I immediately questioned my obstinance.

WE DROVE BY MY favorite place, The Flying Biscuit, but a line of shivering men in heavy coats and thick gloves was curled around the block.

"Well, you would've loved the Biscuit. They actually throw them at you if you piss the servers off."

Steph's eyes widened. "Seriously? They chuck biscuits across the restaurant?"

I nodded. "Yep. It's funny when you get a gaggle of gays packed in there and bread starts whirling about. The squeals can get pretty high pitched … and those are from the musclehead gym rats."

"The ones who strut through the party with their tiny fluffy white dog racing to keep up?"

I grinned. "You know the ones."

"Okay, no food fight. What's our next choice?"

I thought a moment. "It's not fancy."

"Sounds more my speed anyway," he said.

"Careful what you ask for."

We drove the three minutes it took to cross Midtown and pulled into a parking lot beside a building whose massive windows were framed on the top and bottom by several feet of beige brick. A simple sign above its greenish black awning bore simple cursive that read, "Silver Skillet."

"This is definitely more my speed," Steph said, staring out the window. "When we're on the road, these are the kinds of places the guys hunt for. They're not pretty, but the food is usually the best in town."

The parking lot was already packed and we had to circle twice for a spot to open up.

"You just described the Skillet perfectly. Great food, super laid-back, mostly gay boys with a few metrosexuals who haven't realized what time it is yet—oh, and a few older women who just love being around us. They're always here. They think they adopted us, but we actually took them in, bless their hearts."

"Oh shit. You just blessed their hearts. That's twice since I got here. Are they evil? Do they have horns?"

I laughed as I opened my car door. "Nope. The boys are the horny ones. The ladies are real treats."

"Holy cow, this place smells like home," Steph said, an appreciative grin parting his lips as bacon-scented air blasted into us the moment the door opened.

At six foot three and hot as fuck, Steph had barely darkened the door before dozens of heads had turned to check out the new guy. I was used to getting the model treatment. It felt strange to be someone else's shadow, and yet, something akin to pride bubbled in my chest. This was my man. Well, he wasn't *mine*, but he was with me.

That's the same thing, right?

A bent woman of indeterminate post-middle age whose snowy bun only rose to the bottom of Steph's chest appeared. Her royal blue top bore the embroidery of the diner's logo, a circle split across the middle by the restaurant's name with an upside-down pink-and-brown-striped triangle underneath the writing.

"Hey, Jack," she said, leaning to look around Steph. "Who's the new hunk?"

She did the *Karate Kid* paint-the-fence thing with her eyes up and down Steph's body, to the point that I thought she might open her mouth and lick him just to get a taste.

"Hey, Janice. This is Stephan. He's visiting from Memphis. He's a—"

"Happy to meet you," Steph cut in quickly, ending my introduction before I could announce to the world that I'd hooked a professional baseball player.

"Ooh, honey child, you did *good* this time." She gave him the once-over again then craned her head to meet his gaze. "You ever want to switch teams, you let me know."

Steph grinned. "You'll be the first girl I call."

"You keep callin' me a girl and you might get more than just breakfast. I've had a cravin' for sausage lately, and a tall drink o' water like you looks to have a big 'un." She giggled and hooked her arm around Steph's. "You boys come with me. I'll make sure Amanda takes good care of you this mornin'."

Steph walked in front of me, and with each step his ears turned a brighter shade of red. With each table we passed, a new group of gays glanced up; some subtle, others practically handing Steph their numbers. The color spread to the back of his neck.

By the time we reached our table next to one of the massive floor-to-ceiling windows, he looked like he wanted to crawl under his chair, and I was fighting the urge to laugh out loud.

Janice leaned over, allowing her amble, gravity-challenged bosom to dangle before her. "You listen to me, Tall Sausage, if any of these boys bother you, you call me. I'll whop 'em upside the head until they act right." She started to rise, but Newton's laws dragged her down again. "And don't forget my offer. I can ride a bull with the best of 'em."

She patted his fully reddened cheek, then cackled her way back into the kitchen.

I had tears in my eyes when Steph looked up with a desperate, pleading gaze.

"I warned you, Tall Sausage," I said, finally losing my battle with laughter, the tears tumbling down my cheeks. I had to dab them with a paper napkin.

"That's like saying there might be a few waves right before a hurricane."

I grinned. "Janice *was* the waves. You haven't met the hurricane yet."

His face fell, and I nearly doubled over.

"I'm going to make you pay for this … whatever *this* is."

My grin turned lecherous. "I certainly hope so."

Before he could respond, I felt Amanda's presence a moment before she appeared at our table. Clad in a bright pink version of the shirt Janice wore, Amanda's uniform blouse was pulled tight and tied in a knot in the back, showing her slim waist and belly button. A tiny golden hawk dangled from a silver ring attached to the aforementioned umbilical entry.

Despite holding an order book, both hands flew to her hips as she faced Steph. "Eyes up here, big boy, unless you want more from the hawk than a quick peek. In which case, we'd have to leave this dump and get dirty with the bird."

Steph blanched, his eyes flying from her jewelry to me then up to her face. Her blonde hair was pulled so tight in a ponytail that her eyes were yanked back like one of Cher's bad facelifts. The smirk on her face was a work of art even the Mona Lisa would be jealous of.

"I, uh, wasn't … I mean, you surprised me and … uh … I didn't mean to … shit …"

She cocked her head like a school teacher enjoying a good "the dog ate my homework" story, but didn't say a word to save the drowning man.

"Jesus, I'm sorry. You just startled me, and I saw the hawk and wondered if you're a football fan. That's all. I swear."

She relaxed her pose, leaned down, and motioned Steph closer so she could whisper loud enough for me to hear.

"Honey, I am a football fan, love my Falcons, but I'd do almost anything for a man who could punch through my end zone—if you get my drift."

I almost ran from the table, afraid I might laugh so hard I'd wet myself.

Steph's eyes were so wide, I thought they might pop out.

Amanda merely straightened to her full four-foot-nothing height and chewed on the tip of her pen like she was about to milk it for all it was worth.

I finally managed to suck in air. "Amanda, this is Steph. Can you please behave for a minute so he doesn't run away before I've gotten to know him?"

I knew the moment the words left my mouth how badly I'd just screwed up.

Amanda's painted-on brows shot up. "A *new* man! How exciting. And Jack, fuck me running, he's the hottest one yet. Seriously. Is he as hot naked? I'm trying to picture it. Hard abs, big chest, probably hairless like my cat. I bet he has big balls. Do they dangle? I love a good dangle."

Amanda's voice carried and someone at a nearby table howled in laughter.

I snuck a peek to find every table around us eavesdropping without a hint of shame; most stared openly through their own laughter-filled eyes and broad grins.

We gays were funny, snarky, and utterly wonderful. Subtle, we were not.

"Um, can I get some coffee?" Steph blurted out, clearly drowning and reaching for a preserver. "And sausage. I'd like a big sausage."

I thought the whole diner might've erupted in that moment. Steph realized what had tumbled out of his mouth the moment Amanda gripped her heaving uncovered belly.

And then it happened. Hurricane Amanda struck.

She wheeled about, held her order pad to her mouth, and shouted, "This man needs a big sausage. Anyone? Big sausage for table four?"

Hands flew into the air, shouts rang out, a few yelled dollar amounts like they were bidding at an auction. For the briefest moment, I felt sorry for poor Steph. He was getting the royal treatment beyond what was normal. The fact he'd bumbled into it wasn't his fault, but the way he'd failed to recognize the danger, like some teen in a horror flick, and *still* ran down the dark hallway—that was beyond saving.

Just when I thought he might go down with the ship, Steph stood, did a model-on-a-runway twirl, smacked his own ass then waved at the crowd, earning a chorus of cheers and catcalls that echoed off the diner's glass walls.

I swear, in that moment, he'd gone from Hollywood-perp-walk-embarrassed to actually enjoying himself.

As he sat, Amanda leaned down again and said, "That was well played. Guess I'll need to up my game." Then she kissed him on the cheek.

Another round of cheers burst from the crowd.

Steph's hand flew up and cupped his own cheek like he was savoring the kiss, closing his eyes and sighing loudly.

Cheers morphed into laughter, then appreciative applause. I stared in wonder.

When we finally ordered and Amanda left to retrieve our food, I shook my head. "How did you turn that around? She had you down on the mat with both shoulders pinned and her knee digging into your chest."

He shrugged. "I'm a Mango. Making fun of ourselves and doing silly things to get laughs is my day job. Once I got over the initial shock, I just went into Mango mode."

I made a mental note to YouTube the Mangoes when we got home.

"You like performing?" I asked.

"You know, if you'd asked me that five years ago, I would've laughed. All I ever wanted to do was be a baller, to make it to the pros and get paid a lot of money to play a kids' game." He thought a moment. "When that dream died, I had no idea what I wanted to do. I was depressed and scared and … I just didn't know."

Amanda returned with coffee. She seemed to sense the seriousness of the moment and excused herself quickly.

"My agent tried to get me into tryouts overseas, but none of that worked. Once you get the boot here, it's hard to get anybody else to take a look." He sipped his coffee, then set it down and added a couple Splenda packets. "Then the Mangoes came along."

"Were you excited to play for them?"

"Hell no." He nearly spat coffee across the table. "I was a *serious* baseball player, not some circus act. At least, that's what I thought at the time. The Mangoes were some rogue comedy skit. Most of us looked down on what they were trying to build."

"But you like them now?"

"Like?" He shook his head and smiled. "I *love* the Mangoes, more than I ever did playing minor league ball. For one, they're a real family. From the guys to the owners to the staff, they all genuinely care about each other. I had great friends back in the minors, but we knew we'd leave each other one day, either move up or out. On the Mangoes, we know this is probably our last stop in baseball. It's our career now. Once I got over the rejection and loss of the other leagues and accepted where I was, I saw how amazing the team really was. It's unlike anywhere I've ever been."

"You don't miss the bright lights?"

He chuckled. "You think our lights are dim? You should come to a game and see for yourself. We sell out *every* game. There's not a single major league team who can say that.""It sounds like you really love it."

His gaze shifted like he was remembering something and his lips curled into a warm smile. "After every game, the entire team goes out to the pavilion, still in uniform, and we give autographs and take selfies until the last kid leaves. I think it's my favorite part of the game now. You should see some of those kids when they get to snap a photo with us. I can see them falling in love with the game a little more each time we go out there with them."

I found myself mirroring his smile. "I'd really love to see that."

His eyes shot up. "You would?"

"To see what makes you smile like that, of course I would."

He stared, and for a moment I thought he might not believe me, that I would take an interest in his work, in his world. I wasn't a baseball fan. I didn't really watch sports at all, but this was Steph's passion. It was important to him.

In that moment, I realized it was important to me too.

He released his coffee cup, reached across the table and took my hand. "I can't wait to show you. You're gonna love it."

"I would offer you dessert, but the two of you are so sweet I think everyone in here already caught diabetes." Amanda dropped the check on the table then offered the highly mature gesture of sticking her finger down her throat like she was trying to throw up.

Steph didn't miss a beat this time. "Careful, Amanda, stick around us and you might find a heart under that tight shirt of yours."

His look of triumph faded when she replied, "If I had a dollar for every man who thought I had a heart … wait, I *have* way more than a dollar already. I took half their shit."

Her laugh followed her back into the kitchen.

"Can we get out of here?" He squeezed my hand. "If I remember right, my bladder impeded some very important business this morning."

I grinned and squeezed back. "You don't have to ask me twice."

The moment the car doors closed, my hand found Steph's again.

His eyes were fixed on our hands. "I'd never held a guy's hand until this weekend."

It was a little weird at first. We'd known each other, what, a day? Technically, we'd known each other a little over a month, but I wasn't sure two days with Steph as a passenger in my section, followed by a month of texting, counted as truly knowing each other.

Oddly, by the time we'd pulled out of the lot and the tires hit a proper road, we were lacing our fingers. How had something so foreign a moment earlier become so comfortable?

Perhaps odder was that we didn't speak on the drive back to my apartment. Not a single word.

Since the day we'd met, conversation had flowed more freely than the raging waters of Niagara. Eli teased me that I'd become attached to my phone, or that I might wear out the screen if we kept it up.

The truth was that Steph was easy to talk to—and even easier to listen to.

But on that ten-minute drive, we said nothing. And it was the most peaceful, easy silence I'd ever endured.

We weren't at a loss for words. We just didn't need them. Not in that moment. I could sense he was happy. Hell, he smiled the entire way. And if he couldn't feel my own contentment, he wasn't paying attention.

That silence, perhaps more than anything we'd said to each other over the past month, spoke volumes about how I was beginning to feel, about feelings I'd rarely experienced and barely understood. This man, this breathtakingly beautiful man, stirred something in me, a deep longing that tugged at my senses and begged me to get closer to him.

As we parked outside my apartment, he lifted our hands and pressed his lips to the back of mine, his gaze delving deep into my own.

When his lips left my skin, I whispered. "Rufus is probably hungry. I think I forgot to feed him this morning."

He tsked and shook his head, though his grin lingered. "You're a *terrible* father. What am I going to do with you?"

"Anything you want," I mumbled, not meaning to speak the words aloud.

"Let's go feed the beast." Then he winked and added, "We can feed Rufus too."

Chapter Seventeen

Perfect Afternoon

Steph

RUFUS GREETED US THE moment we stepped inside, repeating his mighty yawl like someone was playing a record of a wounded animal and the needle had stuck.

"Alright, mister, come on," Jack said, bending down so the cat could hop onto his shoulder. "Let's get you breakfast. Daddy was forgetful this morning."

Rufus stared back at me through massive eyes as Jack kicked off his shoes and padded into the kitchen. The moment the cat food bag rattled, the fur ball was off his shoulder and circling, his tail whipping back and forth. A purr of anticipation bounced off the cabinet-covered walls.

Jack sealed the bag then set the cat and bowl on the ground. "Well, Dad duty's done."

He didn't have time to find me. I'd snuck up when his back was turned and was close enough to grab his shoulders and slam him against the pantry door.

"Hey!" was all he managed before my lips were roaming his.

Gone was the gentle caress from the night before. Gone was the tentative "should we or shouldn't we?"

I wanted this man so badly I could taste him. So I did.

My fingers slid from his shoulders to dig into the meat of his arms, feeling the corded muscles, stroking the lines of one who worked out hard and had the body to show for it. Everything about his body fueled the hard-on that twitched the moment he'd laced our fingers in the car. That had been a sweet moment, one I savored, but the heat of his skin and the seed of longing planted before we'd left for brunch fanned a flame of passion I no longer controlled.

Our tongues wrestled, as a hand snaked its way inside my shirt. Fire traced where his fingers touched.

With the permission of his hand on my skin, I grabbed the front of his shirt and tugged it roughly upward. He lifted his arms and wriggled free.

His arms still extended, I found his wrists and pinned them against the door above his head. His eyes widened, and I stared boldly, finally unafraid, knowing exactly what I wanted and what he would give me. Hunger, desire, and a desperate need burned in my gaze—and he soaked it in.

"You're *mine*, Jack Sutton. Today, you belong to me. We'll worry about tomorrow when it comes. You okay with that?"

There was barely a pause before his head nodded like a frightened child. His breathing was quick and shallow and I knew I'd thrown him completely off balance. Inky locks of unruly hair fell across his forehead and eyes, obscuring his view. He couldn't have looked more delicious.

There will never be a better time to taste this man, I thought. So I did.

He slammed his head back, smacking the door. Neither of us cared. I dragged my teeth roughly across his skin, scoring lines that marked him for me alone. That thought sent a thrill through me. I wanted this man for myself. I wanted to know him, to feel him, to devour every part of him. Thoughts of Jack consumed me, and I surrendered to them.

My mouth moved from his neck to his collarbone, then across to his shoulder. The musk from his armpit filled my nostrils. He smelled like a man, and that was everything.

I bit down on the meat of his shoulder then teased across his skin with my tongue, soothing the marks I'd just made.

He moaned and strained against my grip. I refused to free his wrists.

I kissed his arms, the crease between his shoulder and bicep, then paused at the swell of his taut muscle. Every line was perfect and defined, a sculpture worthy of a museum.

I breathed him in, running my nose near his skin and filling myself with his scent, his essence, memorizing the aroma I hoped would never leave me.

He craned his neck and kissed my head. It startled me, but told me how much he wanted the same.

I lifted my head and kissed him again, this time deeply. Our lips lingered and parted, then sought each other again. Unbridled passion transformed into something sensual, something deeper, something that scared and excited me ... and offered hope.

My heart threatened to beat out of my chest.

He pulled back. "Can we move to the other room? I'd settle for the couch or floor, maybe the bed, if you're feeling crazy."

Jack made me grin. Every time he opened that stunning mouth, he made me smile. Fucking Jack Sutton.

"Only if we take the rest of these clothes off," I conceded.

Now it was his turn to grin. "In that case, the kitchen counter is on the list too. Maybe the tub. Hell, I have a patio. We could put on a show."

I growled. "I'm a Mango. Don't tease me with a stage."

"Shit," he said. "I forgot. Strike the patio. You'd totally do that."

I wiggled my brows and bared my teeth. "I'd bend you over the balcony and have you screaming at your neighbors. They'd never want to leave this complex."

His eyes bugged. "Who says you get to do the bending?"

I snuck my hand below deck and gripped his rock-hard cock. "He's a big boy. I think he could have anything he wanted. He wouldn't even have to ask nicely."

"Fuck!" He banged his head against the door again. "Let me go so we can get naked already."

"Your house, your rules," I grinned, releasing his wrist and stepping back, my other hand still gripping his dick through his jeans. "Until I decide to break them."

Jack grabbed my hand and led me into the den. Rufus had finished his brunch and perched himself on the kitchen counter, where he could watch whatever his dad was up to. I tried not to look at him as we passed but the little bugger's eyes were so big I couldn't help but steal a peek. His innocence belied what we were about to do, almost comically.

When we reached the leather-clad sectional, Jack sat on the corner of the coffee table, grabbed me by the top of my jeans, and pulled me toward him.

"Shirt off, now," he ordered. Any hint of the scared little rabbit had scampered away.

"So bossy. What happened to the guy who was about to wet himself in the kitchen?"

"I told that wuss to fuck off. Shirt, now."

I reached down and tried to do that crossed-arms shirt-pull-over-the-head model trick that looked so sexy online, only to get my shirt tangled hopelessly around my neck. Jack let me tug and fight for a few seconds before laughing and reaching up to assist.

"Here, let me help before you hurt something."

The moment my shirt was over my head, his hands gripped the top of my jeans, fingers fiddling with the stupid button Mr. Strauss had designed to be harder to open than child-proof prescription bottles.

Jack, apparently, was a master at opening bottles.

My jeans sprung free, and a forest of sandy curls poured out.

"Commando?" Jack's eyes widened. "A man after my own heart."

I reached down and squirmed out of my jeans, letting them pile on the floor behind me. Staring down wearing nothing but my socks, I said, "Your heart isn't what I'm after. At least, not right now."

Without warning, Jack, eye level with the business end of my rifle, gripped my balls and shoved my cock all the way to the back of his throat.

"Oh shit!" I nearly fell over.

His head bobbed so fast I thought I might explode.

I gripped his moppy hair as wave after wave of ticklish, feverish, giddy sensations raced through me. He slammed me into him then pulled back slowly, dragging his tongue along my length, teasing the pulsing vein or artery or whatever that pulsing highway of blood was. I couldn't think. All I could do was feel. When I was nearly out of his mouth, he grazed his teeth just under my head on the spot that may as well be called the "man clit," and the whole apartment shook.

I tugged his hair and shoved myself back into him. The gag that followed was almost as satisfying as his tongue and teeth on my tingly spot.

He pulled back and stared up at me, spittle dribbling from his lips to my cock. The sight made me pulse and twitch. He kissed my tip, sending more pleasure up my length.

"You still have pants on," I pointed out.

"Not my job," he said, his tone playful yet commanding.

"Stand the fuck up then so I can correct that mistake."

I helped him to his feet, then dropped to my knees and attempted the same smooth button removal he'd demonstrated moments before. I was a jock, made to rock and roll. Unfortunately, my fat fingers were not.

"Here," he chuckled. "Let me."

The button flicked free.

Perfectly trimmed black hair appeared and my stomach leapt into my throat. I'd seen Jack naked that morning, but in the light of his den the thrill was even more intense.

As slowly as I could, I edged his jeans downward. This was a show I wanted to last as long as possible. I buried my nose in his fur, sniffing and nuzzling. Then I pulled his pants lower and breathed in again. When the base of his cock revealed itself, his length still caught in his jeans, I dove, shoving my mouth and tongue into the fur-lined groove, not caring how many curls got caught in my teeth.

His body squirmed, and his cock pulsed next to my cheek through the denim.

I pulled his pants lower and he sprang free.

Ignoring his grunt, I ran my tongue up his shaft, tracing the vessels and veins as he had mine. When I reached his crown, I teased him with the tip of my tongue until I felt his abs clench, then I did it again, circling him, taunting him, making him beg me to consume him. His fingers dug into my scalp and still I circled, flicking, prodding, edging, never going above that precious lid where pleasure and release met.

He shivered. His grip tightened. His moans deepened.

"Damn, Steph, you're driving me crazy."

Only then did I lift my head enough to allow his tip inside my mouth.

You would've thought I'd punched him in the chest the way he doubled over. "Oh fuck."

I took only his head, swirling it, letting my saliva coat and drench him in warmth. Sloppy suction sounds filled the room.

His fingers dug. My lips pressed firmer and I wrapped my tongue about his head.

Then I took him all the way down my throat, opening as wide as I could. I wanted him inside me, filling me. I wanted to taste him, to drink him in, to please him in ways that made him plead for more.

"God, Steph, please don't stop. Don't you fucking stop."

I took him faster, grabbing his balls and pulling them down and away, forcing his erection to its fullest length.

His hardness was perfection.

With my other hand, I gripped his chest then dragged my fingers down his sculpted abs. The feel of his muscles excited me further; I tightened my grip, which drove my sucking and slurping faster and faster.

"Steph, you need to stop."

I sped up. I couldn't help it. I didn't want anything to hold me back.

"Fuck!" he called out.

My hand on his abs felt every part of him tighten and resist, but he couldn't hold back what rose within.

The tease of salt tickled my tongue, then his first wave exploded against the back of my throat. I gulped it down, greedily, hungrily, eager for more.

He did not disappoint.

Freed from his chains, he gripped my head and shoved further inside me as one burst after another shot through me. I could barely swallow fast enough; creaminess coated my chin and dripped onto my chest.

He shot again and shivered, so I swallowed the last of him and let him fall from my lips. I looked up at the satisfied eyes of a man who'd just given himself to another.

Holding him upright, I stood and pressed my lips to his, letting him taste himself still coating my skin. His tongue cleansed and thrilled me.

"Your turn," he said.

"No, not yet," I whispered, grabbing his wrist. He would be spent, and I wanted him fully awake when we went further. "Can I just hold you now."

He smiled and smoothed my hair. The look in his eyes stole my breath.

Then he whispered, "You can hold me anytime you want, Stephan Breeden."

Chapter Eighteen

Up, Up, and Away

Steph

Jack dug an enormous plush blanket out of the hall closet and we lay naked on the couch, our legs entangled and his hair splayed across my chest where his head rested. With every breath, the warmth of his cheeks pressed into my skin.

After a moment of channel flipping, we settled on the movie *Dune*—the recent remake, not the original. Neither of us had seen it and sci-fi was yet another topic on which we agreed.

As the final credits rolled, I felt Jack's breathing slow. Brushing his hair back, like searching for the eyes on an Old English Sheepdog, I found them darting furiously beneath tightly closed lids. One of his hands rested beside his face on my chest and his fingers twitched.

I kissed his forehead, let his hair flop across his forehead, then laid my own head back and closed my eyes.

The distinct pricking of needles woke me some time later.

Jack hadn't moved, but Rufus had joined us. The full length of his tiny body pressed against Jack's back, which meant my naked body lay beneath them both. Unlike his dad, Rufus was awake and purring, content to be nuzzled against us. It would've been a most satisfying moment had he not chosen to make biscuits in my arm and shoulder just behind Jack's head.

"Ow. Come on, Ruf, not fair. I'm naked and can't move."

Yawl.

His motor revved at being recognized, as did the intensity of his kneading. Beads formed where his claws pierced the skin.

"You're going to make me wake Daddy, aren't you, you little shit."

"You calling my baby a shit already?" Jack asked without moving. I could feel him smile against my left nipple.

"He's doing the pin cushion thing again, and I've never really been into acupuncture."

Jack pressed his palms into the couch and pushed up. The moment his weight lifted off me, I regretted disturbing him. It had been a perfect afternoon.

"It's probably past his dinner time. How long have we been on the couch?"

I stretched and tapped my phone on the coffee table. "It's almost seven o'clock," I said.

"Wow. The movie was probably two and a half hours, then we slept for another three? No wonder he's making his presence known."

"*Felt* is more like it."

Jack looked back at where my shoulder was dribbling crimson. "Oh crap. I'm sorry." He threw the blanket back and started to hop up. "Let me get something to clean that up."

Rufus, disturbed by the sudden movement, leapt off me and scurried into the kitchen. I reached up and grabbed Jack before he could do the same, pulling him back down on top of me.

"What if I'm not done with you and this couch?" I pressed my lips to his and he melted into my body. I reached up and buried my fingers in his hair, wishing they could never leave their newfound nest. He growled, a deeper version of the purring I'd heard from Rufus.

"God, I wish we could stay right here forever," he muttered.

I kissed his nose, then his cheek, then his forehead. "Who says we can't?"

He cocked his head, eyes twinkling. "You're a professional athlete. You have to eat or you won't be able to swing a bat."

I reached down and gripped his cock, squeezing lightly. "I have a pretty good grip on yours."

"You're terrible." He rolled his eyes, but didn't pull back. "As much as I'd love to lay here naked for the next ... however long ... I do need to feed Rufus before he comes back and does actual damage. You'll learn just how persistent he can be when he wants something."

Jack pushed up and off the couch.

"Sounds like his daddy," I teased, smacking his ass before he could get away.

"Ow. Keep that up and you'll have to give me a proper spanking." He wiggled his brows and scooted into the kitchen, butt cheek reddening and balls flopping. I could've watched him dart around the house like that all night.

Rufus had indeed been hungry. The moment the bag rattled, his purr grew to a cacophonous rumble and he began circling Jack like a lion preparing to pounce.

"Are you hungry? We never really ate lunch."I sat up, letting the blanket fall to the floor. "I'm always hungry."

"I meant for food," Jack said, a smile lifting his voice.

"So did I. Don't get me wrong, I could totally go for a Jack sausage again, but my stomach is as awake as I am now."

"Want to go somewhere or order in? You haven't seen much of the town."

While Jack spoke, I stood and moved into the kitchen and wrapped my arms around him from behind while he watched Rufus eat. I kissed his neck and whispered, "I didn't come here to see Atlanta."

He leaned his head back and pressed his cheek into mine. "Ordering in it is. Chinese, Thai, or pizza?"

"No pizza. The guys order that shit every night on the road." I nipped his lobe. "How about Thai? I haven't had that in a while."

"Thai wins," he said in a breathless moan.

My cock was stiffening, and I pressed it into his backside.

"How long do we have before it gets here?" I asked, circling my hips so a dribble of pre-cum smeared across his butt.

"I have to call it in," he rasped. "It takes …" I licked his neck. "Shit. I mean forty-five minutes, usually."

I slid my cock between his cheeks, not enough to part them, just enough for him to feel it slide up and down.

"You better call it in, then," I growled in his ear.

"I'm trying," he said, gripping my hands holding his chest and pressing his butt back into me, forcing my cock between his cheeks.

"Maybe we should wait to call it in, have an appetizer first?" I pressed the head of my cock against his hole, again not breaching, just teasing. His body quivered.

"Good plan. Fuck food. Thai sucks."

"Not like I'm going to." I bit his neck and wiggled my cock back and forth against his hole. "Couch or bedroom?"

"Bed. Now. Please."

With my arms firmly around him, I turned his body, keeping my cock in his cheeks, then crab-walked us into his bedroom, nibbling his lobe and neck and anything else I could reach along the way.

His bedroom was simple but elegant. A queen-sized bed with a sleigh headboard and footboard was covered in a quilt made of squares depicting stickers one used to put on a suitcase when traveling around the world. It made the whole bed look like a giant footlocker.

The base of the lamp on his bedside table was an airplane, and prints of various fighter jets and commercial planes soaring through clouds covered the walls. In some ways, the room was more flight museum than bedroom, but it suited him perfectly.

He shut the door behind us then freed himself and threw the bed covers back.

We fell onto the bed, a tumble of floppy hair, arms, and legs, all tangled and falling across each other in a perfect mess. He grabbed my face and kissed me like a man dying of thirst absorbing his first drops of water—and I couldn't get close enough to him. He rolled on top of me, pressed his weight against me, and ground himself against my hardness. I felt how much the kitchen prep had excited him as his own slickness smeared across my skin, hot and sticky.

"What do you want, Jack?" I whispered as he trailed kisses down my chest.

"I want to kiss you everywhere." He kissed a nipple.

"What else?"

"I want to lick you everywhere." He licked the same nipple, turning it from sensitive to erogenous. I tried not to shiver and failed.

He smiled and bit down.

"Oh fuck," I said as my cock throbbed beneath his weight.

His eyes brightened and he scooted lower to take me in his mouth. As the night before, his lips were full and wet, his tongue hot, and he knew exactly where to tease and taste and taunt. Hands on my hips, he swallowed me down until there was no length left to take. I stared, caught between electric sensations and wonder at how his throat opened up.

His head bobbed until the skin couldn't stretch across my cock anymore, then he looked up, dick in mouth, and smiled with his brilliant blue eyes.

"What else do you want, Jack?" I forced out.

He let me flop free. "I want you inside me."

I'd been waiting for those words; hoping for them. God, I wanted to be inside this man.

I gripped his arms and hauled him back up so our faces were level and I could kiss him again. I needed to kiss him, to feel him, to feel how much he wanted me and to show how much I longed for him.

Keeping our lips together, I flipped us over so my body hovered above his. Our hands were grasped above his head, pressed into the pillows under my weight.

And still we kissed.

"The drawer." He motioned with his eyes.

I reached out, thankful my six-foot-two frame and gorilla-length arms let me open the drawer without taking my body off his. My hand found only a bottle and a box inside.

Glancing at my treasure, I grinned. "The box isn't opened."

A sheepish grin curled his lips. "Guess I don't do this very often. I got those in case … I mean, I wasn't expecting … just if … you know …"

I grinned wider at how awkward he'd suddenly become.

"I'm glad you thought ahead." I tore the box open and ripped off a condom from the chain, then tore the package with my teeth. "You want to do the honors?"

His grin lost its innocence. "Absolutely."

While he rolled the rubber down my shaft, I grabbed the bottle and pumped cool liquid into my palm, then reached down and dragged my fingers between his cheeks.

He startled. "Oh!"

"Sneak attack," I teased, wiggling my slickened finger against his hole. He shifted, spreading his legs a bit.

Condom secured, his hands gripped the back of my head and he lifted his legs over my shoulders. "I'm yours, remember? All day and all night. Tomorrow will take care of itself."

Jack repeating my own declaration shot fire in my veins, and the passion in his eyes stirred my soul. This man, this ridiculous man, was going to be the death of me.

I slid a finger just past his entrance. His eyes fluttered shut then opened again.

I pulled back and teased again, then slid in once more, this time to the knuckle.

"That feels so fucking good, Steph."

Then I slid in as far as that finger would go. His hips rose off the bed, begging for more.

My finger circled inside him, stretching him, feeling for that precious spot—just there.

"Fuck!"

Then I pulled out and added a second finger.

His muscles resisted, tightened against me, so I eased slowly, spreading him open, prying my fingers apart as they slid deeper inside.

"Yes, Steph, please. I want you in me. Please get inside."

Fingers retreated, I squirted more lube in my palm and smeared it on his hole and across my condom-covered cock.

Then I pressed against him, barely peeking inside.

"Oh, shit, you're big," he said.

I froze. "I'm not hurting—"

His hand flew to my butt and shoved me forward.

I slipped inside, and pricks of light exploded behind my eyes. *So much for gentle.*

He shoved me deeper, controlling me, forcing me all the way in. His finger gripped my ass, squeezed it, his nails digging like Rufus's claws.

I pulled back, then slid in again, just as slow, just as deep.

His grip tightened.

I kissed him. His mouth devoured mine.

He moaned.

I slid out, then back in, no longer slow, no longer gentle.

He cried out.

I shoved inside.

His nails dug. I punished him for it.

He groaned for more. Again and again.

I drove harder, deeper.

I lifted his legs, forcing his ass higher into the air and spreading them wider. I grabbed a pillow and shoved it under him, angling his ass so I could slam into his sweet perfection.

"Steph, fuck me, harder!" he demanded.

I drove him hard into the headboard. He reached up and braced himself, opening his legs further, willing me deeper.

I gripped his shoulders as my weight pressed forward, driving myself into him faster and harder.

The sound of slapping skin, of slippery friction, filled the room. His groans, my moans, the smell of sex and sweat and musk.

I reached down and gripped his cock, my hand still coated and slick. The moment I touched him, his body tensed.

"If you touch me now, I won't be able to … oh shit! Shit, shit, shit!"

I stroked him harder, gripped him tighter, slammed into him faster.

My breathing heaved as my abs tensed and my chest drew taut. He flexed beneath me, and his ass squeezed my cock.

"You grip me like that and I'll explode," I groaned.

His ass clenched. I pushed. Stars exploded.

His eyes flew open and he stared into mine as the last shred of control vanished …

And the first wave of ecstasy shot into him, filling the condom and coating my cock in flame.

Still, I drove into him.

He cried out, spilling himself across his chest, some flying onto mine.

Still, I stroked him.

The last wave of my passion drained inside him, but he wasn't done.

Another shot, then another, then one more, coating both our chests and stomachs, until at last, he shuddered and stilled.

Chapter Nineteen

Cuddle Bear

Jack

We did eventually order Thai food.

By the time it arrived, we were both relaxed to the point of exhaustion and so hungry I thought we might just eat the cartons to get to the food. Our feet rested on cushions I'd spread across the coffee table. The only moment our toes weren't touching or prodding was when we stood to refill our plates.

By the time we'd crushed nearly fifty dollars' worth of basil chicken, cashew chicken, and pad Thai, the tug of sleep was irresistible.

I slept with Steph's arms wrapped around me, the little spoon to his very tall and muscular utensil, more content and at peace than I'd been in a long time. Rufus, having declared ownership of Steph the night before, curled atop his head once again.

The next morning, as the first of the sun's rays peeked through the curtains, I slipped free of his embrace, took care of my morning bathroom business, fed Rufus, and scurried about the kitchen, intent on proving that I could be domestic and provide for my man.

My man.

I giggled as though the phrase had tickled my ribs.

Everything was fresh, and we barely knew each other, but something deep in my gut stirred at the thought of Steph being something special, *someone* special, much more than a one-weekend stand—well, one weekend and three days … and a month of texts … and phone calls … and a few FaceTimes.

I giggled again.

I was a grown-ass man. What the fuck was with the giggling?

"Somebody's happy this morning," a groggy voice drifted from the hallway opening.

I'd been so lost in happy thoughts that I hadn't seen him approach. He was still wearing nothing but his socks.

"Take your socks off and stay a while," I teased, pointing with a spatula to his feet.

He hugged himself and grinned like a little boy given a compliment. "My toes get cold."

A laugh slipped out. "Just your toes? Not your whole feet?"

He nodded. "Especially the pinky toes. They're really sensitive and shy. They get cold a lot."

The cuteness of his words were matched by the adorable, childlike look in his eyes. He wasn't teasing or joking. This was Steph telling me about his little toes and their tiny temperature issues. I wanted to reach out and squeeze his cheeks.

"You sleep okay?" I asked instead.

He nodded again. "You're a good snuggle bear."

God, he *had* to stop.

A sparkle of warmth traveled from my belly button, through my chest, and up my neck. I probably looked like an idiot grinning from ear to ear.

"What's on the agenda today?" he asked, apparently not as distracted by his nakedness as I was. I nearly chopped my finger twice, trying to peek at his Peter while chopping onions.

"It's a surprise," I said, a sly grin teasing my lips. "If you want, you can take a quick shower while I get breakfast ready. We need to leave here around nine."

One brow raised. "A schedule? With times? What have you cooked up?"

I flipped a piece of bacon but didn't look up. "Guess you'll find out soon enough. Hope you're feeling brave."

He stepped into the kitchen, balls swaying in the breeze, grabbed my face and kissed me. "Whatever it is, I'm sure we'll be fine together."

And before I could dissolve into a pile of goo like the Wicked Witch, he turned his naked ass around and retreated to the bedroom.

Chapter Twenty

Valentine's Surprise

Steph

THE NUMBER OF STREETS with Peachtree in the name in Atlanta was bewildering. I liked peaches as much as the next guy, but what was with their allegiance to the fuzzy fruit that inspired so many roads to bear that name?

Jack didn't know. He shrugged it off as yet another layer in the cultural identity of his hometown.

He was unusually quiet on the drive to our mysterious date. It felt as though excitement was threatening to burst through the seams and he was keeping his lips clamped shut to seal it in. Every so often, he peeked at me and offered a tight smile.

We drove through one residential area after another until the split-lane road, its grassy center asleep for winter, merged into a narrow two-lane street. As the car rolled to a stop at a red light, Jack turned to face me and hesitated.

"Everything okay?" I asked.

He gave me that tight, almost nervous smile again. "Do you trust me?"

Well, that's an odd question.

"Uh, sure. At least, I thought so until now."

"I mean *really* trust me? You need to for this next part."

That made my stomach flip. Next part of what? I didn't even know what the first part was.

"Of course I do. You think I walk around in just anyone's apartment wearing nothing but socks and scars from his cat?"

His grin turned sheepish. "Sorry about those."

"The socks or the scars?"

He chuckled. "Both. You really should just stay naked all the time."

"Already planning for this afternoon?" I reached over and squeezed his leg. "What's this all about?"

He sighed. "Don't make me hard. I need my wits for what we're about to do."

Okay, if I wasn't nervous before …

The light turned green and he returned his gaze to the road. I kept my hand on his leg.

"So, you remember I've been taking flying lessons?"

"Yeah, we've been talking about it all month."

He bit his bottom lip. "I kind of finished and didn't tell you."

"What? Jack, that's awesome! You got your license?"

He nodded. "And I was hoping … I mean, the plan today …"

We turned off the road and a small airport appeared out of nowhere.

"Want to see Atlanta from the sky?"

A wave of jitters rushed through me; first, in excitement for his accomplishment, then because I realized what he was proposing. He'd had his license for, what? Days? And he wanted me to get into a plane no bigger than a bucket and hope he remembered what all the knobs and buttons did? It felt like getting in a car with a newly licensed teenager—except this car had wings and would be soaring high enough to splatter my guts if he couldn't parallel park.

Fuck it. The whole thing sounded awesome.

"Hell yeah, dude! I'm stoked. Let's do it."

All the pent-up anxiety he'd held throughout our drive flew out in a laugh as he parked the car beside a giant metal building.

"You're sure? The training plane is tiny, just a two-seater. It's like riding in a racecar. The one I rented is a little bigger, but not by much. You'll feel everything."

I shrugged. "Sounds totally rad, like standing on a board. You can't feel much more than the waves trying to suck you under and crush you."

"Stoked? Rad? You going full surfer on me?" He shook his head. "Alright. Happy Valentine's Day."

My eyes widened and I gripped his arm, stopping him from exiting the car. "What?"

Out of everything he'd said, that might've sent my guts into the biggest tizzy.

"It's Valentine's Day. I thought this might be a good way to celebrate with my ... guest."

"Did you just ask me to be your valentine before taking me on a plane ride then demote me to guest status?"

"I guess I did. I mean, I didn't want to assume or anything." His eyes dropped, then rose again. "Are you okay with that?"

I thought a moment. "I usually celebrate this day by wearing black and mourning those lost in the massacre. It was a terribly sad occasion, often lost to history and bunnies and chocolates."

The horrified look that crossed his face nearly doubled me over. "What massacre?"

"The St. Valentine's Day Massacre. You know, back in 1929. It was terrible. I've never understood why everyone else celebrates with candy and flowers."

He gaped, his mouth open but not moving. I didn't think his eyes could open any wider.

"And I'm perpetually single." I shrugged, struggling to maintain a straight face. "It's not like I've had anyone to celebrate it with. Honoring dead bootleggers who just wanted to drink in freedom seems wholly appropriate, don't you think?"

He blinked, frozen, as if someone had hit the pause button on his body's VCR.

"It's much more fun to celebrate National Singles Day with friends."

He finally moved, cocking his head. "Okay, now I call bull-shit."

"What?" I tried to sound offended.

"National Singles Day isn't in February. Today is Valentine's Day. Tomorrow is Singles Awareness Day. I know that because it popped up on my Outlook calendar when I was checking my schedule."

"I can't believe you just called me out for *my* holiday, the day I celebrate my singleness."

He shrugged. "You've been doing the whole thing all wrong, on the wrong day . . . except for the mourning and wearing black on February 14. You got that part right, for the massacre and all, if you're into that sort of thing."

I laughed. "Oh, I'm definitely into bootlegging and death."

"That's so hot."

"I know, right?" I reached up and flicked a curl off his forehead. It promptly sprang back into place between his eyes.

His phone chimed. "That's our cue. Flight plans wait for no man."

"Aye, aye, captain." I sucked in a breath and opened my door.

Jack led me into a small office at the front of the building. A stunningly beautiful woman in her mid-twenties took his driver's license and had him sign into a logbook, then we strode through a hallway and stepped into a massive open hangar where three planes were parked.

"There she is." He pointed to the third bird in line.

The bottom half, including where the tires attached, was painted white, while the upper half, including the entire tail, shone a brilliant red. I'd been a little queasy in the car when he'd told me the plan, but nothing could've fully prepared me for the lone propeller on the plane's nose.

"Wow, you said it was small," I mused.

"It can actually seat five. We *could* be going up in the training plane. It's only got room for the pilot and a copilot." He pointed to the second plane whose back seat reminded me of the trunk of a Volkswagen Beetle. "Would you rather stay here or come watch me do the preflight checks?"

There was no way I was missing any of this, especially when my life might soon depend on his thoroughness—not that I would actually know if he skipped steps.

"I'm in. Let's check her out."

"You sure she's a girl?" he asked through a playful grin.

How was I supposed to answer that? Were there boy planes and girl planes? Did one have a metallic phallus hanging down somewhere? When pilots "turned Gs" did that mean ...?

"You're thinking too much." He laughed and shoved my shoulder. "Come on. This is gonna be fun."

I followed Jack to the airplane as my stomach did more somersaults than an Olympic gymnast. He walked with the swagger of a fighter pilot. If I hadn't been so flustered, the whole thing would've been a total turn-on.

"Hop up. You can sit with me up here." He opened a door and motioned for me to climb in and sit in the copilot's seat. He then walked around the plane and climbed into the cockpit, which was little more than an anteroom to the passenger seats in the back row.

"Alright, I need to walk through the preflight checklist. This will take ten minutes or so."

He pulled a laminated card out of a pocket next to his seat, then flipped the plane's power on. A whirring sound sent vibrations through the metal, similar to the ones already running through every nerve in my body.

"Power sounds good," he said. "Fuel gauges are at ninety percent. Lights on. Flaps"—he looked behind him as the flaps whirred—"flaps, check."

I got lost in the blur of flips and switches and checks and ticks and whatever else he did. Unlike my car, which barely required a button press to attack the road, there were a mind-boggling number of levers and dials to check and recheck. The computer's compass had to match the magnetic compass on the roof. The horizon level thingy had to actually be in the sight line—or something; he lost me on that one too.

I was at once impressed with everything he had to learn to become a pilot and terrified by the takeoff I knew was only moments away. If I hadn't been so into Jack and unwilling to show him I was afraid, I would've bolted from the building like a politician caught tapping his foot under a public restroom stall.

"Be right back." He leaned over and kissed me, then hopped down to inspect the lights and other important parts. When he pulled out a syringe-looking contraption, I had to stare. Three times, in three different locations, he drew liquid out of what I assumed was the fuel tank, holding it up to the light to examine whatever needed examining. The entire process of getting ready to take off was mystifying.

He reappeared in the doorway and climbed back into his seat, then grinned and said, "No water in the fuel. That's a good thing."

Water in the fuel? That's a thing? Seriously?

Before I could question that terrifying statement, he punched a few buttons and moved a lever. "Here we go. Buckle up."

He didn't have to tell me twice. My fingers flew so fast, I nearly pinched a finger in the buckle.

The plane lurched. I sucked in a breath.

His hand found my leg briefly then returned to the controls. "We'll be fine. Just wait. There's nothing like this."

I stared out the window as we taxied from the hangar. He chatted with the tower, gaining permission for one thing after the next.

And then we sat, staring down the length of the runway. I didn't mean to hold my breath.

The radio chirped in his headset and he shoved a lever forward. The engine roared and the frame rattled. If I hadn't been wearing headphones, I would've covered my ears. It felt as though the entire plane might growl itself apart before we even took off.

This is why Depends were invented, I thought.

And then there was nothing.

The wheels drifted off the concrete and the rattling quieted. The motor still purred, but it was more background noise than sonic attack. And the wind ... wow. I was used to running and hearing wind whipping around me, but this was like nothing I'd ever heard—like slicing through a screen with a knife, more whoosh than roar, a persistent whistle that made it feel as though we were flying even faster than we were.

Reluctantly, I released my white-knuckled grip on the sides of my seat cushion, flexing my fingers to get the blood flowing again. A quick peek at Jack revealed a boyish smile that nearly split his face.

"This is what it feels like to be alive," he said as the airport fell away behind us. "It's a perfect day. Look how far we can see."

The pure joy in his voice stole all my fear—well, most of it. I was no longer worried about peeing my pants. That was progress.

It took another ten minutes for me to fully relax and surrender to the experience. By then, we had traveled well outside of Atlanta, over farms and towns, to soar over mountains I couldn't identify. Browns, whites, and greens blended as wintry trees climbed ragged slopes below. Large lakes added a rich blue.

The view was breathtaking.

I'd flown a thousand times, but this was different. First, it was just the two of us. That was a completely different experience than flying with hundreds of strangers in a giant metal tube. Second, we were in a plane smaller than any I'd even sat in. Jack had warned me about feeling the bumps along the way, but nothing could've prepared me for the constant turbulence of that flight. It felt like a rollercoaster married a go-cart and had an affair with a bumper car ... and we were riding in the unstable love child of that questionable paternity.

Despite it all, I found myself smiling almost as broadly as Jack. There was no denying the rush. Every turn, every shift, drove my senses wild. The idea of soaring above the ground, just the two of us, was invigorating and intimate. Never mind the thrill of the ride, Jack was sharing something deeply personal, something that lived at the heart of his dreams. He'd planned for this day, made arrangements, looked forward to it. That he wanted me to see his world, to experience and understand it, to feel connected to it, made me see him in a different light.

I already knew he wasn't some shallow gym-bunny pretty boy, but to see through his eyes, through his hopes and dreams, it was something truly special.

He looked my way, a twinkle in his eyes. "What do you think?"

I peered out the window at the endless sky. "It's stunning."

He jerked a stick and the plane tilted so my shoulder pressed against the side and the window was nearly facing the ground.

"Better view?" The playful grin in his voice was insidious.

"You're a really, really *evil* man," I called into the mouthpiece. The plane had turned back upright, but my stomach was still on the ceiling, or wherever we had just been.

His laugh sang through the headphones, and my heart soared.

"I love it up here," he said. "There's nowhere in the world I feel more free."

I watched him as he stared out of the windshield. It was like watching a little boy getting to sit on his father's lap with his tiny hands on the wheel of a boat, pretending to steer for the first time. Except Jack wasn't pretending. He was living that little boy's dream. He *was* driving the boat.

"I can't imagine not flying," he said, as much to himself as to me. "It's what I want to do with the rest of my life."

That surprised me—not that he wanted to fly, but that he would make such a bold statement of purpose. He was a flight attendant with a shiny new private pilot's license. I didn't want to diminish that accomplishment—hell, it was more than what most people would ever do—but what would he have to go through to fly professionally? That's what he meant when he said he wanted to do this forever, wasn't it? Was it even possible to become a professional pilot while working full-time?

"Doesn't it take a long time, a lot of classes and stuff?"

"And stuff. Yes. Lots of stuff." He chuckled into my ears. "The flight hours take the longest. It's an entire process. It's why I joined the Guard, remember?"

The Guard. He'd mentioned being a member of the Air National Guard a few times, talked about his weekend duty. I hadn't fully connected the dots from Guard duty to his love of flying. Until that moment, I hadn't even known how deep that passion ran within him. I wanted to ask a million questions but figured it was a conversation better had on the ground.

"Alright, time to turn back. I only rented the bird for an hour."

I gave him a thumbs-up, feeling very *Top Gun*. "Sounds good, Maverick."

"You know that makes you Goose, right?" He winked and laughed again.

"That seems totally appropriate after how hard I goosed you earlier."

He snorted into the mouthpiece and shook his head. "You know the ground can hear us? The guys in the tower?" I felt the color drain from my face.

He laughed. "I'm kidding. I have to press a button for them to hear. You should see your face."

As the airport came into view, my stomach decided to climb back into my throat again. Taking off was the easy part, or so they said in TV shows and movies. Landing was where things could get tricky. I would never learn to fly, but staring down at the runway, I suddenly understood that principle all too well.

"I'll be gentle. Promise," he said, reading my mind. "At least as gentle as you were, Mav."

He was decidedly *not* gentle.

The back wheels touched down and my ass leapt into my chest. We bounced once, then slammed back down. Thankfully, the front wheels chose to stick their landing, earning a solid eight from the Russian judge. She seemed in a better mood that day.

"You can breathe again. We're on the ground."

I rolled my head and stared at him out the top of my eyes.

His shit-eating grin grew wider.

"It won't take long to park and check out. Preflight always takes the longest." Something chirped in the headset, and he replied. The plane rolled to a stop just off the runway. "They're putting us in a different spot. We have a minute while they open the hangar door."

When I turned to respond, his hand found my cheek, and he leaned across the instruments to plant a kiss on my lips. All thoughts of wind or engines or flying or stomachs in throats evaporated. There was only the softness of his lips and the warmth of his fingers on my cheek. When we pulled apart, his eyes were fully opened, brilliant blues staring into me with a breathtaking intensity.

He looked away quickly and asked, "Lunch?"I reached over and laid my hand on his leg, drawing his gaze back to mine. "Sounds perfect."

Chapter Twenty-One

Close Encounters of the Eli Kind

Jack

FLYING WAS A HIGH (pun intended).

Few things in the world got my heart racing and blood pumping like soaring a thousand feet in the air. Add Steph sitting beside me, and I couldn't imagine how Valentine's Day could've gone any better.

We weren't technically valentines, I supposed. Some might say we were still on our first date, though I reckoned it was at least our third, being our third day together in Atlanta. Using proper gay math, we'd had six meals, spooned all night twice, Steph had blown me once, and we'd had wild monkey sex once. Oh, and we flew in a plane. That's at least eleven dates, and I was pretty sure we earned bonus points with the monkey sex. Call it twelve.

So lunch made our thirteenth date. That sounded lucky.

Which was why I wasn't surprised when we walked into Cowtippers in the heart of Midtown to find Eli grinning, arms outstretched, as he completely ignored me and locked in on Steph. The poor boy never saw him coming.

"You must be the sportsball man I've heard so much about," Eli said, flitting toward us faster than the plane had approached the ground on landing, and slamming into Steph harder than my wheels had on touchdown.

"Oh, hi," Steph said, the wind knocked out of him.

Eli pulled back, gripping Steph's arms. "Ooh, look at you. You're a tall drink of water." He rubbed his hands up and down Steph's biceps, then pressed his palms to his chest like they'd been lovers for decades. "And all those muscles. And your nipples are so hard. Are you cold, sweetie? I could warm them up. Dear me, I think you just made me moist."

Steph's eyes darted from Eli to me then to surrounding tables, where men laughed, pointed, and waited for the next Eli-splosion. He was a well-known quantity and his fans enjoyed a good show.

"Eli," I hissed, trying not to be overheard by the entire restaurant. "Leave him alone. At least let me introduce the man before you grope him publicly."

"You're going to let me grope him?" Eli's eyes brightened as he clapped his fingertips together and hopped on his tippy-toes.

"No! Absolutely not. There will be no groping unless I'm the one doing it—and none publicly." I looked up at Steph. "Unless he's into that sort of thing and we haven't talked about it yet. So no, no groping. Period."

"Oh, honey, you're on your period? I'm so sorry. Can I get you a napkin, or one of those things that looks like an ice cream sandwich? I hear they work better. Oh, I know, you probably prefer the popsicle with the string. It's so convenient they come with a rip cord, don't you think so, Steph?"

Steph turned away, a laugh erupting from his lips.

I stared in horror. "Eli, please," I hissed loud enough to be heard on the patio. My face must have been seven shades of red, and I could feel heat from my cheeks to my toes. One glance confirmed that Steph was still struggling to contain his laughter and was enjoying my discomfort.

Eli ignored my pleas, hooking his arm around Steph's and dragging him toward a booth. "You come with me, honey. Let that old puss take care of Aunt Flo. You don't need to see all that, do you?"

I wanted to run back into the parking lot—or smack Eli over the head with one of the server's trays. Yeah, that sounded fun.

But I simply lowered my head and followed them to the booth, like a submissive dog with his tail between his legs.

Eli shoved Steph in then plopped down beside him, practically sitting in his lap. I took the seat across the table and tried not to glare daggers at my best friend.

"My, Stephan, you are much taller than Jack told me. And so blond. I love it. You're a surfer, right?" He didn't wait for Steph to answer. "And you play baseball with that funny team. What are they called? The papayas? No, that's not right. The grapefruits? Oh, I know, the eggplants. You're an eggplant, aren't you?"

Men at the booths behind and in front of us were howling.

Eli stared expectantly at Steph, his eyes blinking like a cat waiting to be fed.

Steph, once again off balance, stammered, "Eggplant? No, I have an ... I mean, I'm not ... no. Mango. I'm a Mango."

"Mango!" Eli shouted, his voice bounding off the wooden rafters. "That's right. All sweet and juicy, and *so* sticky when you're done with them. Umm-hmm. I bet you are."

Steph's cheeks flushed.

"And what do you do on this Mango team?"

"I'm the catcher."

"I knew it!" Eli squealed and clapped. Then his face fell and he leaned across to whisper to me, "I'm so sorry, hon. I know you like to catch too."

"Eli!" I was horrified.

He turned back to Steph. "A real-life catcher, huh? I bet you squat real good, back there behind the plate, looking up at all those men swinging their bats. Oh, and isn't the ump behind you, squatting close so you can feel him rubbing up against you? Does that mean what I think it does? Do you like three-ways? Jack, that's amazing. I get to play with the fruity boy too!"

Steph actually laughed at that.

Encouraged, Eli furrowed his brow. "Let's get back to Mangoes being sticky. That intrigues Aunty Eli. Their juice, I mean, it's so sweet and delicious until it clings like syrup all over your body and in your crack and ... I think I just got moist again. Jack, ask the waiter for an ice cream sandwich, would you?"

"Um—" Steph stammered.

"Let Mama lick you clean, baby. There's no need to be all yucky like that."

"Eli!" I nearly shouted.

One of the men behind me was dabbing his eyes with his napkin as he excused himself.

Eli finally turned to me and smiled. "Oh, hi, precious. When did you get here?"

I rolled my eyes. "I'm going to have Rufus claw your eyes out next time you come over."

"Little Ruf wouldn't hurt Mama and you know it."

I glared. "No, probably not, but I will if you don't behave."

"Fine." He turned to Steph like I'd just slapped him. They sat so close I thought their noses might touch, but still, he extended his hand. "I'm Eli."

Steph's eyes drifted down to the proffered appendage. Reluctantly, he reached up and shook it. "Call me Steph."

Eli raised Steph's hand to his lips and kissed the back of it. "Already asking me to call you by a pet name." He turned to me. "I like this one. Can we keep him?"

I crossed my arms. "*We*? No. But *I'm* thinking about it."

Steph's gaze snapped to mine, and I realized what I'd just said. Heat bloomed in my cheeks. I wanted to crawl under the table.

Eli, never missing anything, patted Steph's arm and whispered, "He can be a real prude, but Jack's a good one. You treat him right, you hear? Don't make Mama spank that perfect, perky, rock-hard ass of yours ... unless you're into that sort of thing, of course."

"Uh, okay?" Steph appeared unsure whether to agree—or what he might even be agreeing to.

Our server, a twenty-something guy with thick glasses and a crooked nose, appeared, a look of annoyance pursing his lips. "Eli, your food just arrived."

Eli stared up at the lad, cocked a brow, then turned to Steph, putting his index finger in the center of Steph's chest. "You have a good lunch with sour puss over there. I'm sure we'll see each other again real soon." Then he turned toward me and blew me a kiss. "Love you, hon."

And just like that, we were alone at our table, shell shocked and unable to speak.

"I'm Dave," the server said in a tone that made it clear how much he hated his job. "What can I get you to drink?"

WE MADE IT THROUGH lunch without further embarrassment, which might not sound like much, but, with Eli around, was a monumental accomplishment. I secretly swore to poison his brownies with X-Lax, or perform some equally juvenile prank, to make up for the torture he inflicted on us that day.

Steph shrugged the whole thing off. In the moment, he'd recoiled from Eli's luminosity almost as much as I had, but as soon as we were freed from his grasp, Steph's focus shifted to his *Flintstones*-sized steak and loaded baked potato. It amazed me that a man as unfairly ripped as he was could eat basically anything and still maintain abs on his toes; while I, a mere mortal, sat before him crunching salad with low-calorie dressing, hold the delicious croutons please.

I wasn't bitter ... much.

The moment we were shrouded in the silence of my car in the Cowtippers parking lot, Steph reached over and grasped my hand—but this was different from the other times. He didn't look at me, or wink, or give any indication it was a special gesture or secret handshake. He just reached over and laced our fingers like it was the most natural thing in the world, which I supposed it was, until I added myself to the equation and then it became something of a calendar-marking banner day.

Don't get me wrong, I dated. One couldn't swing a dead cat in Atlanta without hitting five horny gay men looking to get la—I mean, looking to date—but being with a guy who wanted to hold my hand without any expectations? Because he wanted to be close to me, to feel me with him? To be with me?

Yeah, that was something different. That made my heart flutter in ways I'd thought lost to humanity.

And I lost my battle with a grin—all the way home.

It was two thirty by the time we made it home and were greeted by a rambunctious fur ball. My traitor cat completely ignored the father who'd brought him into the world, fed him, watered him, and changed his litter box, and went directly to his new best friend, curling his entire body around Steph's leg the moment we stepped inside.

"Hi there, little buddy." Steph kneeled to offer a pet and was rewarded with my little climber scaling his arm and perching on his shoulder. "Oh shit. Didn't see that coming."

Rufus shoved his little wet nose into Steph's neck and cheek, purring loudly. Steph, working every angle of my helpless heart without even realizing he was doing it, leaned his head into the cat's touch. Both man and beast had their eyes closed in what was possibly the warmest and fuzziest man–cat moment ever. Unfortunately, my fingers weren't fast enough at opening the camera on my phone to capture it.

"Well, crap," I said as Steph glanced up, his brow furrowing at my fingers flying across the screen. "I wanted a picture of that. You two are adorable."

Steph smiled, stepped forward, and kissed me. Rufus, finally recognizing his dad's presence, leaned over and licked my cheek.

"You're adorable, Jack Sutton," Steph rasped when our lips parted.

My legs nearly turned to jelly on the spot. I *had* to get a grip.

"So, um, it's two thirty," I said, steeling myself. "I, uh, didn't make plans for after, you know, the plane thing, because I wasn't sure what you'd want, you know."

Steph chuckled, then reached up and cupped my cheek. "How about a nap? All that flying and eating has me worn out."

And just like that, my little head made his presence felt ... against my jeans ... several times.

"Sounds like an excellent Sunday afternoon." I stepped forward and kissed him again. "Why don't you go on into the bedroom? I need to check on little man's water then make a quick pit stop."

"Okay." He smiled and turned away.

I couldn't move. I just stared and watched him walk down the hallway and turn into my bedroom.

My bedroom.

"Ruf, what do you think?" I whispered.

Yawl. He nuzzled my neck.

"Yeah, I really like him too."

Chapter Twenty-Two

PANCAKES AND PIGS

JACK

STEPH'S BREATHING WAS SLOW and steady when I made it to the bedroom. I stripped off my clothes and climbed into bed. He lay turned away, so I wrapped my arms around his chest and held him like he'd held me the last two nights.

There was nothing sexual in how we slept. It was like his holding my hand in the car. It just was.

And it was perfect.

We woke around seven, ordered Chinese delivery, and decided to try the first episode of the Paramount Plus original series *Halo*, based on the video game.

Three episodes later, Jack declared it "our first binge series" and instituted a new rule that neither of us could watch future episodes without the other.

It was our first rule. I liked his rules so far.

We kissed good night but again fell asleep sans sex, content in our naked tangle of limbs. Rufus, once again, contorted his body around the top of Steph's head until the sun rose the next morning.

"Hey, you," I said when his eyes fluttered open.

I'd been watching him sleep for about twenty minutes. No, I was *not* a creeper. He was cute when he slept. His feet wiggled and his nose twitched, a little like Rufus when he smelled canned food being opened.

He smiled and rubbed his eyes—just like Rufus in the morning with his paws.

"Hey. What time is it?"

"Around nine."

"We slept that late?" His eyes widened. "Guess I was more tired than I thought."

I leaned over and kissed his nose. "You're cute when you sleep."

A blush crept into his cheeks and he squinted. "You're just cute."

"God, we're syrupy." I laughed, utterly unashamed of the sheer Canadian-ness of our syrup.

He grinned. "Speaking of syrup, I'm hungry. How about pancakes?"

I grunted. "Are you *always* hungry?"

He shrugged. "I'm a growing boy."

I reached down and gripped his cock. "No, no growing happening. You're just a boy."

"Great, now I have to pee." He yanked himself out of my palm and hopped up. I watched his butt cheeks bounce their way into the bathroom then threw my head back on the pillow with a sigh.

"What is today? Monday?" he called over the sound of a healthy stream hitting the bowl.

"It's Singles Awareness Day," I called back.

The stream stopped. The toilet flushed. Then his head appeared in the doorway with a broad grin plastered across his face.

"You remembered?"

I sat up on an elbow. "You celebrated *my* day yesterday. Today's your turn. We can pretend not to know or like each other and just do the same things at the same time. See, we're singles."

Oh shit, had I just implied we *weren't* single on other days? Had I just called us out for being—

"Sounds like a plan. I don't know you, I don't like you, but I want your pancakes. Get your ass up and moving."

I cocked a brow. "So bossy on *your* day. Yes, sir, Mr. Catcher, sir."

He chuckled. "That's a technical baseball term, not a position, just to be clear."

I brushed past him on my way to the toilet, grabbing his junk. "Oh, I'm well aware."

"Although ..."

I nearly tripped and fell face-first into the ceramic altar. "Although what?"

He turned, giving me full frontal and making it absolutely impossible to pee.

"I would be open to playing almost any position on your team."

And just like that, Little Jack hopped to attention.

Steph glanced down and grinned. "Breakfast. I don't have the strength for all *that*, as appetizing as the thought might be."

The six-foot-three wall of muscle who claimed to have no strength sauntered his naked ass out of the bathroom, leaving me hard and unable to accomplish a damn thing. A very long five minutes later, I finished my business and threw on a pair of silky gym shorts. Steph was standing at the kitchen counter, still stark naked, petting an appreciatively purring Rufus.

"Do you just walk around naked all the time?" I asked, trying not to be too distracted.

He maintained eye contact with Rufus. "Pretty much. Clothes suck."

Oh, God, why are you testing me like this? How am I supposed to cook or eat or just walk around my apartment with this man naked everywhere?

"Cool," I said. "I think I have everything to make breakfast. Or we can go out. Your day, your choice."

He turned from Rufus and wrapped his arms around me, his cock rubbing against mine, forcing the silk of my shorts to graze my head and nearly stealing the last of my control. "I'd like to cook with you."

God, I take it all back. Keep testing me. Test the ever-loving shit out of me.

Sorry, didn't mean to curse while praying.

"Sounds great," I said, right before he kissed me, driving my dick into a fit of rock-hard, silk-covered insanity.

He scrambled eggs and flipped bacon while I mixed and turned pancakes. We stood shoulder to shoulder at the stove, and I wondered how he kept from getting bacon splatter all over his ... sausage and eggs. Cooking naked looked painful, but he didn't seem bothered.

As we sat to eat, he asked, "What's the plan today? I'm pretty sure you have one, based on past performance."

"I do like plans, thank you very much." I smiled. "I thought we'd take a brief road trip."

"Really? Where to?"

"Well …" I played with my eggs without looking up. "I *may* have rented a cabin in the North Georgia mountains. And I *may* have already packed a bag with cat food, litter, and a water bowl so the rascal can join us."

His eyes widened. "Oh? An overnight road trip?"

I looked up and nodded.

"Are you planning to take me into the country and go all *Deliverance* on me? Make me squeal like a pig?" He grinned over the rim of his coffee mug. "That might make celebrating Singles Awareness Day challenging; at least, in principle."

Squeal like a pig? Is he hinting that he wants me to test his catching abilities? Wait, what was that about Singles Awareness Day? Is he saying—?

My heart raced faster than my mind.

He reached across and took my hand. "I'm really good with that if you are."

"I, uh … Steph, damn. Yes. I mean, yes, I'm very good … I mean, I'm okay, perfectly okay with that … whatever that is. You squealing. A pig. Like a pig. I love pigs. Pigs are the best. Shit. I didn't mean to say that. Oh God …" I snatched my hand back and covered my face.

He kneeled beside me and pulled my hand away. "Look at me, Jack."

I forced myself to obey.

"I haven't liked a guy in a really long time, and I can't stop thinking about you. I mean, we're together this weekend, but when we weren't together over this last month, you've pretty much been on my mind every day. Talking to you, texting, seeing your face, it's what I looked forward to. Now that I'm getting to know you, it's what I still look forward to even more."

"Steph—"

"I get that I'm on my knees," he said, grinning, "but this isn't a proposal, just a naked guy lightly dusted with bacon grease saying he's kinda crazy about you ... and that he'd totally be your pig, if you're into pork in the mountains."

I stared, struggling to believe he'd just said all that. My overactive brain bounced between him implying we were more than dating and then asking if I wanted him to be my pig. What did that even mean? It might've been the longest string of words he'd put together since arriving in Atlanta. My heart felt like it was about to explode. My cock did too.

I nodded. "I'm really great with all that. Seriously. One hundred percent."

"Even the pig part?" he said with a smirk.

I grinned. "*Especially* the pig part."

He smiled and the room brightened. "Good. I still don't know you, and we're still single. You can't ruin *my* day by being all sweet and shit. Got it?"

I nearly doubled over. "Yes, sir, Porky, sir."

"I'll let that one slide ... this time." He stood so his cock was at an unfair eye level. "Oh, one more thing."

"What's that?"

"I *really* like it when you call me sir."

Chapter Twenty-Three

THE MOUNTAINS

STEPH

"HOW LONG'S THE DRIVE?" I asked as we turned onto the main road from Jack's apartment complex.

"It's really not bad," he said. "Depends on traffic though. We're only going about seventy miles north, but that can take forever if enough people decide to bump into each other."

"Your confidence in your fellow man is admirable," I snarked.

"Fellow men and women are great. Fellow drivers anywhere near Atlanta are another story."

Rufus loudly protested that he was caged in a carrier in the back seat while we chatted up front.

"Will he be okay if I take him out and hold him?" I asked.

Jack grinned. "You really bonded with the little shit, didn't you?"

I reached back and scratched the mesh of his carrier, earning an irritated swipe with his needle-claws for my effort. "He grows on you—like a good mold."

"You just compared my cat to mold."

"You called him a shit."

"We are *so* single right now." Jack laughed. "And yeah, he'll be fine. He'll probably just curl up and sleep in your lap. I use the carrier because it's normally just the two of us and I can't have him making biscuits in my lap while driving."

"And what if I wanted to make biscuits in your lap?"

Jack's eyes widened. "That would not be conducive to a safe journey."

"Probably not," I chuckled, reaching back to retrieve Rufus before he screamed his little lungs out. "But it would be fun watching you try to maintain control while I played with your steering wheel."

"In a plane, it's called a stick."

I laughed again. "Trust me, in this car it's still a stick, especially if I get my hands on it."

"You really are impossible." He shook his head, black curls flopping as he did.

"Something totally wonderful and tubular. I'll take that."

"You didn't just say 'tubular' in my car?"

"Yes, I did. I sure did." I held Rufus to my chin and slipped into baby talk. "And your daddy likes it. He likes it when I talk surfer and piggies and dipsticks, doesn't he, little Rufus."

Jack groaned. "Please don't teach the child bad words. Besides, it's a stick, not a dipstick."

"That all depends on where you put it."

Our mindless prepubescent boy banter continued for another hour. How we managed to come up with so many off-color, juvenile jokes was a wonder ... until I realized we were basically two overgrown boys going on a camping trip with a cat. That put it all into perspective.

The elevation changed quickly. Hills replaced fields, then mountains overshadowed hills. The sun shone brightly in the clear winter sky. Trees, naked and unapologetic, spread in every direction. Our road went from a six-lane interstate down to four, then two, until finally losing its form and dissolving to gravel. Rufus and I stared out the window as Jack's Honda bumped along.

"We're not that far from Atlanta but it feels like we're in another world," I said.

Jack nodded. "We're almost there. I wish you could see this place in the fall when the leaves turn. I never knew so many colors existed. It's really stunning."

"I bet."

We turned onto an even narrower lane canopied by thick trees creating a tunnel of darkness. My joke about *Deliverance* suddenly returned to mind.

"You really are taking me somewhere to kill me, chop me into a thousand pieces, and make a stew, aren't you?"

Jack's shoulders shook as he laughed. "You have one twisted imagination. Besides, you saw the grocery bags and cooler. I brought food to cook. I don't need you. You'd probably be all tough and stringy anyway."

"Hey!" I feigned offense. "I bet I'm delicious."

"A little salty, if I remember right."

I laughed again. "Point to the gentleman. That was a good one."

He did the pageant wave and said, "Thank you, thank you. I'll be here all night."

I stared at him, wondering how much more I could like the guy. The car halting before a two-story log cabin ended my pondering. Smoke billowed from one of three chimneys and warm light streamed through tall windows.

"Home, sweet home," Jack said, turning toward me and smiling. "Come check out the view. The air's a lot colder up here, but you have to see this."

Mountains surrounded us; that had been clear in the ascent. What had not been clear was just how high we'd climbed or how steep the cliff would be only twenty yards from our cabin's porch.

"Whoa, dude. That's insane," I said, peering down the dizzying descent.

He hooked his arm around mine and rested his head on my shoulder. Rufus pawed his way to nuzzle his dad.

"Yeah, I love this place. The closest cabin is about a mile that way. There's nothing but us and nature. It doesn't get any more peaceful."

I kissed the top of Jack's head.

"What was that for?"

"Bringing me up here. The flight. Hell, for inviting me to visit in the first place."

He straightened and freed his arm. "I'm glad you came."

"Me too. It's been great."

Yawl.

"I think the little prince is cold. His fur doesn't exactly cover everything," Jack said, scratching Rufus's head. "Why don't you take him inside. I'll start with the bags."

"Deal," I said, leaning over for a kiss. "Come on, little guy. Let's go scope things out before Daddy comes inside."

Yawl.

THE WOOD OF THE cabin's exterior was rough, giving the appearance of a rustic structure built by the many hands of a hardworking frontier community. The moment I stepped inside, that illusion shattered.

The walls and floors remained the same reddish brown of the exterior, but a crisply polished sheen reflected the light cast by modern fixtures glaring down from the high vaulted ceiling. Lazy leather couches formed a sectional that joined on three sides facing a massive flat-screen television, a much larger unit than either of us owned back home.

I glanced toward the kitchen and my eyebrows shot up. Elegant wooden stools with brass buttons and leather seats nested beneath the lip of a sprawling marble countertop whose surface swirled with blacks, whites, and midnight blues. Matching counters inside the kitchen held shiny silver appliances. My heart skipped a beat when I spotted the coffee maker, which was more of an industrial-sized java factory than any home brew machine I'd ever seen. A baffling array of buttons, handles, and cylinders made me want to drop Rufus and race to play with my new toy.

We strode upstairs instead.

The main bedroom was as oddly rustic and modern as the downstairs, containing a bed with four pillar things on each corner. Posters? Poles? I wasn't sure. They were cool, etched with ornate vines and leaves. The quilt that covered the bed reminded me of the blanket warming Jack's bed but without the vacation theme.

I set Rufus down, and he promptly sniffed a few squares of the quilt then set to making biscuits.

"At least that's not my shoulder," I muttered.

He ignored me.

The main bathroom blew me away. Larger than the bedroom, the master bath made a giant L along the front of the house. Stunning glass walls enclosed a shower made for two, possibly three, maybe even four. The glass below chest level was frosted, but everything above my nipples was clear, allowing a view of the driveway and forest beyond. A flat screen mounted to the wall beside the shower looked like it was built to launch rockets rather than start water flowing. Three frying-pan-sized heads towered above, while waist-high jets poked out from every direction. The whole thing looked more like a car wash than a shower—and I couldn't wait to try it out with Jack.

Across from the shower, three marble steps led to the mouth of a tub large enough for six. I stared at the control panel, pleased to find a button labeled "hot tub mode," as well as one for a "traditional bath." Yet another feature we'd have to try.

A quick peek in the other two upstairs bedrooms revealed similar neat, homely rooms with rustic art on the walls and cozy comforters on the beds.

"Steph?" Jack hollered from below, his voice bouncing off the wooden walls like music off a band shell.

"Up here," I said, walking to the banister that overlooked the downstairs area. "This place is sick. It's not a cabin; it's a wooden mansion."

He smiled up. "A little help?"

"On my way."

We unloaded the car, set Rufus up with water and an afternoon snack in the kitchen, then stepped onto the porch.

"Holy cow, this view really is amazing," I said, staring across the lake in the expanse below. "Look over there. I didn't see that cabin before. There's another one."

We played a quick game of Where's Waldo, pointing out dozens of cabins we'd missed when we'd stood at the mountain's edge earlier. Something about the elevation of the porch made them more visible.

Jack insisted we head into town for lunch. I hadn't spotted even a single lonely gas station, much less a whole town, on our drive up the mountain. There certainly wasn't one visible on any of the surrounding mountains or by the lake below our cabin. When he refused to answer questions about this mysterious village, I knew he was up to something.

Jack was turning out to be a sneaky fella.

It took roughly ten minutes to escape the trees and hit solid pavement again. We passed a couple of other cabins that looked more like model homes where buyers chose their options than places people rented.

"There's a lot of activity up here. Somebody's always building a cabin somewhere, and the ads for land are all over the TV in Atlanta," he said.

I looked around, trying to remember the last time we passed another car, wondering where all this activity might be hiding.

Jack prattled on. "It's pretty cool the way they limit how much can be built. The community up here is determined to protect the natural feel of the place. It pisses off some people who want to make a mint developing the land, but if they weren't so protective I doubt there'd be a tree left standing."

"Huh. That is cool," I said. "From what I've seen so far, I really like it *because* there's no sign of civilization. It's a great place to escape."

He nodded. "Exactly."

A handful of ancient-looking buildings appeared as we crested a hill. Jack pointed. "There's downtown. Fancy, isn't it?"

"Downtown," I snorted. "I guess that's literally what it is, the town down the mountain."

"That's the local joke. Get ready. You'll probably hear it a dozen times before we make it back to the cabin. It's best if you play along and laugh. Otherwise, they'll keep trying and the jokes will get worse. Trust me on this."

"They can't get worse than all your pig jokes."

We were stuck at the town's only red light, which was apparently set to allow all of Atlanta to pass before turning green, when Jack turned to face me, a serious set to his jaw. "I wasn't kidding. You're totally my pig. I'm going to pound you so hard you'll beg for bacon."

I didn't mean to laugh. It just flew out. He looked offended. "I'm sorry. The dirty talk is hot, even with the pig imagery, but 'beg for bacon?' Really? Why would a pig beg for bacon? Is he a cannibal? Jack, that's terrible, even for you."

"Even for me?" he gasped. "What's that supposed to mean?"

The light finally turned green.

"It means it's your turn to go. Gaily forward, my man."

"Ain't nobody gonna be your man makin' fun of his pig jokes like that."

I snickered again. "You callin' me *your* man? Or just trying to mimic the locals to get yourself in the mood?"

He ignored my questions and pulled into an unoccupied plot of gravel on the side of a building whose sign read, "Ma's."

The engine shut off and he turned, one hand on the door handle. "You really better be glad I like you."

"I am." I reached over and patted his leg. "Your jokes ... ehh, we'll see."

He did the most mature thing the moment allowed: stuck his tongue out then exited the car.

We'd given up on adulting for the day.

LUNCH WAS BREADED, DEEP fried, and dipped in mayonnaisey sauces flavored with butter and ten other kinds of fat—at least, that's how it felt as we stepped out of the restaurant.

"Dear God, I'm going to fat camp right now. Take care of Rufus while I'm gone," Jack said, patting his ridiculously rippled stomach.

I chuckled, resisting an eye roll. "Want to walk it off? We could tour the town."

"Sure. I could use a little exercise. Lead on."

We strolled for a half-hour, which was far more time than it took to see two antique shops, one clothing store whose selection had lost its way in the eighties, and to peer into the windows of a church that looked to be hundreds of years old.

"Well, that was exciting," I quipped.

"It's definitely not a tourist trap."

"I'm not complaining about that," I said. "There's something quaint about this place."

"Quaint?" Jack grunted. "Surfer Poo is using new words today. It's cute."

"Hey!" I stepped back with a wide, toothy grin. "I'll have you know I like words ... and shit."

"Wow ... just wow." I shook my head.

"At least I'm pretty."

"That's for sure." Jack scanned me up and down like he was licking me with his eyeballs. "So, big boy, we're stuck in the middle of the mountains with no plans and nowhere to go. We could take a hike, go down by the lake and see what's there. If it wasn't hard nipple weather, we could go out on the lake."

"Hard nipple weather?" I choked out a laugh.

He stared pointedly at my shirt, where my headlights were clearly visible and on the brightest possible setting.

I covered them like an embarrassed girl stepping out of the shower. "My babies are sensitive. Don't stare."

He chuckled. "Your babies. That's great."

I turned away dramatically, as if to shield them from his lecherous gaze.

"Alright, shy one, what do you want to do now?"

His head whipped around, but he kept his headlights pointed away and spoke in an overly dramatic, almost comical tone. "I feel dirty."

"Dirty?" My brow furrowed.

"Uh-huh," he said, his voice lowering to a growl. "So dirty. Filthy, even."

My eyes widened. "Oh?"

"Yeah. But there's a problem."

"What's that?"

He looked around, as if to make sure we were alone. "I can't reach my back, and I'm pretty sure it's dirty too. Think there's someone up here in these darn hills who could help me?"

His faux Southern accent was more valley girl than coal miner's daughter and nearly shattered the steamy innuendo—nearly.

"I think I could help you with that," I said. "I'll be really thorough. Can't have an inch of you feeling dirty. That just won't do."

He grinned. "Let's get back to that cabin before my boner pops the buttons off these jeans."

Chapter Twenty-Four

Bubbles

Jack

THE MOMENT THE DOOR closed behind me, Steph's hands were on my arms, spinning me around and slamming my back against the door. His lips followed, then his tongue.

I nearly lost my breath.

Strong fingers gripped my arms as his body pressed against mine, grinding and sliding, up and down, our chests rubbing and our cocks throbbing.

"I want you naked. Now." There was no pleading, no begging. It was a demand.

I reached up and unzipped my jacket. His hands flew to grip its edges then stripped it over my shoulders and arms. I barely heard it hit the floor.

Steph walked me away from the door then yanked my shirt untucked and pulled it up, forcing me to raise my arms so he could drag it over my head. No sooner had it landed somewhere near the fireplace were his fingers on the top button of my jeans.

"So aggressive," I whispered, as our lips parted for a brief moment.

"You haven't seen aggressive." He unzipped my fly and slid his hands, palms against my hips, into my pants. They were ice cold from our trip outside, but I didn't care. I stepped on the bottom of my jeans and allowed them to fall, then lifted out of them.

"No socks. That's *my* thing," he said, leering at me as he kneeled and removed each sock.

I thought he'd stand and allow me to remove his clothes, or at least strip some off himself, but he stayed on his knees and took my length all the way to my balls.

"Oh shit," I said, startled by the rush of sensation.

His head bobbed, lips pressed, tongue swirling.

He gripped my hips and shoved me deeper down his throat. I felt him open to accept me, allowing my head to scrape new places it never had. His hands reached up and raked my chest. One gripped a nipple in rough fingers, twisting and pinching. Fire shot up my spine.

"Ow!" I shouted reflexively.

His lips left my cock. "No whining."

He pinched again. This time the fire mixed with pleasure and I struggled to remain upright. He braced me as he devoured me, over and over.

"Steph," I moaned.

He released me and stood, stripping off his jacket like it had offended him, tossing it so hard it hit the wall and fell. Then he ripped off his shirt and slipped out of his jeans. Still wearing white socks, he spun me around and shoved his cock between my cheeks, sliding it up and down, teasing my hole.

"Oh fuck," I groaned.

"Careful what you ask for," he rumbled.

His head massaged my hole and my whole body shuddered. Still, he didn't enter. "Did you bring—"

"Bag. Bedroom."

"Move." He gripped my arms and walked me up the stairs like a prisoner he had to secure.

He shoved our packs off the bed, threw back the covers, and tossed me face-first into the sheets.

"Don't move," he ordered.

Steph had been forceful at times, but never rough or aggressive. This was new. A tiny part of me was nervous, but my heart pounded like it might burst through my skin and flee, as a wave of curious excitement thrilled through me. I had no idea what he might do next, how he might act. Everything felt more intense, more real, more raw.

I suddenly craved him in ways I couldn't fully grasp. I wanted to feel him against me, inside me. I wanted him to ravage me and make me his. I wanted to surrender to his will, to give myself to his need.

I wanted to satiate his hunger with my own.

A wrapper tore. A bottle cap popped. Liquid squirted. And his fingers coated me.

"Fuck single. You're mine. You hear me, Jack? I want you and whatever the fuck this is we're doing, and I want it all the time." He shoved into me before I could register what he'd just said. Pinpricks of pain stabbed into my eyes. White-knuckled, I gripped the sheets.

He drew back, then drove himself into me again.

"Oh fuck!" I shouted.

Again.

And again.

His hands gripped my shoulders for leverage and he slammed harder. I felt him rage through me. Skin slapped, but I barely heard it. All I could do was feel.

His fingers dug tighter.

His cock shoved deeper.

I tore at the sheets, gritting my teeth, urging the pain and pleasure to never end.

Then he stilled.

He was pulsing and throbbing inside me. The weight of his body pressed against mine, his chest against my back …

His lips were suddenly by my ears. "Do you know how much I like being inside you?" he whispered then kissed my earlobe.

I shuddered. "Steph—"

He pulled out and my words froze.

What was he doing? Surely he hadn't come. I didn't feel him clench. He didn't holler or grunt. His cock was still rigid and twitching, like a race horse frothing to be released from its paddock.

"I want you inside me now," he said.

And I thought I might die right there.

He raised himself up and turned me over to face him, then straddled my body. I reached up and ran a hand over his chest and down his abs.

"Jesus, you're perfect," I muttered.

He leaned down and pressed his lips to mine, at the same time shifting his weight so my cock pressed between his cheeks. My whole body stirred.

He reached across and tore open another package then glided its contents across me. A heartbeat later, both his ass and my cock were coated, and he was pressing me against his hole.

"It's been a while," he said. "This might take a minute."

"Says the guy who just tried to pack my colon into my lungs."

He lowered himself and I slipped inside him.

"You complaining?" he asked through gritted teeth and a twisted grin.

"Only because you stopped."

His eyes fluttered open. "I thought you—"

"Shut up while I'm fucking you," I said, earning a wide-eyed stare and another grin.

"Yes, sir, Mr. Pilot, sir."

"That's *Captain* to you." And I shoved myself into him.

"Shit!" he screamed.

I was pressed beneath his weight, but did my best to draw back and push upward.

He arched his back, face toward the ceiling, and I thought I might come just staring at his outstretched body, then he lifted himself up and began fucking himself with my cock.

Gone was the "take it slow" from a heartbeat ago. With the force of his body's weight and strength, he drove me into him, faster and harder than he'd done to me.

Sweat dripped across his brow, down his neck, across his chest.

I grabbed his hips. He gripped my chest.

"Fuck me, Jack! Come on, baby, tear me open."

That caught me off guard but I took my cue, grabbing his sides and maneuvering us so he lay on his back. I gripped his ankles and held them in front of me in a wide V.

"What was that about me being yours?" I asked with my first true shove with him beneath me.

His whole body slid toward the wall. "Do it! I'm yours. Fucking claim me, Jack!" he shouted.

So I gripped his shoulders like he'd done mine and rammed into him as hard as I could.

His head lolled back.

I slammed again.

His ass clenched.

I took his legs and folded them over so he lay on his side, leaned down, and dove into him again.

"Oh shit, that's the spot! Right there, Jack. Don't stop. Don't you fucking stop," he cried.

Encouraged by his moans, I pressed deeper and faster.

My body raged. Heat billowed off my chest. My breathing heaved.

His ass clenched again. His hand found his cock and he began stroking. "I want to see you when you come inside me."

I gripped his ankles as before and rested them on my shoulder.

His cock was leaking. That fueled my need.

I stared into his eyes, stared at this man I craved. His gaze never wavered.

He stroked in odd circles, letting his palm rake over his tip with each pass. I memorized the movement, intent on using it on him in the future.

My abs tightened. Pressure built.

"Jack, I can't stop ..." He stroked faster, staring through me, into me.

I slapped his hand away and seized his cock, striking and swirling like I'd just seen.

I pushed harder. "I'm coming!"

My whole body tensed and I shot into him and cried out. Again and again.

"Kiss me, dammit," he shouted.

The moment our lips met, liquid fire shot out of him and coated the skin between us. His body convulsed, shaking with each burst as his lips consumed mine.

"Don't pull out," he whispered, when the last of his pleasure was spent. "Just stay in me as long as you can."

"I'm a mess—"

"I don't care. Don't leave me." He pulled my body against his, wrapping his arms tightly around me, clinging as if he might drown without me.

"Please don't…" he repeated, this time the plea of a small boy.

That's when I felt his shoulders shake.

Chapter Twenty-Five

Under the Hood

Jack

"Hey," I stroked his hair. "What's all this?"

Steph's tears streaked down my shoulder and chest. I kissed the top of his head and held him tight.

The moments of silence that followed felt like they would never end. He wasn't sobbing, but the tears continued to flow, and his uneasy shuddering shook my body as he breathed through whatever pain had found the surface.

"I'm sorry," he finally said. "Everything was so perfect. I mean, *you* were so perfect and all, and I had to ruin it. I'm such an idiot. I'm sorry."

"Steph, stop," I said gently. "You're not an idiot; at least, not for crying on my shoulder."

I felt a weak laugh against my chest, but still, he didn't rise to look at me.

"Talk to me. You can tell me anything. You know that, right?" I kept stroking his hair, hoping the gentle caress would offer some comfort.

Another moment's hesitation.

"I know," he said, again the tiny child I'd heard before. "It's just so hard ... to even think about him."

Him? I was even more perplexed now.

"Think about who?"

"Kyle," he answered without explanation.

I waited. When he didn't continue, I asked, "Who is Kyle?"

A pause. "He was my brother."

Was? My heart lurched at the pain in his voice. A thousand questions sprang to mind, but I held them at bay.

"He died when I was seventeen."

"Steph, I'm so sorry."

Fresh tears slicked my chest as he began to sob, this time losing his battle with grief.

I waited, wondering what had happened in our time together to bring such tragedy to the fore. If his brother died when Steph was seventeen, it would've happened eight years ago. Not that anyone got over the loss of a family member, but it was nearly a decade in the past. Why had it suddenly consumed him?

"We were best friends," he said, finally gathering himself. He propped up on his elbows to look at me. Angry crimson ringed his eyes and tracks of moisture marred his beautiful face. "He was fifteen when ..." He sucked in a breath. "We did everything together. He was big for his age, so they let him play up in summer ball. He pitched and I caught on the same team, the Sutton Brothers. We were unstoppable. He would've made it to the majors. I know it. He was amazing."

A smile of remembrance crept into his gaze. "You look like him. You have that same mop of inky black hair that won't stay off your forehead." He reached up and tried to brush a few curls back. They ignored his effort and flopped back across my brow. He smiled, his eyes distant, his voice even more so. "He was funny like you too. God, he was such a smart ass. We laughed all the time."

"He sounds like a great guy," I said.

He nodded, returning to the present and staring into my eyes with fierce sincerity. "He was the best. Really. I miss him so much, Jack."

I gulped back the emotions that threatened to pour out and cupped his cheek. Seeing him suffer felt like someone hammering a spike through my chest.

I stepped onto thin ice. "Do you want to talk about what happened?"

His gaze hardened, and his head shook. For a moment, I thought he might be angry with me for asking, but then something in him melted and his head fell back to my chest. I didn't feel him crying again, but he struggled to form words.

"I'll never understand, Jack. He was the happiest guy I've ever known. Seriously, I can't remember a single day when he wasn't smiling or laughing or being an idiot younger brother." His grip on my shoulder tightened, then loosened. "Why would somebody like that ... somebody who had everything ... who could be so much ... why would he ..."

Understanding dawned, and my heart panged anew. He pinched his eyes together as though fighting back more tears.

"After he ... you know ... my dad left his job and we moved to Huntington Beach so they could open a surf shop. That had always been my parents' dream, to be beach bums with a shop. They were never really the same after Kyle ..." He paused. "When COVID hit, they lost it all. My mom couldn't take it anymore. Dad got a job doing tech stuff and absorbed himself in work. I think he was running away or hiding. Mom actually ran."

"What do you mean? She left?"

He nodded against my chest. "One morning, we were sitting at the table eating breakfast, Dad and me. She walked in and announced she was moving out. She said she'd be gone by the time I got home from school and wanted to say goodbye. She kissed my forehead, like she did every morning, then just walked out. I've only seen her twice since. She sends a card on my birthday."

"Holy shit."

"Yeah." His eyes fell from mine as tears began trickling down his cheeks again. "When I got picked up by the minors, Dad moved back to San Diego. Our family had already broken into a thousand pieces. Now it lay scattered across the state—and all I wanted was to see Kyle one more time."

He rolled onto his back and stared at the ceiling, though I doubted he really saw anything above.

"I was *so* mad at him. How could he do that to me?" Bitterness edged his voice. "I was his brother, his best friend, and he ... he fucking left me. I'll never understand what was going on to make him do it—it's not like there were signs or anything. He was a happy, easygoing guy. The best. Jack, he was *never* selfish. He might have given me endless shit, but he would never hurt me. If I was in trouble, he always had my back. I never doubted that for a second. How could someone like that just ... just fucking ... *do* that? How selfish does someone have to be to leave his brother behind? To leave me with … to fucking leave me?"

I grabbed him and pulled him back on top of me so I could hold him through his pain.

I lost track of how long we lay there, weeping together. I don't remember when my own tears began. There was no holding them back, no resisting, no being strong for Steph. Neither of us had any strength left, and yet I didn't feel weak, not while holding him. I couldn't feel weak with him in my arms.

Rufus leapt onto the bed. He eyed us a moment, letting Steph reach out and rub his head, nuzzling his hand as he did. Heartbeats later, the scruffy kitten lay on her back, demanding her belly to be scratched. A calm fell over us both as we enjoyed the simple pleasure of Rufus's purrs.

"He would've loved this little guy," Steph said, as Rufus pawed at his fingers for more scratches. "He would've really liked you too."

I hadn't expected that. "Why? I get why he'd like Rufus. He's amazing. But me?"

Steph turned his head and rested his chin on my chest so he could look at me. His answer came so naturally, so easily, as though it was the most logical, obvious thing in the world, and he couldn't understand why I didn't already know it—and yet, when he spoke the words, they stole my breath.

"Because I do."

How did one respond to that? Were there even words? I certainly had none, so I craned my neck and kissed the top of his head. He squeezed himself against me, his warmth flowing through me like the comforting heat of hot cocoa on a wintry day.

"He'd love how much we laugh. I know that sounds dumb but it really was a big deal to us." He hesitated, then a small laugh escaped. "He'd give you shit for your hair, probably nickname you something like Prima Donna or Super Model. You'd never hear the end of it."

I smiled as he talked.

"He'd love this cabin and the whole idea of you renting it as a surprise. He'd get a real kick out of National Singles' Day and you forcing me to celebrate Valentine's Day. Neither of us had girlfriends in school. He was still too young and too absorbed with baseball, and I ... well, you know."

"Yeah, I know."

"And he'd lose his mind over you being a pilot. I mean, seriously, Jack, he'd think it was the coolest thing ever. I would totally lose my seat in that plane."

I smoothed back his hair. "From the quivering in your eyes yesterday, I'm not sure you would've minded giving up your seat."

He chuckled, and a hint of the perpetually cheerful man I knew returned. "Maybe so. Although, if I'm really honest, once I got over flying with a rookie pilot who still had those little fuzzy wings, it was a lot of fun." He lifted his chin in triumph at his own clever turn of phrase. When I didn't chuckle or laugh or even smile, he cocked his head. "What? I know that look. Out with it."

I looked away and mumbled, "Um, I kind of have a confession to make."

"Oh shit. What?" His eyes narrowed. "You're not really gay, are you? This was all just an experiment and you're going back to your eight wives and thirty-two children? Oh no, I know! Are you a closet lesbian? Do you secretly build decks on houses for fun? Do you have a lifetime membership to Home Depot?"

"No, idiot. They don't have lifetime memberships." I let out a nervous laugh. "And I'm fairly certain your ass can attest to my gayness."

"Hmm. I can still feel that lingering soreness. So good." His eyes were twinkling again. "Then what's your confession?"

I sucked in a breath, his body rising with my chest. "You *may* have been the first person I took up after getting my license, and—"

"And? There's more?" His eyes were saucers now.

I nodded. "I, uh, *might've* gotten my license the day before."

"The *day* before? As in, the day before you took my life in your hands? The actual day before?" He pushed himself up so he sat above me, straddling my legs. "You little shit. Were you using a learner's permit on me?"

"No. It's a real license, a full license." I shook my head. "Besides, they don't have learner's permits for flying. You're either licensed or you're not."

"Dear God," he said, clearly not paying attention, or, more likely, intent on giving me shit. "I went a thousand feet in the air with a fifteen-year-old in a Volkswagen Beetle with suspect brakes."

I shoved his chest, tipping him off me and onto his back. "Asshole. I'm a fucking fighter pilot and that was an F-16, not a Volkswagen."

He laughed. "Okay, Goose."

I stuck out my lower lip. "I'm Maverick or nobody!"

He shook his head. "Iceman. You're definitely Iceman. Although, with that hair, you could be the girlfriend. What was her name?"

I planted palms on his chest and flipped us to land on top of him, our noses an inch apart. "You are *so* going to pay."

He grinned again. "That's what I was hoping you'd say."

And right on cue, Rufus yawled.

Chapter Twenty-Six

FIRST GOODBYE

STEPH

Goodbyes sucked.

And not in the warm, tingly way that dribbled down your leg after you popped your rocks.

I mean, they always sucked before, but now they were the suckiest things to ever suck.

We spent Tuesday hiking in the mountains. It's fucking cold in the mountains in mid-February. I'd never been a wimp about weather, but I couldn't feel my toes as the warmth of the cabin flooded into us upon our return.

We made lunch together, shoving, teasing, and laughing like lovers of many years rather than new whatever-we-weres of just days.

That night, we made love on the sectional, then lay naked in our own mess watching one episode after another of *Halo*. Our heads were lolling with three episodes left in season one.

The next morning, we packed up and headed back to Atlanta. Rufus curled up in my lap and slept the whole way.

Being around Jack felt so comfortable and natural, like we were just supposed to be together. I'd never experienced that with a guy. Sure, I'd dated, but most guys only wanted one thing from a pro baller—well, two things, if you counted all the guys who thought players at every level made millions, which was decidedly not the case.

The only guy before Jack to stick around for longer than a couple of romps in the hay had been a military officer. Yeah, men in uniform were hot. They were even hotter when the uniform hit the floor. Unfortunately, that guy—and his uniform—got transferred to somewhere in Europe after our fifth date.

That goodbye sucked too.

Around noon, Jack drove me to the airport. Our hands found each other the moment our seat belts clicked into place. His thumb rubbed back and forth, as if scoring his feelings into my skin. The moment we stepped out of the car, my hand felt naked without his touch.

"So," he said, standing awkwardly on crossed legs in the parking garage like a teenage girl waiting to be asked to prom. "I'd really like to see you again."

I actually laughed out loud.

"What?" he asked, head cocking.

"You're such a dork. You don't have to ask. I'm crazy about you. The only question is when."

His face lit up brighter than the Braves stadium on game night. "Tomorrow? The next day? And the day after that?"

"I like how you think, but that might be tough." I chuckled. "Spring training starts the first week of March, and my life won't be my own after that. And you probably have to get back to work at some point too."

He nodded. "Yeah, unfortunately."

"Hey—" I lifted his chin. "You job is going to let us see each other. Without your flight privileges, I'm not sure I could afford the commute."

He thought a moment. "You want to commute?"

How does he still not get it? Is he blind or just so unsure of himself …? For such a hot, confident guy, he was really a little boy.

"Yes, I will commute to date you, Jack Sutton. We're still single in the spirit of my holy day, but I will sacrifice my commitment to the massacre as often as Delta will carry me to you."

"Or me to you," he said. "I want to see you play."

"Didn't you see that all weekend?"

"Not that!" He spat a laugh, clearly caught off guard, then shoved my shoulder when he saw the grin on my face. "I need to understand this Mango thing. It sounds very fruity."

"You have no idea," I mumbled. "It's a blast. You'll love it, and I can't wait to show you my town. Oh, you'll get to see Coop and Nate again too. I'm sure they'll want a chance to grill you."

"Grill me?"

I nodded. "Sam and Miguel are definitely Mom and Dad in our family, but Coop and Nate are like my big brothers. They're very protective, and Coop is a black belt in taekwondo. He'll probably threaten to kick your ass if you hurt me. He might even say that as he greets you."

"I'll keep that in mind."

"Shit," I said as my phone alarm sounded. "It's boarding time. I've gotta go."

"Text me?"

I laughed again. "We *can* talk, you know. FaceTime works too."

"If we have to." He feigned being put out. "Now go. As much as I'd love to keep you here, missing your flight isn't the way."

"Yes, dear," I teased, leaning down to kiss him one last time. As I reached the airport's glass doors, I glanced back over my shoulder to find him watching me. We waved, that awkward half-wave that said everything we felt, and my heart leapt into my throat.

Goodbyes *fucking* sucked.

Chapter Twenty-Seven

Duty Station

Jack

I zipped up my flight suit, which was basically a drab green jumper with patches. I generally didn't travel in uniform, but the flight from Atlanta to Savannah would barely get me into town in time to drive to the base and report for duty. I didn't want to risk the extra time needed to change once I arrived on station.

Flying on a commercial plane in uniform was a funny experience. People who would ordinarily be absorbed in their own worlds suddenly noticed my presence. I'd lost count of how many times I'd been thanked for my service, had my lunch bought by anonymous diners, or had kids ask to take a selfie with me. They saw the flight suit and immediately assumed I was a pilot. I never disabused them of that notion. They thought it was "super cool," and I was technically a pilot now, so it wasn't really a lie.

Little did they know I was basically a military administrator overseeing some of the base's intelligence operations. My job involved tedious hours managing men and women who stared at maps and satellite images all day. The times I participated in combat mission planning was as close to the excitement as I got.

For now.

That would change when I won my acceptance into the pilot training program. The Guard would then send me to Pueblo for the start of my Undergraduate Pilot Training, then to one of the training bases, and my career as a pilot would finally take off.

I'd used that pun a thousand times. It still made me chuckle.

When I first joined the Guard shortly after graduating from college, they made me shave my head. That was probably the worst day I had in uniform. Thankfully, my current commanding officer and flight leader didn't care about silly things like floppy hair. The other airmen who had to live with stubbled scalps gave me shit, tagging me with callsigns like Pretty Boy and Runway, but I didn't care. I'd take all their crap if it meant keeping my hair how I liked it.

Was it strange that a guy hoping to fly bombers worried over bad hair days? I didn't think so.

The guys at the gate checked my ID, did the mirror check underneath my Uber, then waved me through. I dropped my bag at the barracks, then hauled ass across the base to my office at the heart of the station's headquarters building.

A shrill whistle stopped me mid-jog.

"Where you going, Hollywood?"

I turned to find Major Brandon Sanders grinning from where he leaned against the mess hall's sign. Sanders was one of my closest friends in the Guard and perhaps the most irreverently smart-assed man I'd ever known. In short, we were meant for each other. The only thing keeping us from a lasting, loving relationship filled with insults and barbs was his utter straightness, which included his third wife and six children.

"Hollywood? That's a new one," I said, offering a quick salute, which he returned with a well-disguised middle finger.

"Gotta keep you on your toes, Lieutenant Dimples."

"Nah, that one's a fail. I only have one dimple. No points."

He grinned. "Nothing I do is a fail. You just didn't like it, which makes it wholly successful."

He grabbed my hand in a bro shake, then pulled me into a bro hug, complete with a bro closed-fisted smack on the back.

Yeah, we were bros.

I pulled back, gripping his arm. "As much as I'd love to stand out here farting around with the least respected officer on base, I need to report for duty. You know how the colonel gets."

"I'm glad I don't have to set foot in that building," he said as I stepped away.

Colonel Winston Dyer had been the commanding officer of the 165th for as long as I'd been in the Guard, probably since the eighteenth century. It was strange for a CO to remain in place for as long as he had, but it was also clear that the crusty old airman had no desire to climb the ladder any higher. "Stars are for shooting, not wearing on shoulders," he'd say in private moments, usually with a glass or bottle of bourbon in his gullet.

Colonel Dyer liked to think of himself as a real hard ass, a demanding leader who drove his troops to perfection. In reality, he was just an ass, and we were merely adequate. The thing that kept him in his seat was the quality of his fliers. The pilots of the 165th were beasts, men and women who stood beside the best the air force had to offer. Two had even been accepted into the vaunted Euro-NATO Joint Jet Pilot Training Program. Those slots were the rarest of the rare and required years of specialized training with instructors from the US, Italy, Denmark, and the Netherlands.

ENJJPT pilots were gods in jumpsuits.

My dream was to get into the basic pilot training program, get rated to fly the big birds like bombers and cargo planes, rack up enough hours to translate into a commercial pilot's license, then trade in my jumpsuit for a Delta Navy blazer and a seat in the cockpit. I was years behind the guys who'd done active service, but that was okay. As long as I earned my wings and had a shot at a career before gray hair became a thing, I'd be happy.

"Sutton, you're on time." Colonel Douchebag was sitting on the corner of my desk when I entered, arms crossed, scowl firmly in place. "You know what that means, don't you, son?"

"If you're on time, you're late, sir," I said, repeating his overused mantra.

"Bingo. You're fucking late, and I hate it when people are late."

"Yes, sir. Sorry, sir."

He glared, huffed out a sigh as though I'd just punched him in his slightly protruding gut, then spun and vanished into his office.

"He's such an ass," Technical Sergeant Dombrowski, one of my guys, muttered from a nearby station.

I gave him a *'sup* head bob and half smile. "It's kind of like marriage. Just admit you're wrong and don't let it bother you."

That earned a hearty laugh. "I dare you to say that to my wife."

"Fair point." I held up surrender palms. "Where is everybody?"

The long table that housed six workstations, all of which were normally filled with men and women staring into satellite photos on screens, sat empty. It was mind-numbing work, but necessary.

"No idea, LT. Place was dark when I got here a half-hour ago. The colonel walked in about two minutes before you did."

Great. I'd been one conversation with Brandon away from *not* getting dressed down for being on time.

"You back in the mountains?" I asked, peering over the tech sergeant's shoulder. He'd been tasked with drone footage analysis of a specific region of Afghanistan for weeks. Making sense of that mess was almost too painful to inflict on anyone, but he'd taken it in stride.

"You know it. You'd think they'd offer me tea at some point. That's their thing, isn't it?"

I chuckled. "I'm not sure it works that way. You want me to get you some tea? Is that what this is about?"

He grinned back over his shoulder. "You'd be the best LT ever."

"You know it." I patted his shoulder. "Let me find where everyone else has gone and I'll see what I can do for your craving."

"Thanks, sir. You're the best, sir. Really, the best sir ever, sir."

"Fuck off, Dombrowski."

"Sir, yes, sir. Fucking off, Lieutenant, sir."

I shook my head and laughed. I would miss my team when I finally earned a shot at my wings.

When I got to my desk, a stack of sealed envelopes begged for attention. There was nothing unusual about that. Interoffice memos were a thing in the military—more than a thing, they were life. They consumed much of my first hour of every duty day. This weekend would be no different.

The first four packets contained reports needing analysis. The next was a set of sat photos with tiny rings around unusual objects that someone with a higher pay grade thought were worth tasking resources to study and monitor. We'd see about that.

The next envelope was marked "PERSONAL" and addressed to me—personally.

That was odd. The military didn't *do* personal.

I sliced open the envelope and withdrew three sheets of paper, the first of which bore the wings and torch of the Air Force Pilot Training Program's logo.

My heart began to race.

In bold lettering near the logo, the type read, "Application for Admission."

I'd ordered the packet a few weeks earlier, before I'd actually earned my private pilot's wings. In the excitement of getting my first license, then Steph's visit, I'd forgotten all about it.

Reading the summary paragraph above the instructions, a list of air force bases caught my eye: RPA Flight Screening in Pueblo, Colorado, Euro-NATO Joint Jet Pilot Training at Sheppard AFB in Texas, and Specialized Undergraduate Pilot Training at Columbus AFB in Mississippi, Laughlin AFB in Texas, or Vance AFB in Oklahoma.

My head swam at all the programs and locations. I didn't fully understand what each meant, but knew acceptance meant attending training at one or more of the bases listed on the page.

My palms were sweating as I stared at the paper.

I'd dreamed of becoming a pilot since I was old enough to remember dreams. When I got the job as a flight attendant and they pinned those wings on my chest, I'd closed my eyes and imagined they were handing me a captain's jacket. It was all I ever wanted to be.

As proud as I was for obtaining my private license, it had only been the first step. While there were many paths to the cockpit, most wound their way through the military. Regardless of branch, service in uniform not only gave a pilot unparalleled training, it also offered the eternal hours of flight time required before the commercial aviation world would even consider an applicant.

It was the whole reason I'd joined the Guard in the first place.

Unfortunately, most failed to even obtain acceptance into the Flight Training Program. While official estimates were closely held to not discourage interest, rumor claimed only ten to fifteen percent of applicants ever saw a day of training.

I couldn't think about the odds. They would only frustrate and discourage me.

Like the Wright brothers and so many other brave souls who had flown before me, I would never leave the ground if I let the possibility of failure stand in my way.

So, I shoved my nerves out of the way and pressed pen to paper, taking the next biggest step along my path.

Chapter Twenty-Eight

Preseason

Steph

I GOT BACK TO Memphis around four o'clock. Joggers in skimpy shorts and T-shirts were everywhere, taking advantage of the unseasonably warm weather while it lasted. Lord knew, it never lasted. The weatherman was already chattering on about the next storm system expected to coat the town white over the weekend.

I'd barely pulled into the driveway of my apartment when my phone dinged.

DeltaOne: RUFUS WANTS TO KNOW IF YOU MADE IT HOME SAFELY.

I grinned down at the screen.

ME: TELL HIM I JUST PULLED INTO MY DRIVEWAY AND THAT I'M SORRY FOR LEAVING. I KNOW HOW MUCH HE LOVES MY LAP.

DELTAONE: HIS DADDY LOVES YOUR LAP TOO.

ME: OKAY, THAT WAS GOOD. YOU MADE ME BLUSH.

DELTAONE: WASN'T JOKING. YOUR LAP CONTAINS A BEAST WHO FEELS REALLY NICE IN ALL THE RIGHT PLACES.

ME: AS I RECALL, YOU HAVE A BEAST OF YOUR OWN, MISTER.

DELTAONE: ONLY BECAUSE YOU THREATENED HIS LIFE IF HE DIDN'T SLAM YOU INTO THE 18TH CENTURY.

A neighbor walked by, and we traded waves. She'd caught me leaned over the steering wheel laughing at Jack's messages. I was typing a smart-ass reply when my phone rang and Nate's smiling face appeared on the screen.

ME: HEY, NATE'S CALLING. BRB.

DELTAONE: FINE. I GET IT. MANGOES STICK TOGETHER. IN BUNCHES. LIKE BANANAS.

ME: WE ARE *NOTHING* LIKE BANANAS. DON'T EVER SAY THAT!

I pressed answer and lifted the receiver to my ear.

"Yo," I said, our customary greeting.

"Hey, sweetness," he cooed, straying wildly from the script.

"Sweetness? Really?"

"You just spent five days getting laid in Atlanta. Either you came back all mushy gushy, or you're going to be a raging asshole. I'm used to the latter, but hoping for the former."

"Wow. A guy goes away for a few days and comes back an outlaw."

"You were always an outlaw." He chuckled. "Coop and I love you anyway. So, out with it. How was the weekend?"

I had to fight my inner thirteen-year-old from babbling about how giddy and amazing I felt. "Good."

The phone crackled.

"Good? You're gone for five days, and all I get is one word?"

"Okay, it was really good."

An irritated huff blew through the receiver. "Listen, little brother, we need more than that. Get your sorry butt over here. Coop's cooking, and you'd better not make me eat his shit alone."

"You love Coop's cooking. He's really good."

"That's beside the point," he grumbled.

"Did you miss me? Is that what this is all about? Big bad Mr. Nate missed his little bro?"

"Yeah, that's exactly it. So get over here so I can get my irritating surfer dude fix for the week."

"Yes, dear. Whatever you say, dear. Love you too, dear." I chuckled. "Let me dump my stuff in my apartment first. You can fire up the PlayStation if you want another ass whooping."

"Got a beer with your name on it."

"Sweet. See you in twenty."

I clicked the phone off and quickly switched back to Jack's text chain.

> **DeltaOne:** How's Nate? Did he miss you? I bet he did, his little Surfer Poo. Who wouldn't miss someone with such a cute nickname? Makes me want to squeeze you and do naughty things.

> **DeltaOne:** Okay, shit, now I'm hard, thinking about doing naughty things with you.

> **DeltaOne:** Is it wrong that I just pulled out my dick and started stroking it while looking at your pic?

> **DeltaOne:** Dammit. You're going to get my screen messy.

I couldn't decide whether to respond or wait for whatever might happen next. I'd never been on the play-by-play end of a whack-off, certainly not by text. It was at once exciting and oddly confusing. I suddenly felt cheated on by technology.

> **DeltaOne:** You waited too long. I have no more energy. Rufus is staring at me like I just cut off his tail. I live in shame.

DeltaOne: SHAME! SHAME! SHAME! *ring ring*

DeltaOne: That was the weird nun in *Game of Thrones*, in case you wondered.

Me: I leave you for five minutes and you jack off (pun intended), scare your cat, mess up your phone, and start quoting fictional characters to underscore your own guilt? There isn't a therapist alive who could unpack all of that!

DeltaOne: When you add it all together, it does sound kind of sad.

Me: Like a high school A/V nerd caught with a jar of Vaseline sad.

DeltaOne: Ew. You're sick.

Me: Ha. My hands are clean. Literally. How about yours, Master Debater?

DeltaOne: To think I invited you into my home, flew you around my town, took you to a cabin in the woods, and introduced you to my child! All for what? Abuse?

Me: As I recall, you enjoyed my abuse. Begged for it, even.

DeltaOne: As I recall, you were the one who begged me to "pound the fuck out of you." You won't win this one.

Me: Point goes to Mr. Sutton.

DeltaOne: I'll take it. What are you up to tonight?

Me: Going to Nate and Coop's for dinner. Nate missed me. He's such a softie.

The dots danced then stilled, then danced again. There was a pause, then a chime.

DeltaOne: I already miss you.

I stared at the screen for the longest moment, savoring those words, grinning like a moron.

Me: Miss you too, dude.

DeltaOne: ARGH!

NATE AND I WERE only a few minutes into our first battle when Coop's head appeared in the opening between their den and kitchen.

"Hey, handsome. Welcome home. How was your long weekend?" His tone was what one might expect from a police interrogator who was warming up a suspect, all friendly and smooth.

"Great. Atlanta is cool," I said, like a stupid suspect.

I didn't turn to look. That would've gotten my avatar killed, but I could feel Cooper cock his head and cross his arms. The hound had sensed his prey and there would be no escaping.

"Alright," he said, a mother clearly not buying her child's pathetic excuse. "We'll talk about it over dinner. You boys have fun with your game. Dinner will be ready in twenty minutes."

"Thanks, babe," Nate said without looking up, fingers clicking buttons on his controller as fast as they could move.

"Yeah, thanks, babe," I teased.

Coop snorted.

When his presence no longer disturbed the Force, Nate bumped his shoulder into mine and whispered, "So, how was it? You like this guy?"

I blew out a breath and fired several rounds into Nate's avatar.

"Hey! Friendly fire!" His face contorted at the blood splattering across the virtual sidewalk.

I grinned. "That's for doing Coop's bidding. I know he put you up to asking."

"Did not," he groused, tossing his controller onto the ottoman. I kept my eyes on the screen and my fingers clicking. "Am I not allowed to care about my little brother and want to know if the big, bad, sexy flight attendant spread his legs from Memphis to St. Louis so his massive, powerful plane could make a far-too-rough landing, over and over and over?"

"Ha ha. I think I got lost in that analogy. Whose legs were whose, and who owns a massive plane? I'm lost. Can you translate Nate into English for me?"

"Ass," he snorted. "Just tell me you got laid. I can't take mopey Steph anymore. He's a sorry prick."

"Jack likes my prick."

"Bingo!" He clapped his hands together, then shouted toward the kitchen, "Babe, they totally banged all weekend. I knew Steph was walking funny!"

"Am not," I protested.

"Stephy Poo, that's wonderful," Coop called back, coming up with yet another nickname I would hate. *Please don't let that stick*, I prayed silently. His head reappeared in the opening, a toothy grin parting his lips. "It's so wonderful to see our little boy growing up and sitting on dicks like a big man. Did you remember to breathe like I taught you? To relax? You know you'll get stretch marks if you don't use the good lube and many men will poo-poo your asshole if you have stretch marks … even though poo-poo really is the point of an asshole, but not in the context of you sitting on it. In that moment, poo-poo would be bad, even more so than stretch marks. Still, you need to remember to breathe and relax … and use good lube. Oh, did you think to bleach? Many men like a good bleached hole. Did you do those things?"

I hadn't meant to turn from the TV but Coop's mental splatter coated me like mud on a pig. The sound of my avatar getting mauled echoed throughout the den, and a quick glance to the side revealed Nate staring up at Coop, amusement crinkling the skin around his eyes.

"Uh, yes?" I said, desperate to answer in a way that would not invite more parental wisdom.

"Good." Coop nodded, satisfied his lesson had taken hold. "Now, did you use protection? You know how important condoms are. I mean, we're not worried about you creating little Stephs, even though tiny Surfer Poos running around in itty-bitty board shorts and flip-flops would be the cutest thing ever. I can just see their blond hair flying past as they run around the house. Would their diapers need to be surfer themed? Is that a thing? Nate, we need to look that up, you know, in case Steph decides to pop something other than a non-poopy, non-stretched, well-bleached asshole."

"Dear God, make it stop," I muttered.

Nate was laughing so hard he nearly fell off the couch.

"Dinner in five. Time to die and dine, boys." And Coop's head vanished.

It felt like I'd just been struck by a gay gang drive-by. They wouldn't shoot. No, they would simply re-landscape everywhere, improving the home value to the point you didn't recognize your own house, thoroughly pleasing the neighbors and baffling the owners.

Yeah, that's how it felt.

Over a dinner of chicken baked in Italian dressing, with sautéed brussels and roasted garlic potatoes, Nate and Coop grilled me about every aspect of my time with Jack. As much as I hated getting the third degree, it felt better than I would've ever expected to talk about him. I smiled recalling our easy conversations and endless banter. When I told them about Rufus,

I could almost feel him in my lap, or on my shoulder nuzzling my neck. I could definitely feel his claws digging into my skin.

How could such simple memories cause my chest to swell and feel all tingly?

Midway through dinner, silence fell over the three of us. The only sounds bouncing around their kitchen table were the clinks of forks against plates and the rattle of ice as Coop drank his tea.

Coop, as was his wont, broke the silence. "You're smitten."

It might've been the shortest sentence in the history of sentences spoken by Cooper Hawk … ever … in the history of ever … and sentences.

Nate looked up from his plate, staring at his husband, waiting for more.

Cooper blinked at me.

"Was that a question?" I asked.

Coop shattered his recently set personal record. "No."

I pushed a potato across my plate and tried to answered his non-question, if not for him then for myself. It was actually a good question, one I wanted to resist but knew in my heart was as obvious as the "I know who got laid last night" smirk on the Mona Lisa.

She was such a busybody.

I stared at the potato, then lifted my gaze to Coop. "Yeah, I think I am. I mean, I am. Dammit. I'm so freakin' nuts for this guy."

The smile that bloomed across Cooper's face could've brightened all the lights on every street in Memphis. Hell, it could've powered Broadway and the Las Vegas Strip.

He blinked at me a few times then turned to Nate. "I love seeing him so happy, babe. Look at him. He's practically glow-ing. Wait, do you think he's pregnant? They were only together a few days, but from the sound of things, they did the deed over and over and over. I mean, he never answered my question about using rubbers. What if—?"

"We used condoms. Jesus, I'm not pregnant."

"Whew, that's a relief," Coop said, sitting back in his chair. "I don't think you're ready to be a father. It's a lot of work. Just ask us. We have you, and it's almost more than we can handle."

Nate nearly spat beer across the table. "That's for fucking sure."

"Baby, language at the table," Coop chided. "Not in front of the man-child."

"You two know I'm not actually your child, right?" I said as dryly as I could manage.

Coop covered his mouth with one hand, eyes wide, and turned to Nate. "Did you tell him? Does he know he's adopted?"

Nate sprayed the table at that. Coop and I had to dab our faces with our napkins.

These guys were family, this was true, but sometimes family could be a bit much. I supposed it was like that for everyone, each in their own dysfunctional way.

"Seriously—" Coop dropped his beer-stained napkin on his plate and reached across to grip my arm. "We're happy if you're happy. When do we get to meet Jack? Yes, we met him on the plane, but that doesn't count. Is he coming to visit? We'd love to spend time getting to know him."

For the hundredth time that night, I wasn't sure how to respond. It meant the world to me for Coop and Nate to like and accept anyone I dated, and the more I got to know Jack, the more important that became. At the same time, things with

Jack were still new and fresh, and the last thing I wanted was to expose him to a high dose of Cooper Hawk, which was, in and of itself, a bit like drinking unfiltered pure grain alcohol without any flavoring or ice—not that I'd done that sort of thing … much … on a dare.

"We haven't made plans yet, but he said he wants to come to a game. I was thinking maybe sometime after spring training?"

"That's far too long to wait," Coop snapped. "If you really like this boy, you need to see him more often than once a month."

Coop was right, but still …

"He's got to work over the next couple of weeks, flying all over the place to make up for taking five days off with me. Then we start spring training and I won't own my own life anymore."

"It's not that bad, especially on the Mangoes," Nate chided. "It's not like minors where we lost our weekends too."

"True." The more the guys talked, the more the caterpillars tap dancing in my chest picked up their pace. Just talking about seeing Jack again made the colors in the room richer and the beer taste a little fuller.

God, I was so sappy. What had happened to me? One weekend away with a boy and I'd turned into a walking, talking cotton-candy-on-a-stick-dipped-in-sugary-pellets-with-a-syrupy-grape-flavored-drink.

Yeah, I had it bad.

"Well," Coop said, standing and piling my plate atop his as he began clearing the table. "Make it happen. You know he can stay with us if he's not comfortable in your apartment when your roommate returns."

Roommate. Shit.

In all the excitement, I'd forgotten that spring training wasn't the only thing to return in March. My roommate, Alden, our third baseman, was slated to fly back from his off-season in Wisconsin in two weeks. My home would no longer be mine alone.

I suddenly felt like an eighteen-year-old college kid who couldn't hold down his own shit without a roomie. What would Jack think about that?

Nate must've read my mind. His hand found my shoulder and he said, "If he likes you half as much as you like him, none of that will matter. It'll be fine."

I nodded, focusing on a mental image of Jack holding Rufus on the bed, both their hair swirling in unruly, uncontrollable directions.

And I knew, somehow, Nate was right.

It would be okay.

Chapter Twenty-Nine

MANGO INTRO

JACK

My next flight, an eternal trip from New York to Athens, was scheduled to leave at sunrise. I knew I should get to bed early, but the lingering excitement of Steph's visit had me up packing and cleaning my apartment like a beaver trying to build a hydroelectric dam.

My phone chimed as I carried a basket of clean clothes ready for folding into my bedroom. A quick check of the eighties-style digital clock on my nightstand told me it was 10:15 p.m.

I giggled out loud when I read the text. I hadn't meant to. It just slipped out like a sneaky fart that makes you check your undies for skid marks. The silent ones were always the worst.

Fuck me. I'm hopeless.

ME: HOW'D YOU KNOW I WAS THINKING ABOUT YOU?

SURFERPOO: I GOT HARD. I FIGURED YOU WERE FINGERING YOURSELF.

ME: WOW. JUST WOW. YOU SURE KNOW HOW TO SWEET TALK A GUY.

SURFERPOO: NOTHING SAYS LOVIN' LIKE A DIGIT UP THE BUM. KEEP UP WITH ME, KID.

ME: I'M NOT SURE THAT'S POSSIBLE.

SURFERPOO: SO, I KNOW IT'S LATE, AND YOU HAVE AN EARLY FLIGHT, BUT I WANTED TO ASK YOU SOMETHING.

ME: OKAY. SHOOT.

SURFERPOO: WANT TO COME VISIT ME THIS WEEKEND?

This time, the giggle was inside, like the rumble of a volcano ready to spew lava.

Okay, maybe not that. I wasn't about to spew anything, but I was giddy at the suggestion.

ME: I really, really, really would love to, but I'll be on a flight back to the States from Athens.

> **SURFERPOO:** You know your life sounds so foo foo when you say things like that.

ME: Foo foo? Is that even a thing?

> **SURFERPOO:** Apparently. Did you hear yourself?

ME: My luxurious ass will be working, not sipping champagne like some guys I met recently.

> **SURFERPOO:** I was a guest of a foo foo guy. I was not Mr. Foo, and have never had even a touch of foo in my Poo.

ME: Dear God, he's mixing made-up words with his made-up nickname. I might hurl.

> **SURFERPOO:** Don't spew on your Poo because of his foo. That would be taboo.

ME: I just threw up all over my clean laundry. Thanks for that.

SURFERPOO: I'm here to serve, m'lord. So, how about the next weekend? I start spring training the following week.

ME: Crap. I'm in Paris that weekend. When you left, I didn't think we'd see each other for a while, so I booked a bunch of trips back-to-back. I wish we'd talked about this before you left.

SURFERPOO: Me too. Now I'm really sad. Pouty Poo.

ME: Ha ha. Stop. You can't be Pouty Poo. You're too cute when you smile.

SURFERPOO: You think I'm cute? Aw. My wittle Jacky Poo.

ME: No. Absolutely not. There can only ever be one Poo in a relationship, and you are definitely him in this one.

The dots didn't dance for what felt like forever. I folded three shirts and checked back—still no reply. I reread the last few messages, and my heart sank.

Oh shit. Relationship. I didn't mean to go there.

Was he freaking out? My heart began thumping and I suddenly found myself pacing, phone in hand, staring at the screen.

Come on, dots, do your thing.

Finally, the dots appeared and did their butts-in-a-row-wiggling thing.

> **SURFERPOO:** SO, WHAT ABOUT IN MARCH? WITH SPRING TRAINING, I CAN'T DO ANYTHING DURING THE WEEK, BUT YOU COULD VISIT ON THE WEEKEND. NATE AND COOP ARE GOING TO KILL ME IF THEY DON'T MEET YOU SOON.

I stopped pacing and sat on the corner of the bed, finally breathing again. His closest friends—his family—wanted to meet me. More importantly, he wanted me to meet them. My mood swung faster than a drag queen's cock being chased by duct tape.

I was giddy again.

> **ME:** THE FIRST WEEKEND IN MARCH IS FREE.

> **SURFERPOO:** NOT ANYMORE. YOUR ASS IS MINE.

> **ME:** I LIKE BEING YOURS. MY ASS DOES TOO.

Well, fuck me running. I did it again. Who was this demon speaking out of my mouth? I was not a mushy guy, prone to leap before looking. There wasn't a lesbianic bone in my body. I was not a lifetime member at Home Depot, and I did not rent a U-Haul after a first date. Ever.

I screamed like I'd just won *Drag Race,* then leapt off the bed and threw my hands in the air, forgetting I was holding a phone. It went flying, slammed into the ceiling, then fell to bounce off my mattress and onto the floor.

I paused my happy dance long enough to pick it up, suddenly annoyed that the screen had cracked. By the time I figured out how to swipe without cutting my finger, Steph had left several messages.

He didn't type right away. I stared, holding my breath again.

When he put it like that, it did sound ridiculous, and I started laughing, imagining what he must've pictured as he read my text.

My heart jumped into my throat and I had to stop myself from hurling my already shattered phone again.

ME: I THINK MY BUTT JUST QUIVERED.

SURFERPOO: *GRIN* G'NIGHT. CAN'T WAIT TO SEE YOU AGAIN.

I stared at that last message, ran my thumb over it, then my forefinger, careful to avoid the sharp edges now decorating the screen. How was I supposed to sleep after that? Seriously. I was a generally happy guy, but the level of unbridled bliss bubbling out of me was almost more than I could stand.

So, I did the only thing a mature, stable, clearly *not* in puppy love thing a man could do: I opened my photos and stared at images of Steph until I fell asleep beside unfolded laundry with the phone on my chest.

Chapter Thirty

Alden's Return

Steph

EVERY MANGO WAS REQUIRED to report to the Mangrove on Monday, March 3. On Saturday, two days before the deadline, my apartment door rattled and Alden Whittaker strode in, one lanky arm laden with a pair of pillows, the other with a suitcase the size of a small US state.

"Honey, I'm home," he hollered.

His voice was unusually high pitched for an athletic twenty-four-year-old baseball player who prided himself on bedding more girls than any other man on the team. He was handsome enough, with a square jaw and full head of light brown hair swept back like Leonardo DiCaprio in *Gatsby*. His easy smile and quick wit won him even more points than his hair. Still, everything about him—except for his cartoonish voice—screamed "player," and not the kind who wore a number on a uniform. I wasn't sure I would ever fully understand what it was about him that drove women mad, but they flocked to him like moths to an oddly squeaky flame.

"Dude!" I yelled from my bedroom before rounding the corner and barreling into him, knocking the pillows out of his arm in the process. He barely had time to set the suitcase down before I had him lifted off the ground with his feet dangling in the air. That was a hazard of being the five-foot-ten guy on a team of six-foot-plus beasts. We loved giving shit, and with his voice, we were relentless. "My little hobbit. I missed you, Mr. Frodo."

"Okay, okay. I'm glad to see you too. Can you please not get me pregnant before I unload my luggage."

I dropped him to the ground, a broad grin on my face. "You sayin' you're finally coming over to the dark side? I know plenty of dudes who'd love to knock your fine ass up."

He laughed, sounding a bit like a nervous version of Olive Oyl. "No, there's been no team switching. I still belong to the ladies. We both know many, many women's worlds would shatter if I turned."

I rolled my eyes. "Oh, definitely. Chicks everywhere would just freeze up and lose their shit. Pussies would clamp tight, as though lockjaw had figured out how to work new body parts. It would be like life stopped or something."

"Right!" He pointed at me and nodded. "Exactly."

God, he was full of himself.

"Need help with your stuff?" I asked.

"You really are the best. Let me dump this first."

We spent the next twenty minutes making trips to and from his overstuffed Subaru hatchback thing—again, not a lady magnet, but somehow worked like one. Did it make him look more stable? More dateable? I thought it made him look like a hipster liberal professor who lived on granola and textbooks. Then again, I wasn't his target audience. What did I know?

As we lugged the last of his stereo equipment up the stairs, he said, "You already work out today? I didn't get to this morning and I'm way behind getting back into shape. Coach is going to kill me."

I grunted. "You mean Waldo? He can smell weakness a mile away. Your legs will be wobbly for weeks, almost as if you'd switched teams. You know that's how I'd make your legs feel, right?"

His eyes darted to me then away.

I loved torturing Alden. There was no way I'd ever want in his pants, but he believed *everyone* craved him, so my taunts always held a ring of truth in his ears.

"I hadn't thought about Waldo's Wrath. That's what they call it when he finds out we haven't trained in the off-season, isn't it?"

Waldo Emerson—yes, that was his name—was our athletic trainer. A former Green Beret and complete bad ass, Waldo expected a legionnaire's effort out of everyone and didn't understand why anyone on the planet wouldn't work out four times each day. He bragged about running twenty miles before each sunrise. None of us were even awake by the time he'd nearly run a daily marathon—and he never let us forget it either.

Alden was in serious trouble if Waldo picked up on his lack of preseason preparation.

"We can work out," I said, flexing a bicep into an impressively hard melon. "I've been back at it for about a month now. Feel pretty good."

"I hate you. You know that, right?"

I grinned and mussed his hair like he was a little boy. "You're so cute when you're mad, and your voice gets all squeaky. It really is adorable."

"Fuck off." His voice found a new octave as he flicked me a bird. "Give me a minute to change and I'll be ready to go."

"Cool." I rested a hand on his shoulder. "Welcome back, bro."

"You need me to call a medic?" I quipped. Alden gripped the railing and struggled to climb the stairs. Working out legs had been his idea and I made him pay for it, pushing him far past his poorly prepared limits.

"If I make it up these stairs, I'm going to kick your ass."

"If you make it up these stairs, you won't be able to lift your foot, much less kick anything." I laughed. "I'll go get some ice. You need to soak or you'll be useless tomorrow."

He grunted but didn't argue. No player liked ice baths, but we all knew their value in speeding recovery after a tough work-out. Alden would whine like a baby but he'd thank me in the morning.

I unlocked the door and waited as he hobbled in. "Hey, before I forget, I need to run something by you."

He looked up. "Okay."

"I kind of met someone."

"Steph! You left the apartment while I was gone? That's amazing."

His sarcasm wasn't too far off the mark. I did tend toward being a homebody when there weren't waves nearby. Even then, it was my board and me, not a group.

I shrugged. "Guess so."

He gripped my arm for balance as he walked into the apartment. "Alright, out with it. Who's the new guy?"

"His name's Jack. He's a flight attendant and—"

"Aw, man. You're dating a sky mattress? Have I taught you nothing?"

The look of sincere horror on his face made me pause.

"I've banged plenty of them. So has the rest of the world. They don't get the nickname for their health."

"Alden—"

"Seriously, I know you. You're not a hookup kind of guy, much to my chagrin. I'll never understand why you actually care and want to see someone a second time. That all sounds so complicated, if you ask me."

"You're not convincing me to listen to you," I said, crossing my arms.

"Okay, let me start over. How did you meet this Jack?"

"He was working the flight the guys and I took to Barcelona for the cruise. We talked for hours, then he arranged to work our return flight."

His brows shot up. "No shit. He found out which flight you'd be on and arranged to work it?"

I nodded. "It wasn't hard to figure out. We texted the whole time I was on the cruise."

Alden threw himself onto the couch and rubbed his eyes with his palms. "Let me get this straight—pun intended: you met this guy on the plane headed to another country, gave him your phone number, then he stalked you on your return flight. Now you want to date him?"

"I did spend five days with him in Atlanta."

"He lives in Atlanta?" He threw his head back. "Steph, what are you thinking? And what do you mean you spent five days together?"

"I flew down and we hung out for five days."

"And you got laid?" His voice was a near-whine.

"Fuck yes. Over and over. In many positions and locations."

"Possibly more man love information than I needed." He blew out a breath. "At least my work hasn't been totally in vain."

"He's got a huge cock and a really tight ass, and his tits are rock hard—"

"Enough!" His eyes were bugging. "I'm happy for you, really. Lord knows you needed to get laid. It's good for the harmony of our home. Hell, it's good for the whole team. But I don't need details about cocks and balls and—"

"Oh, man, I didn't even tell you about his balls—"

"Steph!"

I laughed and held up a hand, lowering my voice. "Dude, I'm trying to tell you something here. I really like this guy."

He shook his head. "This guy who lives in Atlanta?"

"Yes, that's not ideal. I know. It sucks, actually. But we're figuring things out. It's all really new but I think there's something here, something worth giving a shot."

He stared a moment, like seeing a spider climbing the wall and deciding whether or not to swat it with his shoe. "When do you see him again?"

I ran a hand through my hair. "That's kind of what I wanted to tell you. He's coming next weekend and I'd really like him to stay here, if you're okay with it."

His features softened, then he chuckled. "You asking me for some privacy? You don't want to hang a necktie on your doorknob or anything?"

"I would never ask you to leave your own apartment."

He held up a palm like I'd done to him a moment earlier. "You don't have to ask. I see how important this is, even if I have my doubts. I'll get one of the guys to put me up for the weekend. The last thing I want is to have to listen to you two screaming and moaning all night."

Now it was my turn to laugh. "It never stopped you. I think you scream louder than your women, and a hell of a lot higher pitched."

He flicked me another bird.

"Thanks, dude. Really," I said.

"You got it, brother. It's good to be home."

Chapter Thirty-One

Arriving in Memphis

Jack

Athens, New York, Atlanta, Miami, Barcelona, Miami, Rio, Miami, Atlanta, New York, Paris, New York, Atlanta.

By the end of that two-week run, I barely knew where I was or what time zone I was in, and I couldn't remember ever being so exhausted. Unfortunately, there was no way to plan a day of rest between returning from Paris and flying to Memphis. I was excited to see Steph, more than I could've imagined possible only a few months earlier, but that childlike exuberance was muted by my body and mind's desire to pass out.

Steph suggested I sleep on the plane. Of course, to a normal person who didn't fly for a living, that was a logical suggestion, but my body and brain were wired to be "on" the moment I stepped aboard a metal bird. It was like some twisted Pavlovian thing where the dog's eyes were kept open by tiny bits of raw steak waved under its poor nose—and in this case, I wasn't sure whether I was the dog or the dead meat about to be eaten.

Magically, the weariness of the past weeks ebbed the moment I stepped through the "point of no return" at the airport and spotted Steph. He was staring at the electronic menu, not paying attention. I made it halfway across before he turned and saw me.

I swear, it was like someone flipped a switch and lit up his whole being. A brilliant smile bloomed, and his entire aura glowed. I could practically feel his eagerness from across the terminal.

And then, just like the six-foot-three goober I knew him to be, he raised his hand and waved. The boy in the man's body actually waved at me, and my insides threatened to twist into knots. It took everything in me to avoid recreating the movie scenes where two lovers see each other across a crowded airport, drop all their belongings, and run into each other's arms. Seriously, I wanted to. Despite the chill outside, he wore a tight-fitting short-sleeve T-shirt. Arteries bulged like a roadmap across his perfectly sculpted biceps. I wanted him to wrap those arms around me and never let go, right there in front of a pair of airport cops and the ancient woman selling Elvis bobbleheads.

Instead, my inner six-year-old responded by raising one hand and waving with just the fingertips. The only thing I didn't do was giggle and squeal or flick my hair. Although, I might've done one flick, but only one, and it was a good, just-walked-under-a-fan-and-it-blew-in-the-breeze flick. The muzak playing over the speakers didn't do the moment justice.

"Hey, you," he said, our customary greeting, before stepping directly into my path, grabbing my shoulders, and planting a kiss on my lips. I'd never kissed a man in a crowded airport, and, while I wasn't shy about flying the rainbow flag, it was my workplace.

But his lips were soft and his grip was so firm. I reached up and felt his biceps and nearly melted.

A group of snow-topped ladies sitting at a table in a nearby restaurant facing the walkway applauded. One whistled and called out, "Kiss him like you mean it, baby!"

We laughed and released each other, eager to spot our cheering section.

The moment we glanced over, the women stood, cheered, and waved their hands in the air like we'd just scored a touchdown at the Super Bowl. I looked back at Steph and realized maybe I had … I mean, in my own way, in a gay dating Super Bowl playoff thing.

Okay, it wasn't the same, but it felt the same.

"Wanna get out of here before they ask for autographs?" Steph asked through a blushing grin.

"Yeah, I left my Sharpie at home."He reached into his pocket and produced a purple Sharpie. "I'm a Mango. I never leave home without one. Would you prefer to greet the ladies?" "Let me quote a great philosopher—" I cleared my throat. "Take me home or lose me forever."

His grin widened. "I still don't think that's how that quote goes."I shrugged. "Then take me to bed."

"You don't have to ask me twice. After you." He motioned toward the exit.

The moment we settled into his car, two things happened. First, his hand flew faster than a pissed-off cobra, gripping mine like he thought it might fly away. That made my heart do a somersault. The second was far less thrilling. My Disney-esque, romantic-dream-fueled adrenaline wore off. Steph was as chatty as a room full of auctioneers, but I had to fight just to keep my eyes open.

At some point during the drive—and I honestly don't remember when—he peeked over and said, "Why don't you lay your head back and close your eyes? We'll be home in a few minutes."

I knew I should've argued, insisted that my rebellious eyes remain open and available to see him, but the Titanic was going down and there was nothing anyone could do about it. A heartbeat—or fifteen minutes later, I really had no clue which—Steph's meaty paw pressed into my shoulder and shook me awake.

"Hey, Flyboy, we're here."

"Flyboy?" I said blearily. "I like that. It's cute."

"You're cute, especially when you sleep. Did you know your nose twitches like a rabbit when you dream?" He raised my hand to his lips and held it there a moment, his eyes glittering with amusement.

"It does not," I tried to protest, only ending up yawning and making a sound eerily similar to a Rufus yawl. "Besides, you're the cute sleeper. Your feet wiggle and your fingers twitch."

He kissed my hand again. "Come on, let's get you inside. Alden's staying with some of the guys so we have the place to ourselves."

"That's nice." I yawned again, then looked over his shoulder out his window. "Who's Alden? And what time is it? It's dark already. How long did I sleep?"

"You were only out for about ten minutes," he chuckled. "Open your door and try not to fall over. I'll grab your bag and take you inside. Oh, and it's half past eight."

"So early." I yawned again, opening the door. "I'm sorry I'm being a pooper."

I climbed out of the car and righted myself, bracing against the door. It was remarkable how wobbly and sleepy I felt.

"I guess all that traveling finally caught up with me," I said to the car next to us. Steph was opening the trunk and didn't hear me.

A moment later, his arm wrapped around me as though I was a drunk friend being escorted from the bar.

"Are you hungry?" he asked as he stepped past the kitchen to drop my bag in his room.

"A little, I guess. I should be. I haven't eaten since lunch, but I'm really not that hungry."

He reappeared, grabbed my hand, and led me around the couch. "Have a seat. I'll whip us up a snack. What would you like to drink? I have beer, wine, iced tea, milk, water … and that's about it."

"What are you drinking?" I punted the first question.

"Beer. I'll pour you wine. I got that cab you like."

"Wine will put me right out. I should probably drink water if you want tonight to—"

He dropped to his knees in front of me and held both my hands in his. His eyes were the deepest blue. I knew that, of course, but I hadn't remembered just how blue they were. I felt myself getting lost in them.

"All I care about is being with you." He smiled. "If you fall asleep, I get to hold you all night and feel you breathing against my chest. Do you know how many nights I dreamed of you doing that again?"

My heart tried to swoon, but it didn't have the energy. I gave him a weak smile and said, "I can't wait."

He leaned forward and kissed my lips. My eyes closed and I felt the world all warm and cozy, wrapping around me like the plushest blanket, tucking around my arms and under my chin and just over my feet so my toes didn't get cold.

When I woke to Steph's voice sometime later, he'd literally covered me in a fluffy blanket and tucked it in all the right places.

"Want some cheese and meats? I figured charcuterie was a good light snack." He held up a small plate half filled with sliced meat and squares of different cheeses. He'd eaten his fill and left the rest for me. "Your wine's on the table. I'm pretty sure it's had time to breathe."

I blinked a few times and yawned again. "How long was I out that time?"

"One full episode of *Press Your Luck*. You missed a woman from Idaho rack up three hundred thousand dollars, mostly cash, and lose it all on her last spin. The whammy was a bastard tonight."

"Sounds like it." I reached out and topped a slice of meat with a hunk of gouda then grabbed the wine. "Mmm. That meat is good."

He nodded. "I love it. It comes in little packets, pre-sliced in round discs. I cut those in half and it goes a long way. When I was in the minors, we had to make food stretch."

I made another meat and cheese bite, then sipped the wine.

Elizabeth Banks's perky voice announced that the next set of contestants were about to be tested with the first question round, so I settled into the nook under Steph's arm and ate and sipped until nearly falling asleep again during the bonus round.

I didn't remember him helping me into the bedroom. For all I know, he carried me. He definitely undressed me without any assistance. I woke at some point in the night to find his arm securely wrapped around my chest, our bodies nestled as close together as possible without actually being connected. Steph's breathing was slow and steady. I listened as long as I could stay conscious, enjoying the comforting rhythm of his chest rising against my back.

It hadn't been the evening either of us had pictured or planned when we arranged our rendezvous, but in that moment between waking and sleep, as hot breath tickled my skin and the touch of his twitching fingers teased my chest, I knew it had been the perfect night.

Chapter Thirty-Two

Good Morning, Sleepyhead

Steph

MY BACK TINGLED AS my eyes fluttered open. An uncontrollable shiver raced across my skin, though in the fog of waking, I couldn't fathom what had caused it. Then the haze lifted and I felt Jack's fingers tracing my shoulder blades and vertebrae, as though creating a stencil with a coarse-tipped pen. My first instinct was to roll over, to welcome the morning with his gaze and the smile that would surely creep across his lips, but the finger-tracing thing felt too good. I didn't want it to stop.

So, I pretended to stay asleep.

"I know you're awake." I could *hear* him grinning behind me.

"How?"

"You shivered all of a sudden. Then you shifted."

"I didn't shift. I stayed perfectly still," I said, sure I'd been clever.

He chuckled softly. "My fingers are on your back. I felt you shift. Good try though."

Maybe he had me there. Either way, I wasn't about to respond and bring this finger massage to a halt.

"You don't have to play possum for me to keep doing this. I'll rub your body all day if you like."

And just like that, my morning wood grew into a rigid, pulsing bar of steel.

Perhaps most pleasantly, I felt his own sword, already unsheathed, clang against my butt cheek. He shifted his hip so it rubbed up and down my crack.

"Not fair," I groaned. "Fingers only—unless you want more than you bargained for."

His lips grazed the back of my neck. "I didn't bargain. I bought. And I want it all."

Fuck me. How did I get so lucky to find this guy?

With one hand still tickling my back, his other reached around my waist and began the same teasing graze along my cock, almost hovering above the skin without touching it, just enough to make me tremor all over.

"Really not fair," I moaned, my voice still carrying a note of sleepiness.

His lips pressed into my neck, then his tongue drew a line down my spine from my hairline to the top of my back. His fingers closed around my shaft and gripped.

I was about to turn when his teeth dug into the soft spot between my neck and shoulder, the spot he knew sent my blood boiling with barely a kiss.

"Jack," I groaned.

His cock slipped between my cheeks and teased against my hole. "I want in there," he whispered.

"Uh-huh," was all I could say as he began tickling the now hyper-sensitive head of my cock. The first hint of moisture slipped free, and he quickly lapped it up with a finger and smeared it across my shaft.

"Nightstand. Middle drawer."

My cock suddenly felt cold as his hand lifted and his whole body turned away from me. The drawer slid open and shut, then I heard the pop of a bottle cap and a loud squirt. He rubbed his hands together for a moment, then heat and wetness pressed against my hole.

"You heated the lube for me?"

He kissed my neck as his fingers threatened entry. "Of course I did."

I shivered again, more at the man than his touch.

Then one finger slid inside, and I was wide awake.

"Mmm. Careful back there."

"I've got you," he breathed. "Just relax."

I pressed my butt back, forcing him deeper. "I'm not worried about you hurting me. It's early, and your little miner might get coal on his cap."

His finger froze and I felt his chest heave against my back as he laughed. "You choose *that* moment ..."

His laughter grew, and his finger popped out.

I rolled over to find him on his back, laughing at the ceiling, shaking his head. I propped up on an elbow, grinning from ear to ear, resisting the urge to laugh with him.

"What? I'm just looking out for your welfare. Poop on your pee-pee is a mood killer."

"Poop on your pee-pee? I'm dying." He sucked in breaths between laughs.

His laughter took on a higher pitch as he lost control, which made me join in until tears dribbled down my cheeks.

A few minutes—and even more deep breaths later—his head turned toward me, a wry grin warning of sarcasm to come. "I'm pretty sure your comment killed that mood long before your poop could."

I chuckled, swallowing down another round of giggles. "That's called 'fair warning.' I could've just let you play butthole roulette."

His eyes widened, and he burst out laughing again. "Butthole roulette?" he wheezed. "Did you just make that up? That's priceless."

"Not as priceless as keeping your pee-pee clean."

And just like that, both of us were crying and laughing and very much avoiding each other's gaze ... for a good half-hour. I wondered if he'd sober up and make another move in an attempt to get our sexy time back on track, but he never did. When a heartbeat of satisfied silence lengthened, I reached over and ran my fingers through his hair.

"So," I said. "We have dinner at five but no other plans. How about we get cleaned up and go find some breakfast? Afterward, I can drive you by Graceland and Beale Street. We can play tourists for a day."

"Sounds good." He nuzzled his cheek against my arm, his scruff scratching my skin in the most pleasant way. If he'd been a cat, he would've purred. "We have plans for dinner?"

I grinned and nodded. "Yep. I'm taking you to meet the fam. You might want to brace yourself. Nate's easy, but Coop ... he can be a lot."

"He's the karate kid?"

Steph snorted. "Taekwondo. Please, for the love all that's holy, don't call it karate."

He grinned. "Oh, okay."

"Trust me. Coop almost made the Olympic team. Now he owns his own gym, or dojo, or whatever they call it. I still can't remember all the terms. He's super passionate about the sport and ..." I struggled with how to describe one of my dearest friends.

"What?"

"Well ... he's Cooper. You'll just have to experience him yourself." Jack's eyes narrowed, so I quickly added, "It's nothing bad. Hell, Coop is one of the kindest, most genuine people I've ever known. In fact, his, um, *uniqueness*, is one of the many reasons we love him so much. There's really no one quite like Cooper Hawk."

Jack quirked a brow. "Uniqueness. Okay. Duly noted."

"You'll see. You're gonna love the guys, trust me. And I know they're gonna eat you up."

"I hope so," he said quietly.

I scooted forward and pressed my lips to his. "They're gonna absolutely love you. You're freakin' amazing."

Now he leaned forward to kiss me. "You are."

I kissed him back. "No, you are."

We went back and forth until sweet intentions turned into tickling and a round of light wrestling. With the advantage of twenty pounds and two inches of height, I had him pinned in no time.

"Trying to wrestle me?" I grinned, shoving his wrists deeper into the mattress.

He stopped struggling and smiled up at me. "Nope, just trying to get you on top of me. See, it worked."

I leaned down and kissed him. "All you ever have to do is ask."

"I know," he said, squirming out of my grip, planting palms on my chest and shoving me off him. "But that way was a lot more fun."

He hopped off the bed and fled into the bathroom before I could grab him again, leaving me lying there staring at the closed door and grinning like a fool.

I'M NOT SURE HOW breakfast turned into lunch at a hole-in-the-wall barbecue place off Beale Street, but the beer was cold and the food was amazing.

"We're going to smell like smoked meat all day now, aren't we?" Jack asked, sniffing his shirt.

I nodded. "Just wait. When we get home, you'll shower and still smell it. I think the stuff gets in your pores or something."

He grunted. "Tastes great though. Totally worth a little stink."

"That's not what you were saying this morning."

His eyes popped wide; he grinned, then tossed a wadded napkin at me.

"Abuse!" I pretended to shout for help.

"You'll get your abuse right before that shower."

"If I'm lucky." I was on fire, not missing a beat.

He shook his head. "How am I supposed to keep up with you?"

"I'm a professional. You can't. Just enjoy the ride."

"I plan to, right before that shower."

I groaned. "Point to Mr. Sutton."

He placed a hand over his chest and bowed, first to his right, then left. "Thank you very much."

The winter sun was already well past her peak when we left the stinky joint and drove toward Graceland.

"Don't get all excited. You're not going to see Elvis. He's at McDonald's."

Jack snorted. "Good to know. Will we spot any shag carpets?"

"Only if we go inside. Do you want to?"

"Nah. I think the outside is fine. I like Elvis as much as anyone, but it's just a house."

I nodded. "Most people who do the tour come out a little underwhelmed. There's only so much sixties burnt orange and brown one can take before their stomach starts to sour."

He chuckled. "Fashion advice from a baseball surfer. Who would've thought?"

"Dude! My board and shorts always matched. It was my jam."

"Wow. I'm not often speechless, but damn."

I turned and did a Groucho brow wiggle, earning another eye roll and grin.

"Oh, here we are," I said, slowing the car. "To your left, past that fence and between those trees, is the former home of the King of Rock and Roll, currently in residence at a Happy Meal near you."

"You are so irreverent. Show the man some respect," Jack scolded. "Whoa, cool fence."

The iron front gates were adorned with black musical notes across white lines spread between two brick pillars. A long drive curled up toward the large home, where Southern columns held an elegant white portico aloft.

Jack whistled. "That doesn't look like bad shag and bean bag chairs."

"It's actually really nice," I admitted reluctantly. "Some of the stained glass separating rooms is pretty gaudy, but most of the house is reasonably well done, even for the sixties."

"So why does everyone talk it down?"

"I don't know. It's one of the big visitor attractions in town. I guess people make fun of anything tourists like."

Someone behind us honked.

"If you don't want to go inside, I guess that's the end of the tour," I said.

Jack reached over and took my hand. "I'm good. How much time do we have?"

I glanced at my phone. "By the time we get back, we'll need to shower, change, and head on over. The day slipped by quicker than I expected."

"Sounds good. I'll scrub your back," he said.

"Just my back?"

A firm squeeze of my hand was his only reply.

Chapter Thirty-Three

Close Encounters of the Cooper Kind

Jack

An hour later, we pulled into Nate and Coop's driveway. Thick, neatly trimmed bushes surrounded the red-brick two-story home. Black shutters framed large windows on either side of a stately entrance. The house didn't scream wealth, but it clearly fit in with the more affluent areas of town.

"Nice place," I said, peering up through the windshield.

"Not nearly as nice as Coop could afford. He inherited a shit ton of money, but you wouldn't know it. These guys are as down-to-earth as they come." Steph leaned across and gave me a peck on the cheek. "Come on. You're gonna love them."

The moment our car doors slammed behind us, the mahogany front entrance to the house swung open and an athletic man nearly as tall as Steph stepped out. He wore a deep navy shirt with the sleeves rolled up, revealing impressive forearms, but what struck me dumb the moment we approached the one-step landing were his eyes. They weren't just gray, they were like staring into pools of quicksilver, deep and rich and somehow clear at the same time.

"Good to see you again, Jack," Nate said, reaching a hand out for me to shake. I snapped out of my pupil-induced daze, stepped forward, and gripped his palm. It was like shaking an iron clamp. His eyes never left mine as we shook and I had the sudden feeling of being examined in the very depths of my soul.

Steph's shoulder brushed mine as he leaned toward my ear to whisper, "His eyes creep a lot of people out. Don't let him do that Jedi mind trick thing."

"Are you telling him about the mind trick?" Nate said, releasing my hand and turning toward Steph.

"You know it." Steph grinned, then grabbed Nate's wrist and pulled him off the step to wrap him in a warm embrace.

"Good to see you too, little brother," Nate said through a surprised grunt. "Come on in. Coop's working on dinner so we have a little time to catch up. Want a beer?"

"You asking me?" Steph replied.

"No, actually, I was asking the only person here who still qualifies as a guest." The Eyes of Sauron shifted toward me.

(I know, it was the *Eye* of Sauron, but that's how his eyes felt, all judgy and never resting.)

"He prefers wine," Steph said before I could speak.

Nate's brow rose. "Answering for him already?"

I opened my mouth, but Steph got in first. "If you heard what I said about *you* before we got here, you'd just get the wine and behave."

Nate laughed and shook his head. "You see how this ungrateful child treats his dad?

"You're not my dad—"

"That's Sam, right?" I said. "He's Dad, and Miguel's Mom. That's what you called them on the plane, isn't it?"

Nate's eyes widened almost as much as his grin, then he stepped forward and clapped me on the arm. "Keep putting Steph in his place and you're going to fit in great around here. Let's get you that wine."

He pulled me forward, leaving Steph to bring up the rear.

"Stop staring at his ass," Nate called back.

Steph reached out and pinched my butt. I nearly tripped up the step.

Nate braced me. "Boys, boys, can you two behave, or do I need to show you where the bedrooms are so you can fuck it out of your system?"

I didn't know how to respond to that.

Steph didn't hesitate. "That'd be sweet. You and Coop can watch if you want, maybe video the whole thing. Jack fucks like a champ."

I stepped through the door and actually tripped this time, nearly tumbling into the back of the couch.

"Ooh, he's a graceful one," Nate said behind me.

Steph rushed forward to help. "You okay?"

I turned and tried to hide the color spreading in my cheeks. I'd so wanted to make a good impression.

"Aw, look at you, being the concerned boyfriend," Nate said. "I can't take it anymore. I'll be back with drinks."

Boyfriend? Had I heard Nate right? Was that what Steph told him I was? My mind spun faster than a porn star on a cock.

"You just have to laugh and roll with them. They're harmless, I promise." Steph's hand rubbed my back gently.

I nodded, not trusting my voice. There were a million questions I wanted to ask … well, not really, only one, but there was
no way I was asking it in Nate and Coop's house as Steph helped
me to my feet.

How was I supposed to get through this night, to look at
Steph and not wonder what he thought of me, what I was in his
eyes, what we'd become. Then I chided myself for being silly and
letting my mind run away. We'd known each other, what, two
months? Okay, three now, but we'd only really been together a
few times … unless you counted the days and meals separately,
which was an entirely legitimate form of dating math …

"You look like you've seen a ghost." Steph cupped my cheek.
"You sure you didn't bang your head?"

I stared into his eyes, lost in pools of blue that always stole my
breath. Did I want to be boyfriends? Maybe that was the question I should've been asking. Until we could talk, I wouldn't
have a clue what he wanted, but I could definitely sort out my
own feelings. Who cared how many dates we'd been on? We'd
known each other three months. That was a perfectly acceptable
time frame in which to lose oneself in the sheer perfection of
another person.

Shit, I had it bad.

"Beer for you, and wine for you, sir." Nate passed out one
bottle and a delicately stemmed glass for me. "I wouldn't know
a good wine from gasoline, but Coop says that one is medium
to dry with a nice bouquet—whatever that means."

I took a sip and immediately knew Cooper and I would be
fast friends. "It's great, thanks," I said, still afraid to meet Mr.
Mercury's gaze.

"Why don't we go in the kitchen? Coop laid out some meats and cheeses to munch on while he's finishing dinner. We can hang out and make fun of his apron while he spits in our food."

I glanced up to find Nate's warm and welcoming smile. His teasing had been in good fun, and there wasn't a hint of resistance to greeting the new guy with anything other than open arms and sincere affection. I'm not sure how I read all that into a smile but it was there, clear as Steph's hand squeezing my ass.

He rasped into my ear, "I'm gonna tear that thing up when we get home tonight, pick up where we were before the whole coal miner's daughter conversation."

Nate vanished into the kitchen, so I turned and whispered, "As I recall, where we left off would not have *you* doing the tearing up, mister."

He grinned. "Even better. Think you can fuck the smart ass out of me?"

My cock twitched against my jeans, and I knew we needed to move before it became obvious. "I think Nate is—"

Steph grabbed my crotch and squeezed. "He's mine and I want him as rough as he can give tonight. You got it? I want you to pin me against the wall and—"

"Nate," I called out, far higher pitched than I'd intended, then pulled away from Steph and darted into the kitchen. Steph's low rumble followed ... along with the rest of him.

I was now fully erect and pulsing. Dammit.

The kitchen was beautiful, with marble countertops and stainless steel as far as the eye could see. My eyes scanned the room, searching for a counter to hide my inappropriate erection behind, only to find Nate leaning against the far counter staring pointedly at my zipper.

"Hey, babe," he called to Cooper, whose back was turned as he attended something on the stovetop. "I thought you said we were having pasta."

"We are," Coop answered without turning.

"But Jack brought a sausage—a really massive one too. What's that for?"

Behind me, Steph coughed and beer splattered across my neck and back. Nate looked past me and I was sure the pair's eyes met. Nate doubled over. Cooper turned, eyed Nate, then Steph, then scanned me, landing in exactly the same spot Nate had found.

"Well done, Steph. Wow. He's a *big* boy ... and twitchy. That's an impressive range of motion, especially in jeans," Coop said.

So much for a polite meal where we told tales of our child-hood and laughed politely at jokes that skirted the line of polite society.

I covered my crotch with both hands like I was holding a fig leaf.

It couldn't have been less obvious if I'd just taken off my jeans and wiggled around the room.

Nate and Steph lost it. Cooper hesitated then snort-laughed his way back to the stove.

"This was my fault," Steph said through gasps, clearly trying to help but throwing fuel on the fire.

Nate pounced. "Oh, there's no doubt about that. Were you trying to rub one out on my couch? Are you sure you don't want me to show you the bedroom before dinner?"

Coop turned and slapped Nate with a spatula, though his own laugh said he was enjoying my torment as much as the others. "Nate, you boys treat Jack right. We can't afford to scare him off when he's the first man you've brought home to meet us in, well, ever."

"Let's go sit at the table." Steph's arm wrapped around my shoulders as he guided me across the kitchen. He whispered, "They won't give you shit all night. They just have to get it out of their system."

Then he kissed my temple like I was ten and had a boo-boo—which I kind of did.

Nate followed and sat across from us, still grinning like a boy who'd just told a fart joke.

"So, Jack," Coop called from across the kitchen, waving his spatula like a wand. "You're going to have to start from the beginning and tell us your life's story. Steph is a man of few words, which means *no* words most of the time, unless those words involve giving us crap or playing video games or talking about baseball, which doesn't really need words because it's Mango ball, which is hilarious and cheeky and totally for the kids, which again, needs no words, just laughs."

I felt my mouth open but couldn't bring myself to answer whatever that was. Was there even a question in all that?

Slowly, I turned my head to find Steph and Nate grinning and waiting, as though they'd fully expected Coop to shoot salad at me and couldn't wait to see how I responded.

I looked back at Coop, who was still facing me, wand at the ready.

"Uh, okay. Um, I was born in Orlando, grew up there, moved to Atlanta for college and stayed there afterward. Now I work for Delta, but you knew that. What else would you like to know?"

Coop and Nate exchanged a look, each man grinning at the other, then Coop turned back to his dinner preparations.

"Orlando, huh?" Nate said. "Ever work at Disney?"

I laughed through a sip of wine.

"What's funny about that?" Nate asked.

"*Everybody* asks that. The minute I mention Orlando, every-one assumes I wore a mouse outfit."

"You didn't?"

"Nope. Never wore the mouse head. I was Aladdin."

Steph's head snapped up.

"Aladdin? Really?" Nate asked.

Then Coop shouted over the hum of some mechanical cook-ing device, "As in, the guy who rubbed the lamp and flew on a carpet? I loved that movie. Aladdin was such a cutie with his black hair and big eyes; oh, and he wore that vest showing his chest and arms. That really didn't translate into hot in the cartoon, but I've seen an Icecapades version with a real man with muscles and he's freakin' delicious. Did you wear that vest? And did you have those arms back then? Do you still have the vest? Have you and Steph role played? He could be your Jasmine. He acts like a princess most of the time. I bet the boys lined up to sit in your lap. Did they sit in Aladdin's lap or was that just Santa? I'd totally rather snuggle with Aladdin. He was hot."

Again, my mouth did not work. And again, Cooper turned away and resumed cooking.

Steph snickered beside me. "You'll get used to it, I promise."

"Don't listen to him. I've been with Coop for years now and I'm still caught off guard. There's no preparing for word vomit." His words were sarcastic but his voice was filled with amused affection—and the way he looked across the kitchen at Cooper made my heart skip a beat.

"I bet you got stuck with Aladdin as a nickname," Steph said.

I nodded. "A lot of my high school class forgot my name was Jack."

"I might have to change how you're listed in my phone. This is too good," Steph added.

"Don't you dare—"

"So? Were you wholesome Aladdin or stripper Aladdin?" Nate asked, leaning forward with his elbows on the table.

I snorted, forgetting whatever I was going to say to Steph. "I don't think there is a role for a stripper Aladdin at the Disney park. There definitely aren't any poles for him to work on. Maybe in one of the bars downtown, but not on the main campus. But to answer Coop's question, yes, I wore the vest without a shirt. It was part of the costume. My arms and chest weren't as big back then, but for my age, I was pretty hot."

"Got any pics?" Nate asked almost before I'd finished speaking.

Steph leaned forward, mirroring Nate's elbow lean. "Yeah, I'd love to see you rockin' the fez and vest."

"From high school?" I shook my head and laughed at the pair. "Do either of you have pics of yourself when you were seventeen on your phone?"

Before they could answer, Coop yelled, "I do. I have lots. Want to see them? I was a really cute kid, but my hair was really big and puffy, and when it was hot and humid outside, I looked like a wilted Chia Pet, all limp and stringy. Is that where the band Limp Bizkit got their name? I always wondered about that. The biscuit part still doesn't make sense, but anyway, sometimes my hair would stick to my forehead and look really gross. Has that ever happened to you? Your hair is kind of big and wavy. I bet humid days suck for you."

I wasn't exactly paralyzed that time, but I did need a moment to decide which question to tackle.

"You have pics when you were a teenager on your phone? Really?" Nate said, cutting off any response. "Why have I never seen these?"

Coop glanced over his shoulder, toothy grin beaming. "Because you never asked. Grammy insisted I keep them. She had the paper copies turned into digital ones for my birthday. I think it was my twenty-first. She said memories like those were too important not to keep, so I kept them."

Steph leaned over and whispered, "His grammy died a few years ago. She pretty much raised Coop."

"And she's responsible for all this." Nate waved around the kitchen. "That woman was a fireball, from what Sam says, but as sweet and generous as they came. She set Sam up pretty good with a luxury suite at Sounds Stadium too."

"Her real legacy," Coop shouted, having heard every whisper despite the guys' best efforts, "was funding college for kids and taking care of her friends and funding charities, most of which never knew the money came from her. Before she died, she spread millions all over the place and never asked for a word of credit or praise. I hope I can be half the person she was."

I didn't know Coop well and I'd never met his grandmother, but the way he spoke nearly brought tears to my eyes. I think that was the moment I realized how amazing Cooper Hawk was. He might be quirky as hell, but that side of him was already worming its way into my heart. The quality of his character made me want his friendship and approval more than anything. He was at once endearing, charming, and inspiring.

"You okay?" Steph laid a hand on my arm, startling me out of my thoughts. I'd been staring into space in Coop's direction for a long moment.

"Oh, yeah, sorry, was just thinking. I'm good."

"Careful, thinking gets people in trouble in this house." Nate's easy grin made me smile.

"Alright, kids, dinner's ready," Coop called, heading toward us holding a casserole dish with two mittened hands. "Hope you're hungry. I don't know how to portion control."

I nodded. "I am, and Steph's *always* hungry."

"Hey!" Steph elbowed me.

Nate chuckled. "You just described anyone who wears the Mango jersey."

"Damn straight," Steph agreed.

Coop set the dish on the table, then planted a hand on my shoulder. "I'll protect you from the big, bad Mangoes. Don't worry."

And just like that, I was family.

Chapter Thirty-Four

After Party

Steph

"Well, I'm pretty sure you passed all the tests."

Jack and I stepped back into my apartment around ten o'clock. Nate and Coop hadn't exactly grilled him in a cement room with a single lamp shining in his eyes, but he had been the subject of most of the evening's conversation. To his credit, he played along and answered pretty much anything they asked.

"I'm not sure there's much more they could want to know," he said, gripping my waist and spinning me to face him.

"It's funny," I said, then paused.

"What?"

"I don't know. It just feels like … like I've known you a lot longer than three months."

His lips brushed mine, just barely making contact. "I know what you mean."

I leaned in and did the lip brush thing to him, pulling back when he leaned in. Two could tease.

"Nate got me thinking," I said.

He cocked a brow. "Didn't he say that was dangerous?"

"Only when in their presence," I chuckled, brushing a stray curl from his forehead. It rebelled, as always, and fell right back. "I give up on that hair."

He flicked his head and the darn thing stayed back. "You just have to know how to talk to it."

I pulled his body tight against mine and smiled. "Is that right?"

"Uh-huh." He kissed me, letting our lips linger and breath mingle. "What were you thinking?"

"Oh, uh ... " His tongue teased my skin. "I can't think when you do that."

"Good."

I pulled back, putting a few fingers' distance between us.

Jack's smile smoothed into a line. "What is it?"I looked away then back toward him. "I don't know how to say this or even if I should. I really suck at this part. I've never actually done this before."

His brow scrunched. "Done what?"

I stared into his beautiful eyes and lost myself in his gaze. My heart raced like a thoroughbred chasing a rabbit.

"Steph, what is it?" Concern now crossed his features.

"Fuck it." I stared a moment longer, then sucked in a breath. "Jack, I'm crazy about you.""I know, me too—"

I pressed a finger to his lips. "Let me get this out before I lose my nerve."

He nodded once.

"I'm so fucking nuts about you, Jack. I think about you all the time. I mean, we text all the time, but when we're not texting or talking or whatever, you're on my mind. I see you everywhere. Nobody's ever haunted my thoughts like this."

"Haunted? That's—"

"I'm freakin' falling for you, Jack, and I'm scared shitless. There, I said it. Fuck."

I turned to flee toward the couch but his hands grabbed both my shoulders. His eyes searched mine, like they sought the deepest mysteries of the universe. I felt like I might wilt under that gaze, simply dissolve into a puddle of nothingness right at his feet. He didn't waver and his grip didn't ease. He kept searching.

"I don't know what this is, Steph, what we are, and I sure don't know what we might turn into, but I do know one thing."

He paused so long I had to ask, "What's that?"

"I want to find out."

My heart tried to claw out of my chest.

Jack cupped my cheek. "Nate said something tonight, and I know he was joking and didn't really mean it, but he told you to bring your *boyfriend* into the house, or something like that. I couldn't stop thinking about it all night. I know it's stupid, but every time I looked at you after that, I couldn't help but ask myself, 'Are we?' I didn't know how you would answer, but about halfway through dinner I realized I already thought of you that way."

"As your ... boyfriend?" I could barely believe what he was saying.

He nodded, tentatively once, then firmly, as if affirming a decision. "I don't want to date anyone else, Steph. I can barely think about anybody else, and I don't think I'll be able to until I see where this goes—where *we* go."

I stared, openmouthed, still not fully comprehending—or maybe believing—what I was hearing. I wanted Jack so badly it hurt. I dreamed about him, and not just the sexy dreams that ended in having to clean the sheets. I dreamed about being with him, waking up next to him, listening to him talk about flying or Rufus or whatever he'd done that day. I craved being near him a way … in the way I craved being on a baseball field … and nothing, certainly no one, had *ever* made me feel that way.

What I couldn't fathom was why he felt the same about me. I wasn't anything special, just a dumb jock who didn't even make it in the minors. What did I have to offer? He was handsome, kind, crazy-smart, and on his way to being a pilot. He'd make it, I knew he would. He'd earn his wings and get hired by Delta or some other major airline and his life would soar.

When he did, why would he want to be with a beach bum like me? It made no sense. I would only hold him back. He would eventually see that and—

"Hey, look at me." He brought my eyes back into focus. I hadn't realized how far I'd wandered. "Don't let me push you into anything. I know this is fast, probably so fast it's stupid, but I know what my heart feels and I know what I want."

"And that's—"

"You, silly. I want *you*."

I stared at him. He'd said these words several times in several ways, and they still hadn't sunk in. None of it made sense. My own feelings were out of control because he was incredible. Who wouldn't fall for Jack?

Shit, had I *fallen* for him?

My heart knew that answer. What a stupid question. Of course, I had. I'd fallen so hard I might never get up. Truth be told, I didn't want to get up. All I wanted was for him to lie down next to me and hold my hand.

His other hand pressed into my cheek. Both now held my head firmly in place. Jack's gaze was a beacon whose light sliced through the deepest night, guiding me toward him.

"I'm falling in love with you, Steph."

My first tear fell, and it took everything in me to resist reaching up to wipe it.

His thumb did it for me. "Say something, please. You're killing me here."

He was so intense, so unsure. What the hell? Why would he ever be unsure?

"Jack, I'm head over heels. I have been since I first set foot on the plane, the *first* plane, that first day. God, I'm so helpless—"

His lips crashed into mine and our tears flowed together, mingling as one in beautiful, salty happiness. I wrapped my arms around him and held him so tight I worried he might not be able to breathe.

Our kisses weren't hungry or needy like they so often were. There was no urge to drop to the floor or shove each other against a wall. Waves of emotion poured through me, foreign thoughts and feelings I'd known existed for other people but never dared dream would fill my soul. All I could do was cling to Jack, to hold his lips to mine, and to know they were enough to weather any storm. His caress, his warmth, his constant strength, they were enough.

They were more than enough.

They were everything.

I surrendered the last of whatever stubborn defense still remained, giving myself to the moment and to him. He gripped the back of my head and drew our foreheads together. I couldn't take in enough of him, his scent, his taste, his touch.

God, was this what it was supposed to feel like? Was this how Nate and Coop, or Sam and Miguel, saw each other, how they felt when they kissed?

Again, I already knew the answer. Of course, it was. I'd seen it time and again over Christmas. Their love was deeper than any sea we'd crossed and plainer than the beauty of the Greek Isles.

And now I felt it for Jack. For us.

"Can I make love to you?" he whispered, his voice a perfect song on a distant breeze.

I stared into his eyes and nodded, unable to give voice to everything racing through me.

We walked into the bedroom and I sat on the edge of the bed. Jack stood before me, a statue of perfection incarnate.

My statue.

He reached up and slowly unbuttoned the top button of his shirt. Then the second, then third. His eyes never left mine as he reached the last one and deliberately pulled the fabric over one shoulder, then the next.

My eyes fell to his chest and down to his stomach, as though seeing him for the first time.

His fingers found the top of his jeans and the button sprang free.

I reached up, but he pushed my hand away. "Just watch."
So I did.

The zipper's hum tickled my ears and he wriggled out of the denim, stepping out of one leg then the other.

When he straightened, naked, before me, he stood and stared down. "Do you like what you see?"

My eyes rose. "God, yes."

"Now your turn."I reached for my shirt, but his hand stopped me. I cocked my head. "Stand up and do it, like I did. Take your time."

I nodded and let him help me to my feet.

As I repeated the ritual he'd just performed, his eyes consumed every motion, every detail.

He didn't touch me. He didn't even reach out. He simply watched. I'd never known how intimate a gaze could be until that moment. His eyes caressed me in ways no man's hands ever had.

When I stood naked before him, he smiled. "I love your body."

After everything we'd said that night, I still had to fight off blushing beneath his praise. I couldn't speak.

His fingers rose and teased the tiny hairs on my chest, barely touching, wandering aimlessly for the simple pleasure of their own exploration. His other hand joined, fingers searching the other side, making my skin pimple in their wake.

"Are you cold?" he asked.

I shook my head.

"Good."

He took a step toward me.

Our cocks were so close, almost banging together. Our chests were inches apart. I could smell him, feel his breath, taste the wine on his lips.

I wanted him so badly but knew better than to shatter the moment.

His hands drifted up to my collarbone, then to my shoulders. They teased then pressed then squeezed. They trailed down my arms, feeling the ridges of my biceps and triceps, then rose from my skin to brush only the hairs on my forearms.

He clasped my hands, his grip now firm, and raised them both to his lips, kissing one, then the other.

He stepped closer, and our bodies met. Heat flowed between us. Excitement throbbed against my cock, and I knew he wanted me as much as I yearned for him.

Still, he moved slowly.

So slowly.

He kissed my cheek. Then my chin. He held his lips before mine and sucked the breath from my mouth, holding it in his own, showing me he wanted me living inside him. When our lips met he released the breath, letting it flow into me, mingled with his own. I sucked it in, a dying man desperate for air.

His lips kissed. His tongue grazed. Our breaths grew shorter and quicker.

Still, he moved slowly.

So slowly.

His hands gripped my arms again, and he walked me backward. He gently laid me on my back, guiding himself atop me. The weight of him, the press of his heat, it drove the air from my lungs, and I didn't care to breathe.

He kissed my neck gently, so softly. His tongue traced circles and lines. His teeth teased my tender skin.

My body shook beneath him.

He held me. And he kissed me.

He lifted my hands above my head, kissing my curled biceps then burying his nose in my pit. I hadn't bathed since morning, yet he wallowed in my musk, drank it in.

His lips found one nipple then the next, and fire burst to life in the center of my chest.

My cock stiffened and jolted. Blood raged and pulsed.

Still, he moved slowly.

So slowly.

When his tongue pierced my belly button and his scruff scraped the last vestige of stomach that bordered what lay below, I thought I might lose my mind. My fingers dove into his curls, tangling within, pulling and gripping. Everything about this man drove me mad and I never wanted this moment to end.

Then he …

He took me in his mouth, and my breath caught.

Dear God, he took me into him so deep, so wholly, so completely.

His rise and fall, his lips so tender, so soft, so wet …

His tongue swirling and prodding, then curling and …

One hand gripped my balls, while the other, one finger slickened and wet, pressed into my hole.

I sucked in a breath and held it. I wanted to see, to look down, to watch him consume me, but I couldn't move or think or breathe. All I could do was feel.

He tugged as his finger pressed and his mouth dove. I arched. He rose.

His finger vanished, then his knuckle pressed, then he was inside me as far as his hand allowed.

"Jack," I called out.

His grip tightened. A second finger entered. His head drove me further into his throat.

I gripped the sheet, then reached back and clung to the bedframe. My body stretched and clenched.

Still, he moved slowly.

So slowly.

I don't know when he found the lube. My mind had failed and senses piqued.

He lifted my legs and pressed himself into me, and, for the first time in forever, I opened my eyes and saw him, staring down, his gaze never wavering. He slid deeper, slowly, deeper, a caress of my heart through the entrance that was now his. I felt him in my chest, my head, my arms and legs. I felt him throughout and within. I felt his gaze fill me as his body merged with my own.

And I begged for this never to end.

He bent over me, sliding in and out slowly, kissing my lips while gripping my cheek. I pressed into his touch, leaned into his kiss, arched my back and offered him everything my body would give.

And he took it all.

He kissed me deeper, gripped me firmer, pressed himself as far as any man could.

And it wasn't enough.

"Don't stop. Please, Jack, I want to be yours. Only yours."

I was yearning, knowing my words were more promise than plea, for him to take me, to make me, to shape me into whatever his mind or heart or will desired.

I longed to be his, to belong to him.

And he made it so, again and again.

Still, he moved slowly.

So slowly.

When, at last, his hand gripped and his body clenched, our moment was close. He stroked me, tenderly, gradually, teasing the senses already alight with passion and desire. His body moved with each stroke, as if we were each inside the other.

He shuddered.

I flinched and jerked.

He cried out as I flowed over him.

He was hot inside me, one burst, then another, and again. And then we stilled.

Him inside me, me still in his palm, his weight a blanket across my body.

"I'm falling in love with you, Steph. I don't care how scary it is, or how crazy or fast or whatever. I can't stand being without you. Please, say you feel the same."

My mind whirled, overwhelmed, unsure yet somehow certain.

I started to speak, then bit back the words. I chewed the inside of my cheek to hold my tongue in check.

This was insane. I shouldn't feel this way. *We* shouldn't be moving so fast.

He would leave. Jack would leave. He would find a reason, be it his work or a guy who lived closer, someone with a better job or who was smarter or cuter or had his shit together better. There were a million reasons he would leave, but all that mattered was that he would.

I knew it with absolute certainty.

Everyone left me in the end. My mom did. My dad did. Kyle

...

Oh God, Kyle ...

I can't trust anyone with my heart. Never again. Not family, not friends, definitely not some guy I barely know.

I just can't.

It doesn't matter how incredible this feels or how much I want Jack in my life, or how he always says and does the right thing to make me feel safe and warm and loved.

I just can't.

And then, despite all my efforts, my protestations and guards, all the fighting and dithering and questioning, despite all the

years of pain and longing, words I immediately knew would
forever be true slipped free, and I was at peace.

"I love you, Jack."

Chapter Thirty-Five

Afterglow

Jack

SUNDAY CAME TOO QUICKLY.

Sleeping with Steph's arm wrapped around me was the most comfortable, safest place in the world. I couldn't get close enough. His heart beat against my back, and my mind added melodies to his timpani. That made me smile.

I don't know what changed, what made him suddenly say words I'd only spoken a few times outside of family. Steph, the happy-go-lucky surfing baseball player, the guy who smiled easily but rarely shared his true self ... *that* Steph had said he loved me.

I wanted to laugh out loud, so full was my heart.

Instead, I gripped and kissed his hands, wishing we could never leave that bed, never be apart.

His lips surprised my skin, and a shiver ran down my spine.

"Good morning," he mumbled through a mouthful of neck.

My grin was so wide it hurt. "Morning, mister."

He squeezed me, his strong arms drawing my body into him. "Did I mention that I love you?" he asked.

And I giggled. "I think you might've said something like that in passing."

"Well, let me say it while lying naked with my cock against your back. I love you, Jack Sutton. I fucking love you."

I squeezed his arms, willing the moment to stretch, dying to jump and scream and run and …

"I love you too."

His breath stilled. The moment stretched.

"Really?" a small voice asked.

I rolled over so our noses were an inch apart, so close it was hard to focus.

"I love you, Stephan Breeden, in the tips of my toes and all the way to my chest. Every part of me loves you and I can't wait to see what this life might bring for us."

He blinked, his face an unreadable mask, then moisture pooled in his eyes. "I'm sorry." His gaze drifted downward. "I'm being stupid—"

I reached up and lifted his chin with my fingers. His eyes resisted, but eventually found mine. "Steph, do you believe me?"

"Of course. I mean, yes. I think so. I want to." He blew out a frustrated breath. "I'm sorry. I suck at this."

"At what?"

"At accepting whatever … good things, I guess."

I smiled and cupped his cheek as he often did mine. "One day at a time, okay? We said some pretty big things last night, and that can be scary. We're still not picking out curtains, and we can still wear black and celebrate Singles' Awareness Day."

He snorted. "Asshole."

I wiggled my brows. "Last time I checked, you liked my asshole."

His eyes widened with his grin. "Oh no, Jack Sutton, I *love* your asshole, and nothing about that scares me."

We laughed and I shoved him back so we lay beside each other staring up at the ceiling, two boys searching for stars before the sun consumed the night sky.

"I wish I didn't have to go home today," I said without thinking.

"Me too."

"You know, the distance thing sucks, but with my flight schedule and your road trips, we wouldn't see each other much more if we lived in the same city."

"True," he grunted. "It just feels ... I don't know ... like you're far away. I'm not complaining, it is what it is, but still ..."

We sat in silence and his hand found mine, entwining our fingers. I could practically hear his mind racing, darting from one fear to the next, probably wondering what lay at the bottom of the cliff he'd jumped off last night.

I wanted to soothe his fears, to tell him I would always be there, that he needn't worry, but I couldn't say any of those things.

Neither of us knew what the future would bring. As close as we'd grown in such a short time, we still had much more to learn about each other, and about us. We were expressing hopes and aspirations, not promises or commitments. We weren't ready for those, not by a long shot.

Still, my heart ached to wrap around him and keep him safe.

"One day at a time," I whispered. "We'll figure it out."

Reluctantly, the small boy yielded. "Okay."

BREAKFAST WAS QUICK—TOASTED BAGELS with blueberry cream cheese and coffee. My flight departed at noon, so time was tight. I'd only arrived Friday evening, giving us one full day together before I had to board yet another craft.

It wasn't enough time.

Steph drove in silence, holding my hand, his thumb circling, never stilling.

I stared out the window at Memphis passing by.

As we turned onto the exit that announced the airport, a quiet voice said, "I miss you already."

I thought my heart might melt right there in his car. "You stole the words out of my mouth."

His smile was tight, his lips barely curling at the corners. He raised my hand to his lips and held it there until we reached the departure area. That might've been the most intimate thing he'd done all weekend.

When the car stopped, we faced each other, and his hand rose to fight with his favorite curl, a battle he lost yet again.

He scrunched his nose in mock frustration. "I will make that thing stay one day."

"You talking about my hair or me?"

He cocked his head, then his smile widened, finally his true self shining through. "Maybe I mean both, smarty pants."

"That's *Captain* Smarty Pants to you, bucko."

He chuckled. "I'm a surfer. Call me Corkscrew."

That caught me off guard, and I nearly doubled over. "That's terrible. I will *not* call you that."

Someone tapped on my window. I turned to find an annoyed airport cop giving us the universal "hurry your asses up" signal.

"Guess I've gotta go," I said.

He reached up with both hands and pulled my face across and kissed me, letting our lips linger.

"I love you, Jack Sutton," he whispered as we pulled apart.

"I love you too, Surfer Poo."

His grin was worth all the flights in the world. I clung to that image as I gathered my bag and stepped into the airport.

Chapter Thirty-Six

THE SEASON

STEPH

Unlike the pressure-packed minor league season in which every player was on stage hoping to perform well enough to catch the eye of their senior club's management, sometimes wondering if they were doing enough to just keep their job, the Mango season kicked off with singing, dancing, and fireworks. Literally, fireworks.

When the owner proposed a whole new brand of baseball designed to be fun and interactive, the city of Memphis frowned. When he named his first team after a fruit, the papers panned the whole thing as a waste of time and money. On opening day of the first Mango season, with overflowing stands and a thousand fans watching on a massive television in the courtyard, Mango Nation gave all those doubters a friendly wave of the middle finger.

In the eleven years since the team's founding, only four games had failed to sell out, and each of those coincided with unusual natural disasters or earth-shattering news that distracted Memphians who would've otherwise darkened our doors.

The Mangoes were a massive success.

And the show, which was as hilarious as it was clever, had scaled with the growth of the franchise. Rather than rewarding the first five hundred who entered with some token bearing from our mascot, Milo the Mango, *every* child under the age of twelve received a gift as they passed through our gates. The pregame entrance and dance routine grew from just the players to a cast of hundreds of dancers, kids, and local supporters who enjoyed being part of the craziness. The postgame fireworks, now a staple of every game, had grown from a backyard embarrassment to a display of brilliance to rival the city's annual Independence Day celebration.

And at the center of it all was baseball—and the players.

Everything else was fluff designed to put the crowd in a good mood and make them laugh, but we were the main attraction. We had to be funny and outrageous, but we also had to play the game well, to showcase how great baseball could be so the kids in attendance would dream of one day donning a uniform.

It was a tall task, being all those things, but I'd never had more fun playing the sport than when I became a Mango.

In college and the minors, the guys on a team were unified around winning games and championships. We worked to be the best at the sport, both individually and as a group. The whole experience of playing competitive ball was a rush. Every game was important. Every play carried weight. Screw up more than a few times and a season would end before it began. For some unfortunate players, careers ended that way too.

Where competitive ball was all about the win, Mango ball revolved around putting smiles on tiny faces and making a genuine connection with the next generation who would carry the sport forward. The pressure of lip-syncing to Miley Cyrus was greater than the consequences of a missed fly ball. Don't get me wrong, miss too many of those and there would be a problem, but routine baseball wasn't generally an issue. Social media likes and followers were.

So we recorded videos. We posted. We wore silly outfits, sang ridiculous songs, danced to players banging cymbals, and bore our chests for the mamas (and more than a few of the papas). When the team began, no one knew our name; but at the start of this season, we had more than twenty million followers on TikTok, a loyal fan base that liked and shared virtually every silly thing we slapped on the web.

God, I loved my job. And I couldn't wait to share it with Jack.

He flew me down to Atlanta for another quick weekend at the end of March, but we weren't able to arrange a single visit in April, which sucked.

In May, Jack came to Memphis twice. His first visit was a quickie the first weekend of the month. The first flight available was Saturday morning and he had to return Sunday afternoon. We packed as much quality time into those few hours as possible, but it wasn't nearly enough.

He flew back at the end of the month for Memorial Day weekend, which was amazing because we got a bonus day together. The downside was that I had games every day that weekend, which consumed solid chunks of our time. Jack attended the games with Coop, which gave them time to bond. By the end of that weekend, the pair had become so close I started to wonder who my boyfriend liked more. I'd known the guys would love him but it still made my heart swell to see how quickly Jack had become part of our family.

The June and July calendars sucked worse than April had. Between my game schedule, his flight time, and his Guard weekends, our options were sorely limited.

FaceTime became our best friend. We still texted like teenagers, but seeing his face and that stupid lock of hair I loved wrestling with was more satisfying than a million text messages.

Being apart was hard.

When August rolled around, something special and unexpected happened: Jack took the whole month off.

He packed several enormous suitcases, stuffed Rufus into a crate, and flew to Memphis. In an odd, beautiful way, it felt like he was moving in, which, I supposed, he sort of was. Alden accepted his presence with all the grace a Mango could muster, quickly realizing Jack could take his shit and would fight back whenever he needed his not-so-humble feet returned to the ground. The pair of them didn't become fast friends as had happened with Coop, but they tolerated each other well.

It took Rufus all of two minutes to find the bed and claim my pillow, making biscuits until the pillowcase was knotty then nesting his tiny body so far down he looked like a patchy black yolk inside an egg.

Those first few days hadn't felt real.

I kept waking up expecting the pillow beside me to be empty, that I would reach out and find empty air where my heart once lay, but each morning, Jack was there. Sometimes he'd be facing away so we could spoon all night. Other times, I would wake to the deepest pools smiling at me as I wiped the sleep away. I caught him watching me sleeping a lot. It was adorable and made my heart flutter every time.

It's funny, we were truly together at last, and it wasn't the grand gestures, fancy dinners, or big events we might attend that left their mark; it was the simplest, humblest moments: making breakfast together, feeding Rufus, racing each other to the bathroom and getting our shoulders stuck in the doorway, then laughing until neither of us could hold our pee (yes, we actually did that one morning).

It amazed me how Jack's gaze never wavered or changed. Well, that's not true, it did change. It lingered longer. It felt deeper and more intimate, like he was looking into me, not at me. It became so familiar I could close my eyes and see every line and color of his. It became part of me.

In my twenty-five years of life, I had never known such un-bridled love from another person—with the exception of Kyle. We had been like twins, born two years apart. I still felt him. He watched over me, cared for me, laughed at the stupid things I did. In his heavenly way, he made fun of me and showered me with love to comfort and strengthen me. I knew it.

The closer Jack and I got, the more I missed my brother, and the more I felt his presence. He would've loved Jack. Kyle was as straight as a boy could be, almost as annoyingly so as Alden, but he was of the generation that didn't care who one loved. He didn't need words like gay or straight. Labels weren't important. I was his brother and that was the only thing that mattered. If Jack was important to me, he would be important to Kyle too. I hated that the two of them would never experience each other.

In the doggiest days of August, the Mangoes played every night and most weekends. Each player was granted one night off per week, which meant Jack spent an inordinate amount of time sitting in the stands behind home plate, sweating his balls off under the Memphis sun. He never complained. Never once did he ask to skip a game. I offered, begged even, but he refused, saying, "If this is where you are, it's where I want to be."

The first time he said that, I nearly choked on my own tears.
The tenth time he said it, I finally believed him.

This man was from another planet. He had to be. There's no way he was one of us. Though he was half of *us*.

In the second week of his visit, my teammates hatched a plot. There were no secrets among Mangoes. We spent far too much time together for anything to remain private. Hell, our privates weren't even private. I'd seen every cock, ball, and ass the team had to offer hundreds of times.

So, after the Tuesday evening game, as Jack waited patiently in the courtyard outside the gates, my sneaky brothers of the Mangrove crept out of the locker room while I was showering and assaulted my boyfriend.

They didn't *actually* assault him, but I did walk out to Jack standing in the center of a ring of Mangoes performing a horrendous rendition of Celine Dion's "My Heart Will Go On," complete with Camry, our insane left fielder, and Alden, my ungrateful roommate, assuming the position at the front of the ship with their arms outstretched, as though the wind was whipping through their hair and the stars were twinkling above.

I worried it might've been too much or crossed some invisible line that would send Jack packing, but, true to form, he laughed and flicked his hair like Rose in the movie, then called out to one of the players, making him Jack, begging him not to give up and sink.

The entire team roared when the player swept Jack off his feet and planted a kiss on his cheek, calling him "Steph's fallen Rose."

I gaped from outside the ring, loving every moment, not fully believing it was real.

Waldo, the crusty team trainer, filmed the whole thing and posted it on Instagram with the caption, "Surfer Poo finds love off the field." Jack and his backup singers got more than a million views, likes, and comments, one of the top posts in Mango history.

We were an internet sensation. That's when I knew he'd been accepted into my "other" family.

After that night, Jack and I had dinner after nearly every game with a group of the guys, just like I would've done had he not been in town. There wasn't a single awkward moment or sideways glance. He'd become a Mango by extension. The gang even foisted Milo-branded hats, shirts, and other gear onto him, insisting he needed to look the part if he was truly going to be as fruity as the rest of them. He donned them immediately and with a smile that could've powered the lights of a small nation.

And just when I thought that moment couldn't get any better, he turned and gave me a private smile, smaller than the first but clearly intended for me alone. It wasn't like he made some secret sign or winked or anything, he just looked at me, and I knew that gaze was special and only for me.

I thought I might die right there. It would've been a good death.

Was it even possible for life to feel this good?

THE LAST WEEK OF August arrived far too quickly.

I rolled over and smoothed Jack's hair, savoring the softness against my fingers.

"Hey, you," I said when his eyes opened.

He gave me a groggy smile. "Hey."

I stared, amazed at the man who continued to lay beside me and the life I knew we were building together. Any doubts I had about either of our intentions had evaporated in the summer heat. We were more than boyfriends. At least, we were on our way to being more. It was an unstoppable force, some construct of physics or chemistry or nuclear science that couldn't be halted.

What did I know? I was a baseball player. I never studied any of that stuff.

What I *did* know was that I was so in love with Jack Sutton that I couldn't imagine life without him, and I was fairly certain he felt the same about me. He'd said as much.

That's another thing. We'd stopped dancing with words. Something clicked after Nate and Coop took Jack in, then the team's little performance. It wasn't a decision we discussed or made. It just happened. We spoke our truths, what was in our hearts, without hesitation or regret or fear—or anything but courage and compassion.

There was something inexplicably freeing in speaking one's truth without fear.

I couldn't tell Jack "I love you" enough. I could never say it enough. I could never hear it enough, either.

"Do you know ..." I began dramatically. "How much I love you?"

The skin around his eyes crinkled as he smiled. "No. I have no clue. Tell me."

Now I grinned. "I love you more than Rufus loves sleeping on my head."

He laughed, his eyes drifting up to the Daniel Boone cap I still wore, despite the sun rising an hour earlier.

"That's a lot of love," he said. "Ruf is all about some Steph head."

My eyes widened. "Speaking of Steph head—"

He shoved my shoulder. "You're impossible. I don't think I've ever met a hornier guy."

"And you love me for it."

"Maybe. A little." He cocked a brow. "But I have to pee."

I tried to reach for him, to hold him back so he'd suffer when I tickled him, but he slipped away and raced into the bathroom, slamming the door behind him.

"Ruf, what am I going to do with your daddy?"

Yawl.

"Ow!" I jerked upright. "No making biscuits on my head."

Yawl. Yawl.

He stood, stretched as far as his stubby legs would reach, arching his back and yawned, then lazily strode to the edge of the bed and leapt off.

"Fine. Leave me alone in this bed. I see how you two are."

I grinned up at the ceiling, not really seeing the popcorn staring down at me. The sound of Jack's pee splashing into the bowl was oddly satisfying. It meant he was here, with me, in my apartment. Alright, enjoying another guy's pee was weird, but it wasn't *because* of the pee or the sound or the splash, it was what it represented.

Forget I brought up Jack's pee. The whole thing sounded creepy when spoken aloud.

"What do you want to do today?" I yelled through the door.

The toilet flushed, then water ran, then the towel rack squeaked.

Jack appeared in the now opened doorway. "I need to talk to you about something."

The way he hesitated and didn't look directly at me sent my stomach to the floor.

"Okay," I said slowly, shoving a pillow behind my back and sitting up. "What's up?"

Jack walked to the bed and sat, but not close to me like he normally would. He stayed on the edge where I couldn't reach him. It felt like there was a chasm between us suddenly.

"I need to tell you some good news."

I let out a breath. "Okay. Good news is good."

He nodded but still didn't look me in the eye. His focus was drilling into his hands.

He opened his mouth, then closed it, then looked out the window, then at me, then back to his hands.

That's when I noticed his phone.

When had he grabbed it? I'd missed that quick snatch as he ran to pee.

The screen was still lit with what looked like an email. It was too far and obscured by his hand to read.

I scooted to his side of the bed and rested a hand on his arm. "Babe, just tell me. Whatever it is, we'll figure it out."

"You know that pilot training program I've been working for?"

"Yeah, the Guard thing."

"Right." He nodded and drew in a deep breath. "When I got my private license earlier this year, I put in my application for the program. It's so competitive, I really didn't expect to hear back."

"You got in." It wasn't a question.

He hesitated, then nodded without speaking.

When silence lingered, I unfolded myself and took his hand. "Babe, I don't understand. This is amazing. It's what you've been working so hard for, right?"

He nodded again, then looked into my eyes. There was something in them I hadn't seen before. Doubt? Uncertainty? *Fear?*

"What am I not getting?" I asked.

"The training is intense," he finally said. "It lasts a year, sometimes more, depending on the class. There are three bases where the training takes place: Mississippi, Texas, and the one I've been assigned to, in Oklahoma."

My head spun. I couldn't wrap my mind around any of this. It was fantastic news that he got into the program, but what about his work with Delta? What about Atlanta? What did Oklahoma mean?

"I have to report to Vance Air Force Base the last week in September. Delta put me on leave for the entire length of the program, so my job will be waiting for me when I'm done. It's why they gave me this month of vacation. My boss gave that to *us*. But ... I have to move to Oklahoma almost as soon as I get back home."

"Okay, that's fast." I gulped back the emotional bile that threatened my bedcoverings. "But ... we can still visit, right? You'll be living on a base doing training and shit, but you'll get time off. They have to give you time off, don't they?"

He nodded. "I'm sure I'll have time off. I just—"

"Just what?"

"After the year of training, I'll probably have to fly for the Guard for a year, maybe two or three. That will get me the flight hours I need to finally land my commercial license, but I'll be at the mercy of the military. They'll send me wherever they need me. I don't have any clue where that might be."

This was his dream, the future he'd been working for since he started flying lessons, since *years* before. It's what he'd wanted to do since he was old enough to see the sky and clouds and imagine what might be beyond. And here he was, one step closer to living that dream, only it would steal him away for, what? A year, two, more? We already lived hundreds of miles apart, and I couldn't see a clear path to that changing anytime soon, but to look three years down the road and know there would be no hope of a life together, of a life resembling anything remotely normal ...

Of all the things he could've said, of all the challenges we could've faced, I was *sure* there would always be an answer, a way to fight back or rearrange things or something we could do to make things work. We loved each other and that had to be stronger than anything that could fall in our path. It had to be, right?

His eyes fell and he muttered, "I don't know how this is going to work."

I stared, stunned.

His eyes lifted, and I swear there was moisture pooling in them. Kyle's face flashed in my mind; I pulled my knees to my chest and hugged myself, clutching for comfort or safety, I wasn't sure.

My heart became a thousand-pound weight in my chest. What was he saying? He couldn't mean what my stupid head was hearing. Not after this month. Not after this year, after everything we'd done and said and felt ... after every guard I'd let down and every fear I'd overcome.

He couldn't possibly mean—

Chapter Thirty-Seven

What Now?

Steph

I BALLED MY WHOLE body against the headboard.

"Steph, why do you look like I just killed Rufus with a baseball bat?"

The ridiculousness of his question startled me out of my downward spiral. "You're leaving?"

Jack gaped but didn't answer right away.

I knew it. I knew what he was thinking, what all this meant. I was such a fool for thinking anyone would ever be true or loyal or whatever the fuck made people stick around for years with another person. Heartwarming happy endings might happen in books or fairy tales, but we didn't live in either of those. We lived in my miserable life where everyone always left, one way or the other.

"I'm moving—"

"No, you're leaving." I stared into his eyes, fire blooming in mine, anger welling in my chest like volcanic pressure. "You're leaving *me*."

He looked shocked, like I'd slapped him, like I reared back and punched him in the gut—in the way I wanted to in that moment but never would.

So I did it verbally.

"You're not just moving, you're leaving me, aren't you? After everything we've said and done, all the promises we've made, after I bared my soul to you in ways I've never done with anyone … I can't believe it." He tried to speak but I cut him off with clipped words. "I fucking knew you would. I knew it from the beginning, and I was too stupid to walk away. I'm such a *fucking* idiot."

Jack's eyes widened and he shot forward, both hands reaching for my arms.

I pulled away as far as the headboard would allow, but he still gripped me. "God, no! Steph, babe, look at me." His voice was pleading, yet insistent.

Slowly, I lifted my gaze to his.

"I will *never* leave you. Never. I love you with all my heart. You are everything I want in this world, more than I could've ever hoped to find. I want to build a life with you and grow old and make fun of our friends who don't age as well."

I wanted to be *so* angry, to hold on to my rage, but his declaration, so plainly spoken, so sincere, stole my wrath.

I didn't smile, though one did tease my lips.

His eyes wrinkled at the edges as he went on. "I just mean … and I'm probably screwing this all up … I'm so sorry. I didn't mean to scare you like that. I would never … I just meant the training and living in Oklahoma and whatever they make me do after ... and seeing you and your season. It's all so much and so complicated. And I'll be there a year and then wherever for who knows how long. Steph, it's fucking *years*. We've sort of lived together a month, if you count this visit like that, and already I want a lifetime of this. What's a year—or three—apart going to do to us? I'm not leaving you, but ..."

As his voice fell away and his gaze faltered, I realized what he was truly saying, what I'd been too pigheaded and wrapped in my own insecurities to hear.

He was worried *I* might leave *him*.

My hand reached up and cupped his cheek, and the first of my tears trickled down my cheeks. "Jack, I'm with you, right now and always. I don't care if you're in Europe or Russia or get sent to the moon. I'll be right here, by your side, *with* you."

"It's not ... too much?" His voice was a pained whisper.

"Too much? Shit, Jack, we already live in different cities and are making it work. I'm more in love with you today than I was a month ago. The distance between us didn't stop my love from growing. What's the difference between Oklahoma and Atlanta?"

A tiny curl formed on his mouth. "Besides Midtown? I don't think Oklahoma has a gay mecca."

A laugh escaped and it felt like I'd breathed for the first time after suffocating for days.

"Yeah, except that, but I'm pretty sure you and I are gay enough for the whole state. We'll cope." My thumb brushed his cheek as I held his face. "Will you still get to do the Delta thing?"

He nodded, fear receding. "They put me on a serving-in-the-military leave that doesn't stop my flight privileges. I checked on that before applying for the program. The company really is amazing to employees who serve. It's a perk of being in uniform."

"Okay, so we can still fly to see each other. Jack, I don't get the issue here. Yes, the distance sucks. Yes, you might get sent to Zambia to fly planeloads of military-grade bananas or whatever. So what? Why were you so worked up about this? It sounds like incredible news."

"Zambian bananas?" He grinned, shaking his head. Then his face smoothed and he looked down, then back into my eyes. "I just … I don't know. Everything has been so great, so perfect. My gut told me you'd run when you found out I was going to be moving."

"Me? You thought *I* would be the one to run?" I laughed, a deep, rumbling roar that shook my shoulders. "I've never run from anything, not even your ugly-ass cat's claws."

Yawl! Rufus made his presence known from the doorway.

"Shit, that reminds me. There's one more thing," he said.

My face fell. *Oh crap, there's more?*

"What's that?"

He glanced down at Rufus and something I couldn't identify clouded his face. "I can't take him with me."

It took me a second to follow his gaze to the smudge of fur blinking up from the bottom of the doorframe. Jack and Rufus had been together for years. He hadn't said how many, but it sounded like a long time. The look on his face was his heart breaking. I could feel it. He had to move away from more than just me, he had to leave his little buddy behind too, if he wanted to follow his dream.

"Babe, shit, I'm sorry. That's awful for both of you."

He nodded, still staring at Rufus, like it might be the last time he saw his sidekick.

"What are you going to do? Can Eli take him? They seem to get along well."

He shook his head slowly. "No, Eli's roommate is allergic to cats, and as much as I love him, he's not exactly responsible one hundred percent of the time. I wouldn't let anyone take him who I didn't trust completely."

I ran a hand over my head and spoke before thinking. "I... could take him."

Jack's head whipped up, and a spark flickered in his eyes.

"Really? You would? You'd seriously take Rufus?"

"I've never had a cat, but we had a dog growing up. I can't imagine he's harder to take care of than a golden retriever." I nodded, looking from him to the cat. "Besides, it would be like having a piece of you with me when you're far away."

Jack blinked. A tear escaped. I reached up and wiped it.

He smiled and pressed his face into my palm, like Rufus nesting in the pillow. "I love you so much, Steph."

"Love you too, Jackson Pollock." He grunted a chuckle as I scooted forward and wrapped my arms around him. "But I *really* need to know one thing."

"What's that?"

"Does this mean we're still single?"

He laughed into my shoulder, his forehead rolling back and forth as he shook his head. "Hell yes. Single and free. I wouldn't have it any other way."

"But single together, right?"

He shoved his nose into my neck and nuzzled. "Single together."

Rufus chose that moment to hop onto the bed, bound into my naked lap, and dig his claws deep into the skin of my legs.

His love could've been a little less forceful.

I KNEW DRIVING JACK to the airport would be hard, but given the length of his stay and the conversation we'd had about the future, it felt like driving a condemned man to the gas chamber—assuming there was a drive involved in going from death row to wherever they did that sort of thing.

We rolled to the same spot we had a number of times before at the departure doors and Jack leaned over, just like he always did. He cupped my cheek and kissed me deeply.

The same guard who'd sped us along before tapped on the window and made the same grumbling, "get the fuck out of my lane" gesture.

"Guess I'd better go," Jack said.

"I should come to Atlanta before you move, help you pack things up."

He smiled. "I'd like that."

"Okay, we'll make it happen. Help me with Rufus?"

I nodded and kissed him again, then we climbed out of the car and unloaded his luggage. We were only a few feet from the curbside check-in desk, so Jack wheeled his bags to the desk while I unloaded Rufus's carrier.

Yawl! Yawl! Yawl!

The prince was not pleased at being locked up. Needle-like claws poked at me through the mesh.

"Ow. Be nice," I scolded.

Yawl! He was totally pissed.

"You two need a counselor?" Jack said, stepping back toward us with his baggage claim ticket in hand. "Looks like a bad argument. Should I be worried?"

I handed the carrier to its owner. "Nope. My job here is done. He's your bloody problem." I held up a dripping finger to emphasize the point.

Jack chuckled.

"Cop's coming back," I said. "Gotta go."

Jack leaned in and kissed me. "Love you."

"Love you too. Fly safe. Don't let the little shit stab you."

He stepped away and the Memphis airport absorbed him into her belly.

Chapter Thirty-Eight

LEAVING ATLANTA

STEPH

On Friday, September 20, I flew to Atlanta for the last time. It was strange thinking of the trip that way. Atlanta was Jack's home, but it soon wouldn't be. We'd both have to adjust to that reality. Maybe we'd like Oklahoma. Stranger things had happened.

However, before we called Jack's new base home, we'd both determined to make this the best weekend ever, pledging to not speak about his move or the future until I returned to Memphis on Sunday evening. After that, I was fairly certain most of our conversations would be consumed with his move and what followed next.

There was one other odd thing about that weekend's visit: I beat Jack home.

He had accepted one last long-haul trip from New York to Paris and back, and wouldn't land in Atlanta until around eight o'clock that evening. My flight had me arriving at four o'clock, which meant I would Uber to his apartment, feed Rufus, and start dinner while waiting for him to arrive. While that was unusual, I rather liked the idea of making dinner for him while he was hard at work. There was something beautifully domestic about that mental image.

What I had not expected was to find Eli sitting on the couch, cat in lap, when I stepped through the door.

"Hey, Jackykins!" His singsong voice drifted through the apartment like a fart with wings.

"Eli, dude. You scared me to death," I said, gripping my chest.

"Clutch those pearls, baby. Clutch 'em tight!" He cackled, clearly enjoying the sneak attack more than I had. "Don't mind me. I just came over to make sure Ruf was fed. Jack knows his employer isn't always on time and didn't want the little guy waiting to eat if you got stuck with a delay."

I doubted any of that was true. My flight was a direct from Memphis to Atlanta, which lasted a whopping one hour and twenty minutes. The skies were clear in both places, and Delta had a fabulous on-time record.

Eli was up to something.

"Okay, thanks for that. I know Rufus enjoyed the company."

Yawl. A tiny head with massive ears and eyes nearly as large peered over Eli's shoulder. In a blur faster than I thought the cat could move, he bolted free of Eli's lap, bounded onto the back of the couch, and leapt across the room to plant himself on my chest, claws first.

"Motherfu—"

"Stephan Breeden! Language. Not in front of the child," Eli chided.

"Sorry," I said as I pried tiny daggers out of my flesh.

"You really should learn to watch your fucking language."

I looked up in time to catch a smirk teasing his lips, his eyes glittering. Then he unfurled himself and stood, straightening his thick black-rimmed glasses.

"Jack said he'd be home around nine, assuming, you know, the bird flies fast. He asked me to stock the pantry and fridge so you have lots of goodies to make." He stepped toward me, gave Rufus a scratch, then gave me a peck on the cheek. I was so startled by the gesture that I nearly stumbled backward. Laughing, he wiggled his fingers and floated to the door. "See you tomorrow."

And just like that, Rufus and I were alone.

Yawl.

"I agree. He's a strange one."

Yawl.

"You said it, little man." I scratched Rufus's head, earning a nuzzle for my effort, then set him on the couch and dragged my rolling bag into the bedroom.

Jack had already started packing for his move. Unassembled cardboard boxes leaned against the far wall, and a few already filled, taped, and labeled were stacked in the corner. He'd refuse, but I would offer to help pack while I was in town. As much as I hated the ritual of moving, part of me wanted to participate, just to feel like I was part of his adventure.

Jack's ancient alarm clock flipped to five o'clock while I stood there, so I decided to abandon my suitcase and check out what Eli had supplied for dinner. Something about Jack's best friend worried me when it came to domestic responsibilities. I had no basis for that judgment, just a hunch.

The first thing I saw when I stepped into the kitchen was an unopened bag of Oreo cookies.

"Great. At least he hit one of the major food groups," I mused, moving to the fridge.

Opening the door, I may as well have heard angels singing "Ahh" and a light beaming down from the heavens. Eli had, indeed, outdone himself and soared well past my limbo-pole-like expectations.

Three bottles of white wine, already chilled, stared back from the door rack. There was fresh milk, OJ, a case of bottled water, and a pack of raspberry-flavored iced tea I knew to be Jack's favorite. A quick check of the meat drawer revealed a pair of stunning ribeye steaks, a pack of chicken, a pound of jumbo shrimp, and what looked like some kind of fresh sausage. The veggie and fruit drawers were equally well stocked.

I moved to the pantry where Jack kept staples, pleased to find boxes of pasta, cans of diced tomatoes, and other necessary elements of my quick-dish repertoire.

I had misjudged poor Eli. He'd set us up.

The shrimp and sausage called to me, and I quickly decided to make a play on jambalaya. Jack and I both liked spicy food, and pasta sounded comforting to my rumbling tummy.

In the immortal words of the great philosopher Yoda, "Airplane snacks a meal do not make."

I popped the cork on one of the white wines, poured myself a healthy glass—well, a tea glass filled to the rim—and dumped the rest into a saucer to reduce. After another ten minutes of chopping and prep, there was nothing to do with dinner but wait until closer to Jack's arrival time, so I grabbed my tea glass o' wine and plopped down on the couch.

Rufus joined me almost immediately.

News. News. Infomercial. News. Radical news. News in Spanish. Liberal news. Conservative news.

Apparently, it was the news hour.

My game of TV remote roulette stopped on the sci-fi channel, where reruns of *Star Trek: Next Generation* were playing on a loop. Will Riker had just grown the beard, and Captain Picard was making Earl Grey tea in his ready room. I hadn't heard enough notes to "name that tune" yet but would soon be able to identify every aspect of the episode. I'd seen them all about forty-two times.

I'm not sure how long I sat there. When I woke, my wine glass was empty and Rufus lay curled on my chest. My phone was buzzing.

"Shit, I forgot to turn the ringer on after the flight," I said to no one in particular.

I flicked the screen to find the time was eight twenty-seven. There was one message in voicemail. It was Jack.

"Hey, babe. We're about to take off from New York. Looks like the flight's on time, which means I should be home a little after nine. Can't wait to see you. Love you."

I smiled at the screen like a dumbstruck teen, then realized I only had thirty minutes to make a meal that needed to simmer and develop. I moved Rufus to the couch and raced to the kitchen, chopping, sautéing, assembling, and stirring faster than the chefs on *Chopped*. By the time the door creaked open at nine-fifteen, the apartment was filled with a mouthwatering mix of garlic, sausage, and Cajun spices.

"Wow, something smells amazing." Jack's voice wound around the corner and into the kitchen. His keys rattled as they hit the dish, then his suitcase thunked as he set it by the door.

I was stirring freshly cooked rice into the meaty, veggie-filled sauce when Jack's hands wrapped around my waist and his lips pressed into the side of my neck. I laid my head back, propping against his forehead, and savored the moment.

"Missed you," he whispered.

"Missed you more."

He bit into my neck.

"Ow," I said in faux outrage. "What's with you and your son trying to damage the goods today?"

Rufus chose that moment to rub against Jack's leg. His purring was loud enough to rise above our simmering dinner. Jack bent down and held him before his face.

"Were you mean to the scary man? Did you protect Daddy's apartment? That's a good boy."

I grunted a laugh. "Excuse me while I spit in your dinner."

"Don't threaten me with a good time." He bumped my butt with his hip then fled the kitchen with Rufus. "How much time do I have? I smell like the inside of a 747 turbine."

"Dinner could use a little simmering. Want to take a shower?"

"Yeah, I won't take long." His voice faded as he moved further back into the apartment.

"Be there in a second."

His head popped out of the bedroom. "What do you mean?"

I grinned and pointed a wooden spoon in his direction. "Didn't think I was gonna let you shower without me, did you?"

A smile bloomed. "Better hurry, I'm almost naked."

I turned the eye down, tipped the lid so steam could exit, and tossed the wooden spoon onto the counter. By the time I stepped into the bedroom, the shower was running and steam was pouring out of the bathroom. Jack liked water so hot it nearly scalded his skin. He looked like a beach bum who'd fallen asleep in the sand after most of his showers.

I tossed my shirt and shorts in the corner, then stripped off my socks and raced into the bathroom. The outline of his naked body shone through the foggy glass. As many times as I'd seen the man nude, I still couldn't take my eyes off him.

"You coming in or just creeping outside?" His voice was light.

I slid the door open and stepped in.

By the time we cleaned up the second time, the water had turned cold and the glass was no longer foggy. Only Jack's palm prints remained on the glass.

Chapter Thirty-Nine

Our Day

Jack

THE NEXT MORNING, I snuck out of bed while Steph slept and made breakfast, surprising him with a tray filled with omelets, toasted English muffins with butter and jam, bacon, coffee, and orange juice. I even added a single rose in a tiny vase like some of the fancy hotels did to their room service trays.

Steph sat up, rubbing his bleary eyes, and grinned from ear to ear. "You are the sweetest boyfriend ever," he said.

"I know." I pecked him on the forehead. "Now, eat up while I get ready. We have to be somewhere at one o'clock and traffic in this town sucks."

His eyes followed me as I walked around the bed and headed into the bathroom. "Where are we going?"

"Nope. Not gonna tell you. It's a surprise."

He grumbled something through a mouthful of bacon, but I'd already turned on the shower and couldn't hear. By the time I was toweling off, he'd finished his breakfast, returned the tray to the kitchen, and was brushing his teeth. He glanced at me in the mirror, his eyes squinting with a foamy smile.

"What?" I asked, hanging the towel on the bar to dry.

His eyes traveled up and down, then he moaned through his toothbrush, "Yummy."

I spanked his butt, earning a tiny hop and an "Ow!" then darted out of the room before he could retaliate.

Freshly showered, shaved, and dressed, Steph offered to help me pack before we went on our mystery drive. I hadn't wanted either of us to work over our last weekend together in Atlanta, but there really wasn't anything else to do for a couple of hours, so we folded clothes and packed boxes.

My phone chirped at noon.

"Alright, time to pack up and go—pun intended," I said.

Steph rolled his eyes. "No lunch?"

I laughed. "Are you *always* thinking with your stomach?"

"Have you met me?"

I chuckled and shook my head. "We'll eat when we get there."

"Wherever *there* is," he mumbled, earning a playful slap on the shoulder.

"Oh, I almost forgot," I said, an evil gleam in my eye. "You need to wear something."

He cocked his head then followed me into the bedroom. I pulled a Mangoes jersey—*his* Mangoes jersey—off a hanger. He'd given me one of his when I stayed with him in Memphis. He didn't want me going to the games in regular "civilian" clothing, as he called it.

"Why am I wearing my jersey when I'm not playing?"

I grinned and tossed it to him. "You'll see."

"Why aren't you wearing a jersey?"

I planted my fists on my hips and glared like a school teacher about to explode. "Because I don't play on a team. Besides, this is *my* evil master plan. Your job is to do as you're told. Got it?"

He grinned and nodded. "I really like it when you're bossy. Makes me kind of wish we didn't have plans so I could slam you into the shower glass again."

I shoved him so he tripped and fell backward onto the bed. "Later. Now quit lying around and let's go."

He found a balled-up sock next to the bed and hurled it into my back as I strode out of the room. We shoved and laughed all the way down the stairs to the car, two rowdy, untamed little boys going on an adventure.

Steph stared out the window, his eyes darting from one building to the next, as he tried to guess where we might be going. When we entered the interstate, he surrendered and sat back … until traffic became a logjam of cars flying Atlanta Braves flags in their windows.

"Are we going to a Braves game?" he asked, the excitement of a child strumming through his voice and widening his eyes. I glanced over, grinning, and nodded.

He was literally vibrating. I could feel it in the seat. Despite our crawling pace, he sat forward, hands on the dash, as though we were flying through town at light speed. When we finally pulled into the fancy parking lot closest to the stadium, I thought he might leap out before I found a space.

"Babe! I haven't been to a major league game in years. This is awesome. One of the guys I used to play with in the minors is a Brave."

"Oh?" I switched the car off. "Who?"

"Yeah, Brody. He's their shortstop. He's a freakin' stud on the field. I bet he wins a Gold Glove this year."

"Maybe you'll get to see him today," I said.

"I wish. We would've had to arrange that with the front office way ahead of time. It would've been awesome though. He's such a cool dude."

We joined the river of fans headed from all directions toward the cathedral of sport. Uniformed police stood on every corner, directing cars and ensuring an orderly flow of attendee traffic. We passed through the gates, then wound around until the entrance marked on our tickets appeared.

"Where are we sitting?" he asked.

The entrance could take us to the nosebleeds or down to the premium seats directly behind home plate. There was no way to tell from the sign above the entrance which way we'd ultimately go. Steph stared, waiting for my answer, and I had to chew my lip to keep from laughing.

"We're going down."

His eyes widened. "How far down?"

I shrugged, like it was no big deal. "All the way."

"No freakin' way! Babe!" He actually hopped and clapped his hands. An image of an eight-year-old Steph attending a game with his dad flashed before me, and I lost my battle with my lip, laughing with the purest joy at his reaction.

"Come on!" He grabbed my wrist and pulled me toward the usher checking tickets. "Let's get down there. I might be able to yell at Brody in the dugout."

By the third inning, Steph had downed a burger, two hot dogs, three slices of pizza, and two beers. He'd also relaxed and was no longer trying to press his nose through the protective netting.

He did manage to get Brody's attention. The lanky shortstop, who looked more like baby Bambi trying to run on too-long legs than a pro athlete, came over to visit between innings. It was fun seeing old friends reunite.

While he finally calmed, my nerves were beginning to rise. My palms started sweating and I couldn't stop my leg from bouncing.

Thankfully, Steph didn't notice.

When the top half of the seventh inning rolled around, Steph stood.

"Going somewhere?" I asked?

"Nope. It's the seventh-inning stretch. Everybody's gonna stand up. You'll see."

He'd barely finished mansplaining when the announcer came over the PA. "Ladies and gentlemen, get out of your seats and stretch those legs." A second later, he continued, "Did you know today is a holiday?"

A confused murmur raced through the crowd as fans tried to guess what holiday it might be. The Braves often found excuses to celebrate or give away prizes to attendees.

"It's National Singles' Day!" the announcer proclaimed. "If you're single, congratulations. Wave your arms if you're unattached and watch the JumboTron."

Steph grinned down at me, then motioned for me to stand. As soon as I rose, his hands were in the air, waving with thousands of others.

Fan after fan, laughing and waving, appeared on the massive screen.

The announcer continued. "It's tradition we sing 'Take Me Out to the Ballgame' right now, but we have a very special seventh-inning stretch tonight. There's a Mango in the crowd!"

Like an invisible version of the wave, a thrill traveled through the crowd from one end to the other as heads around the stadium whipped about, searching for the Mango. Clearly, these fans knew all about our beloved Memphis fruits. One of the Mangoes' highly recognizable theme songs blared through loudspeakers. Raucous laughter and silly dances broke out on every level.

When a cameraman appeared beside us and Steph's stunned face splashed across every screen, a thunderous cheer erupted. A fan sitting behind us reached down and patted Steph on the back, then gave him a thumbs-up. Even the Braves and their opponents peered out from their dugouts and clapped.

But he gathered himself like a pro and waved, a toothy smile parting his lips.

"Let's give Mango catcher Steph Breeden a warm Atlanta Braves welcome!"

The crowd cheered even louder.

"And folks," the announcer boomed, "this Mango has a question to answer."

Steph looked to the cameraman, but there wasn't an interviewer with him. He glanced around, but no one stepped up. Confused, he looked at me.

I sucked in a breath, then raised the microphone I'd been handed to my lips and dropped to one knee. The crowd exploded, a combination of cheers, applause, "oohs," and "awws."

"Steph, I love you, more than anything in the world. I know this is your holiday, but I don't want to be single anymore. In fact, I don't ever want to be single again. Will you marry me?"

Steph was gulping back tears by the time I finished. When he nodded, unable to get a word out, the world around us burst into flashing lights and music and noise that quickly morphed into the ringing notes of an organ and thousands of voices serenading us with one of his favorite baseball songs.

I barely heard any of it as we embraced. We were lost in a melody of our own making.

LEAVING THE STADIUM TOOK forever. Fans flocked around us, wanting to high-five the Mango and offer their congratulations and well wishes. When an usher appeared offering to guide us through a private path, I saw a light at the end of the tunnel … until we entered an actual tunnel and I realized the usher was leading us further into the depths of the stadium rather than out of it.

Brody and two other Braves stood outside the double doors to their locker room, still wearing dusty uniforms and tired expressions. They perked up the moment they saw us approach.

"Wipeout!" Brody's voice echoed off the tunnel walls.

Steph beamed. I glanced sideways, curious about this nickname I'd never heard.

The guys embraced, then Brody introduced the other Braves whose names I didn't recognize. Steph appeared starstruck. Apparently, the two willing volunteers Brody had recruited to meet Steph were among baseball's elite.

After several moments of baseball guy talk, Brody turned to me. "Jack, that was awesome. Was it what you were looking for?"

I nodded. "You guys are the best. Thanks for helping pull that off."

Steph's eyes widened, as his gaze bounced between Brody and me. "You two—?"

Brody's grin mirrored my own as we nodded.

"Well, fuck me runnin'," Steph said.

"Later," I answered, then realized the very straight, very well-known baseball players were listening.

One of them blushed, the other laughed.

Brody gripped my shoulder and grinned. "Wear his ass out. Somebody's got to keep this one under control."

"Hey!" Steph protested.

I nodded gravely. "It's a tough job, but I'm on it."

"Or you will be later," one of the other guys joined in the fun, and we all laughed.

Steph nearly fell over, shocked that a hero was making gay sex jokes involving *him*.

The pair of sidekicks congratulated us one last time, then excused themselves into the locker room. I leaned against the wall and watched Steph and Brody chat like a pair of teammates who still played together rather than guys who hadn't seen the same field in years. The smile that seemed permanently pinned to Steph's lips made all the effort I'd put into arranging the day worth it.

The boys finally said their goodbyes, promising to stay in touch, and we headed back up the long corridor.

"Hope we can find our way out," I thought aloud.

"We'll run into a guard or usher or somebody on the staff who can point us out."

He gripped my hand and stopped walking, turning me to face him. "Thank you, babe. This day ... I don't even know how to describe how awesome it's been. Like, you blew me away. Totally."

My heart sang at his praise, but my mind couldn't resist a jab. "Did you just go full valley girl on me?"

"For sure, dude. Like, totally." He snorted. "Now hurry up and kiss me before somebody shows up, Mr. Fiancé."

It took a second for my brain to register the word, and then to shut down completely as his lips melted into mine.

Chapter Forty

Departure Lane

Jack

The next morning, we slept in, ate bagels for breakfast, and lazily made our way to the airport. Steph's flight departed at one o'clock, so there wasn't much time for anything else. I tried to stay upbeat, to enjoy the fact we'd had an amazing weekend and got engaged, but the trip to the airport felt something akin to driving in a procession with a hearse as pace car. My heart had climbed into my throat about the time we left my apartment and it refused to sink back where it belonged. From the way Steph's fingers fidgeted against my hand, I suspected he felt the same.

"At least you'll get home at a decent hour," I said, grasping for anything to break the silence.

He nodded but didn't speak.

"You should be able to put Rufus in the seat next to you. I checked, and your flight is only half full."

"That's good."

We'd packed up what food remained in Ziploc bags. The litterbox got a thorough cleaning. We wrapped it in several layers of plastic wrap to keep the cat pee smell off Steph's clothes. It fit neatly in the bottom of his suitcase with clothes stacked inside.

Rufus sensed something. His own nervous energy came out in added affection, barely leaving either of us alone all morning. The only way we could get him to stop crying in the car was to move his carrier to the floor between Steph's feet.

"When do you leave for the base?" Steph asked after another interminably long moment of silence.

"Thursday."

"That gives you plenty of time to pack." Steph's voice was oddly businesslike. "How will you get your car there?"

"The Guard is having it transported. Their move package wasn't like corporate, but it did cover that. I'm not looking forward to driving the truck for twelve hours."

"You're stopping halfway, aren't you?"

I nodded. "Yeah, no way I would make that whole trip in one go. It'll probably take fifteen or sixteen hours when you add in stops and meals."

"That sucks."

The sign for the airport appeared, and my heart sank.

Steph's hand lifted off mine. I suddenly felt empty, hollowed out.

"Pull into short-term parking," Steph said, altering our well-established routine.

Numb, I did as instructed.

We parked and turned to stare into each other's eyes, each waiting for the other to speak.

Yawl. Rufus was braver than either of us.

Steph glanced down at the carrier, his grin more a tight line than a smile. "We're going to make this work, Jack."

"Of course we are, babe." I reached across and reclaimed his hand, startled by the way his lower lip suddenly quivered. "I love you, Stephan, more than anything in this world. We can make this work. As soon as I get to the base, I'll find out my schedule and we can plan our next visit. Okay?"

He nodded, his eyes brimming as he looked back toward me.

"I miss you so much already." His voice broke as he fell toward me and I wrapped him in my arms.

There weren't any more words to be spoken. Nothing we could say would shorten the distance between us or the time we'd live apart. We hadn't even talked about what would happen after my training and possible service. My career was still centered in Atlanta, his in Memphis. Delta wasn't moving its headquarters, and the Mangoes were a Memphis staple. That question had kept me awake nights, but I vowed, in that moment, to let it wait. There was at least one year, possibly more, before we had to cross that bridge.

His phone chimed, an alarm telling him to get moving. As he pulled back, I forced my face into a smile and cupped his cheek. "You get Rufus. I'll grab your bags."

He nodded and reached down for the carrier as I opened my door.

We waited in the bag check line together, then strolled toward the security line, stopping a few yards from where the last passenger waited. Rufus was restless, wriggling and mewing loudly.

"Guess you'd better go before he breaks out of jail," I said.

He nodded and pulled me into one final hug. "I'll call when we land."

"Love you," I whispered.

"Love you more."

Chapter Forty-One

A Trip Around the Sun

Steph

The Mango season ended a week after Jack left for Oklahoma.

Perfect timing, right?

My dear roomie left two days after the season ended, determined to get home before football and snow arrived in Wisconsin. Apparently, both were big deals up there.

That left me home alone, bored out of my mind and staring at a cat that reminded me of Jack every waking minute of every day.

I adored Rufus. He continued sleeping on my head, which was oddly comforting each night. His steady breathing and rhythmic purring vibrated through me as I dreamed. But a cat, no matter how cute, was no substitute for a hot fiancé.

Jack's smell lingered on his pillow. There was an impression where his body lay in the bed beside me. The mug he'd used for coffee, insisting the one with Milo the Mango was the only mug he would drink from, still carried the imprint of his lips on its rim.

Yes, it was a little gross that I hadn't cleaned his mug or changed my sheets. Maybe it was a little weird too, but I missed him. Smelling that pillow and seeing that mug made me feel like he was near somehow.

I was probably losing my mind. That's what Nate said. Repeatedly.

Coop remained sympathetic, wrapping his arms around me and holding me tightly, telling me Jack was one in a million and all my loneliness would be forgotten once we were finally together.

I wanted to believe him. Really, I did.

But a year felt like forever, especially when it had just begun.

Jack and I FaceTimed at night, but texts throughout the day were scarce. I got it. He was in training and couldn't exactly look at his phone while military commanders stared over his shoulder. While there wasn't a time zone difference, the military's tradition of starting the day before any human should be awake represented all the differences necessary to keep Jack from wishing me a good morning each day.

Rufus never missed a chance to make biscuits as the sun rose, and my scalp had the pinholes to prove it.

Our first visit came in late October. Jack flew into town and we spent nearly all of our two and a half days naked. It didn't matter which room we were in, whether we were showering, cooking, or watching TV, we almost never wore clothing. I had always been a nudist, preferring to let nature flop freely in the breeze, but Jack took convincing. He blushed most of that first day, which only made me want to hide his clothes even more. By the morning of our final day together, he acted put out by the act of dressing and I knew I'd won him over to the dark side.

The only time we left my apartment that weekend was to attend a mandatory dinner at Nate and Coop's house. The boys were in rare form, fawning over Jack like he was the prodigal son returning after a lifetime of debauchery.

If only they knew. The debauchery part was definitely true. The prodigal thing, not so much.

The training program shut down for a week between Christmas and New Year's, giving us our first extended period together since our month-long respite in August. After that, there were few breaks. Jack's training picked up steam and the Mango season kicked into gear. We were burning our respective candles at both ends, which meant the meaty part in the middle didn't get enough love.

Yeah, that was a bad candle metaphor mixed with a cock reference.

One might think the missing Jack thing would subside, that I would get used to the distance and weird contact patterns, that life would take over and speed by—but none of that happened. In fact, as spring turned into summer and the baseball travel season kicked into high gear, I found myself missing him more than ever.

It didn't help that Rufus had to stay behind, fed and cared for by Cooper, when I went on week-long roadies. He was my one living reminder of Jack, and here I was, leaving him for weeks at a time. From April through July, we managed only one visit that lasted a ridiculously short day and a half.

I never washed his pillowcase.

In fact, I was so pitiful that my teammates nicknamed me "Slush" after the mopey Slush Puppy mascot with the giant floppy ears and perpetually pouty voice. The day they presented me with a new jersey with those letters stenciled on the back, I knew I had to get myself together.

Alas, the fates had other plans.

The video of Jack proposing at Braves' Stadum went viral on all the Mango social media outlets, earning more than ten million views on Instagram alone. Every Mango fan alive knew my name—hell, they knew Jack's name too. We became the couple representing an entire Mango movement, and the team's ownership played it to the hilt. Virtually every time I stepped up to the plate, the scene from Atlanta flashed on the screen and Jack's voice blasted through the speakers. I couldn't have been prouder that our love was celebrated in such an unashamed, public way, but hearing Jack speak to thousands of others while I sat at home most nights wishing we could talk was beyond hard.

Still, he was flourishing in his training, earning top marks in everything he did. I was so proud each time he spoke of winning another award or being recognized for excellence by the program's leadership. I wanted to fly out to Oklahoma and holler across the base, "That's my man!"

That probably wouldn't have gone over well, so I screamed it to myself, on the inside, where no one could hear. And I screamed it to Nate and Coop. Okay, I didn't scream it, but I did repeat it until Nate threw something to make me stop.

It was in one of those exact duck-and-cover moments in July, as Coop was serving up an Australian version of pavlova he'd seen on one of the cooking channels, that the boys shifted the conversation toward the future.

"Any idea what the Guard will do with Jack after he graduates? His program ends in a few months, right?"

I savored a bite of pillowy goodness followed by the sweet crunch of strawberry. He'd hit a home run with this dessert.

"Yeah, graduation is slated for September 27. We're finally marking the days on the calendar. It's become our nightly ritual."

"Huh," Nate grunted. "Our nightly ritual usually involves Coop's cock and balls—"

"Nate!" Coop scolded.

I groaned. "Please don't talk sex. My balls are so blue you'd think I stole them from a Smurf."

"That speaks more to their size than their color," Nate quipped. "I'm sorry for you, brother, and for Jack. It's his loss, really."

Coop snorted. I glared.

Nate took another bite, unperturbed.

"No word on duty after graduation," I said, my voice resigned.

Coop stared a moment, then asked, "You okay?"

I shrugged. "I'm as okay as I'm gonna get. It's not like I can do anything about it if they send him to Zaire."

"Wasn't it Zambia last week? The whole banana scandal?" Nate waved his spoon.

"Fuck off. And yes, Zambian bananas are a very real thing."

"They sound frightening," he mocked. "All long and thick, probably veiny. Do you think they're cut or uncut?"

"God, I hate you."

He grinned. "No, you don't, which is why you keep returning and eating my food."

"I'm eating Coop's food, thank you, and it's fantastic, Cooper."

"Thank you." Coop offered a sitting version of a Victorian bow.

"So no clue about post-graduation?" Cooper asked again, clearly unsatisfied with my previous answer.

I stared into my bowl a moment, then said, "His success makes me worry. I mean, he's killing it, scoring at the top of his class in everything. I knew he would. He's amazing like that. But it makes me wonder. What if he did so well the brass thought they'd need him flying missions in Uganda?"

"Not Zambia?" Nate grinned.

"Or Zambia. Either one. Bananas not included."

Coop reached across the couch and rested a hand on my leg. "There's no sense in worrying about what you can't change. You don't even know there's something to worry about yet. He might not be sent anywhere. Life has a funny way of working out for the best."

That last bit sounded like bullshit they taught on the last day of parenting school when most of the students were cutting class because their kids were acting up, but I understood what he meant and the spirit in which it was said.

The boys were my rock.

"Have you started planning the wedding?" Coop asked, surprising me with the sudden change in topic. We hadn't talked about a wedding since Jack proposed, and I was embarrassed to say I hadn't thought about it either.

"Uh, no, not really. I mean, it's kind of hard to plan when we don't know where he'll be."

"Nonsense," Coop said, sounding more like I thought his grandmother might than the thirty-year-old man sitting before me. "You shouldn't wait to get married. It's too special. Besides, who knows what might happen if he's deployed. You don't want to regret … never mind. I didn't mean—"

"It's nothing I haven't thought about." I blew out a breath. "How do military families do this? He's not even in harm's way and I'm worried sick about what might happen. If he actually got sent somewhere dangerous, I don't think I'll be able to focus on anything."

"Yes, you will," Coop said firmly. "And that focus will get you through it all."

"How can you be so sure? You don't have any family in the military, do you?"

He shook his head. "No, but I focused my entire life on being the best martial artist I could be to escape an unbearable home life. When I was on the mat, training or sparring, I wasn't thinking about how miserable my life was back then. It will be the same for you. I promise."

"I hope so."

Nate leaned forward. "If not, the rest of us Mangoes will beat you up until you smile. You're too pretty on camera to be sad all the time. Our social team needs you. And that shit hurts me to say."

I chuckled. "I bet. You aren't usually one for compliments."

"Especially when they involve your ugly-ass face."

I laughed. "There's the Nate I know and love."

Coop stood and took my bowl. "You boys play a game or something. Try to let Steph live for a few minutes this time."

Nate laughed well past Coop disappearing into the kitchen and into the first moments of our game … when I died … quick-ly.

As Nate reset the game, giving us an equal chance to swiftly kill my avatar, my phone chimed. I glanced down to find a text from Jack.

DeltaOne: You around? Can you talk?

Two things made my blood pressure spike: one, we didn't text much these days. He would FaceTime or call. And two, he *never* asked if I could talk. He just called.

Me: Sure. I'm just hanging out with Coop and Nate, getting my ass kicked in four directions.

The phone rang almost before I could hit send.

"Hey, babe. Are you okay? What's going—"

"I got my orders."

My breath, my heart, my everything froze.

Nate mouthed, "What's up?"

I ignored him, trying to gather the strength to ask the logical next question. "So?" I asked artfully.

"What's the worst thing you could think of? Be creative."

I squeezed my eyes tight. This was bad. My life was flying away from me and I couldn't stop it. I wanted to scream and yell and punch something all at the same time.

"I ... I don't know. A war zone with no return timeframe."

His breathing was heavy in the receiver, like he'd just run laps.

"Yeah, that would be about the worst," he said. "Good thing it's not that."

"Jack!"

I swear he laughed but covered his mouth.

"Okay," he said. "What else? Think shitty posting for us."

"The North Pole with no airport nearby."

He grunted. "That's evil. Shit, that would suck."

"But it's not it?" I asked, more hope than question.

"Nope."

"Jack, you're killing me here. I don't know the military or posting or missions or shit. I'm a fucking baseball player whose husband—"

"To be."

"What?"

"Husband-to-be. You haven't put a ring on it yet."

I didn't know how to respond to that.

This time, he laughed and didn't cover it up. "I can't torture you anymore," he said. "Babe, are you ready? Are you sitting down?"

"Um, no ... and yes."

"I'm not getting activated at all!"

I sprang to my feet. "What?"

"I'm going home to Atlanta, to resume my job and life and everything. I'll still have Guard weekends, and there's a chance I'll get called up later, but for now, I'm going home, babe."

I wanted to cry and scream. So I did both.

Coop flew into the room. "What happened? Are you alright? Is Jack alright?"

By then, I was so overwhelmed by the year of bottled-up, miserable, frustrating emotions that everything I'd felt came tumbling out in a messy, wet, slobbery mass of man mush. Jack tried talking to me, but I was sobbing so loudly I couldn't make out his words.

"I'm not a crier, dammit," I shouted at no one in particular before wailing like someone stepped on Chewbacca's tail ... if Chewbacca had a tail ... which he didn't.

Coop snatched the phone out of my hand, shoved it at Nate, and pulled me into his arms, where he became little more than a giant Kleenex for my disgusting, tear-fueled slobberfest.

"Jack, it's Nate. You've turned your husband—"

Jack must have cut him off.

"What?" Nate listened as Jack spoke. "Fuck off. That's a detail. Call him your bitch for all I care. You've turned him into a blubbery mess and I want to know why. I'm putting you on speaker."

Jack was laughing so hard, I could see him holding back a bladder explosion.

"Jack, this is Cooper. I think you'd better tell us what's going on before Nate combusts and Steph turns into a slug after you've salted him."

"Ew," I said, wiping my snotty nose on his shirt.

"Ew yourself." Coop pulled away, his face contorted as he tried to look at his shoulder where I'd left a snail track.

"I'm not getting called up or deployed," Jack's voice rang through the speaker. "I'm moving back to Atlanta."

Nate and Coop burst into a cheer. I just sobbed, still unable to gather myself.

Jack waited patiently, but the mayhem on our end of the line continued so long he finally said, "I have to pee. Call me back when you can talk."

And the line went dead.

Chapter Forty-Two

Pits

Steph

August promised to be a scorcher. It rarely failed to keep its promises.

August also happened to be the busiest month for team Mango. Schools were out, families were vacationing, and money flowed freely from parents' pockets into ticket booths and souvenir stands. It was the perfect time to be in the entertainment business, especially when that business coincided nicely with the well-televised and highly popular Little League World Series.

We were not only sold out for every game, but more than two thousand fans packed the courtyard to watch on the giant screen and hang around hoping to meet players after the game. We would, they knew, come out in uniform, sign autographs, and take photos until the last little fan departed with a smile on his or her rosy cheeks.

The guys were in a festive mood most nights, recording ridiculous TikTok skits. Each night, they donned a more outlandish outfit than the last, and their on-field antics reached epic proportions. Team management left us alone, satisfied to let us be our silly selves and count the cash behind closed doors.

It was, therefore, rather odd when I received a summons to visit the front office before our Tuesday night game on the third week in August.

Bobby West, the general manager and head field Mango, stuck his oversized head into the locker room as I was lacing up my cleats.

"Breeden." His booming baritone cut through the mayhem of nearly thirty players close by prepping for a game.

My head flew up at the familiar voice. "Sir?"

"Boss's office. Now."

Every head turned and looked at West, then turned and stared at me. The moment the GM vanished, the whispers began.

"What's going on, Steph?"

"Are you getting canned?"

"What did you do?"

"You're not going into management, are you?"

I didn't have any answers. I hadn't called the meeting. So, I did the only thing I could: I grabbed my cap and glove and headed upstairs.

The original office of the owner of the Memphis Mangoes was tattered and torn. His desk had been a card table that was missing a leg, so he and his wife found a folding chair to serve as the fourth support. His desk chair was another folding chair, in slightly worse repair than the chair-turned-leg. There were no break rooms or coffee pots. There was barely a working restroom on the same floor as his office. And he made it work.

That night, I walked into a mahogany-paneled palace fit for any major league owner, complete with trophies that towered above my head and a minibar to rival most of the actual bars in town. The richly etched wood of the sprawling desk that sat at the far end exuded power and prestige, which was funny when the guy sitting behind it was still in his pink, yellow, and orange circus ringmaster outfit.

David Boyce, head Mango in charge, loved his team, but he loved his role leading our craziness on the field even more. In the years I'd played for him, he'd never missed a single game. The guys loved him for his support of our sport, his willingness to fight for his players, and, most of all, because he still thought of himself as one of us, despite his excessive change in fortunes.

"Steph, come in," Boyce said, his voice warm and welcoming as always. "Want something to drink?"

"Uh, no, sir. I have to play."

"Oh, right," he said, as if he could ever forget anything about his games. "Have a seat. I need to run something by you."

"Me, sir?"

He smoothed back his thick brown hair and beamed a smile in my direction. "Yes, you, and please stop calling me 'sir.' I'm only a few years older than you. You make me feel like my granddad."

"Yes, si—"

He cocked a brow.

"Okay." I blushed and slumped into a high-backed leather chair that probably cost more than my car.

"Steph, you've been a Mango for a long time."

I nodded.

He waited.

I stilled.

"You're a team leader," he went on. "And the stuff you do online drives engagement at nearly double the rate of any of your teammates."

I grunted a laugh. "You can thank Jack for that."

"Yes, Jack. Nice guy. I like him." His eyes glittered at the mention of my soon-to-be. I didn't know he'd actually met Jack though. That must've happened on the night when I was playing and Jack was in the players' box. "So, Steph, I'd like to get your opinion on something I have cooked up. It's big, and a little crazy, but you know how I like crazy, right?"

I grinned, still unsure where this was going but absolutely knowing how much our fearless leader loved crazy. He was the king of crazy town.

"Alright," I said, not sure how to tell my boss's boss's boss to proceed.

"How do you like peach pits?"

"Excuse me?"

His grin widened. "Peach pits. You know, the hard things inside a peach. You like them?"

I couldn't have been more confused if he'd pulled up Microsoft Excel and tried to make me program a spreadsheet, if that's even what you called working with one of those Satan-spawned things. Peach pits? What the hell? I was starting to think somebody had bonked him in his peach pit.

"Uh, sure. Why not? I love a good peach pit." I really was talking out of my ass.

He nodded firmly and stood. "Excellent. That's what I wanted to hear."

Chapter Forty-Three

NEWSFLASH

STEPH

AN HOUR LATER, THE Mangoes were beating the Party Beasts by three. It was the sixth inning. I'd been given the rest of the night off.

I stumbled, numb, into the locker room and unlaced my shoes. There was an eerie silence to the place, like its soul had left when the guys walked on the field. In a way, that was accurate. The players were the soul of any team.

My head spun from the conversation I'd just had. It felt like getting hit by a corporate bus—a real one, with a metal bumper.

My first thought was that I had to call Jack. I grabbed my phone and pressed send. His was always the last number I'd called.

It rang. And rang again. And rang some more.

Then Jack's voicemail picked up.

"Dammit, Jack. Call me as soon as you get this. Code red. Red alert. Whatever the fuck you military guys say when shit happens. Say that, and call me."

I set the phone down, then picked it back up. Two swipes and a button press later, Nate's phone rang. And rang again.

His voicemail picked up on the third ring.

"Fucking fuckety fuck. Call me. Now."

That was any baseball player's equivalent to a code red or red alert. He'd know what I meant.

Then I realized Nate was on field playing. Crap.

I picked up my phone again and dialed Coop. It rang. Then rang again.

I was about to throw a towel when Coop's voice said, "Hey, handsome. Shouldn't you be torturing kids with baseballs or something?"

Ignoring his jibe, I went on the offense. "I need you now. Can I come over? It's urgent. I mean it. Not bad, just urgent. Oh. My. Gawd. Coop, I'm freaking out. Help me, Obi Wan. Please."

Coop was laughing by the time I came up for air. "Get in your car and try not to crash. I'm at home."

"I'm on my way."

THE TWENTY-MINUTE DRIVE TO Coop and Nate's house might've been the longest drive of my life. I burst out of the car like the Kool-Aid pitcher into a commercial. Coop had the door open and was stepping aside when I blew past him.

"Coop, holy crap, you're not going to believe what happened tonight." By the time he closed the door and turned to face me, I was pacing the full length of their den like a panther in heat.

"Do you want to sit—"

"No! I may never sit again. This is so freaking amazing. Never in a million years ... Oh, God, I'm going to pee. Hang on. I'll be right back. Don't move."

Coop's laughter followed me into the restroom. Thankfully, the rest of him didn't.

I hoped a good wee-wee would calm me down, give me a moment to relax and breathe, but it only freed me up to be more anxious. I was practically shaking when I stepped back into the den.

"Why don't I get you a drink?" Coop said. "I know you like beer, but how about a whiskey; neat, maybe a double? You can shoot it, like when you were in college. I won't tell."

I stared, cocked my head, tried to process, but nothing registered. My brain wasn't receiving inputs, at least not until it gave an output.

"No. At least, not yet. I need to get this out, then maybe we can drink. Hell, I might drink everything you've got after I tell you—"

"Steph, spit it out. I'm usually the one who can't get to the point. You're being me, and that's a scary thing to be unless you actually are me, in which case it's perfectly normal and expected because, well, I really am me. Does that make sense?"

I blinked. Coop had succeeded in shutting me up.

Only Coop.

Then my phone rang and my heart turned back into an overheated, sweaty, possibly angry bull locked in a cage, about to break the lock and escape.

I answered without checking to see who it was.

"Jack, are you alright? What's going on?" It was Nate.

"I'm fine. I'm at your place with Coop."

"What? Why aren't you here? Why'd you miss—"

"Shut up and listen. I'm putting you on speaker. I just got here and haven't been able to get my news out because I had to pee and was excited and then there's Coop and you know Coop, right?"

There was a second of silence, then Nate said, "Yeah, I know Coop, but I know you too, and this is weird. What's going on?"

"Alright. Here we go." I sucked down a deep breath and gripped Coop's hand. "So, I got called into Boyce's office tonight, right?"

"Yeah, it's all the guys could talk about in the dugout."

"Nate, you can't tell any of the guys what I'm about to tell you. This is super-secret shit. You know how the boss likes to make a show of everything, especially announcements."

"Got it," Nate said.

"Who's Boyce?" Coop asked.

"The owner," Nate and I answered in unison.

"Oh," Coop said, raising a dramatic brow.

"Anyway, Boyce called me into his office. I'd only been in there one time, the day they hired me. Nate, the place is sick."

"Steph, get to the point. What did he want?"

My phone beeped. I held it away to check. It was Jack.

"Shit, hang on. It's Jack."

I pressed a button. "Hey, babe."

"Steph, are you okay? What's going on?" He sounded terrified.

"Babe, I'm good. I mean, great. Hang on. I've got Coop here and Nate on the other line. Let me get us all together. If I lose you, I'll call back. Don't go anywhere."

Before he could reply, I pressed a few buttons.

"Jack?"

"I'm here."

"Nate?"

"Present."

"Good. Okay, where was I?"

"Boyce," Nate said.

"Who's Boyce?" Jack asked.

Coop chuckled, as I put my face in my palm. "Okay, nobody talks but me. Just for a minute. I know you people can do it. You're accomplished and proud and whatever else. Just stop talking."

Silence reigned, perhaps a first for our little family.

"Good. Boyce is the owner of the Mangoes. He founded and funded the team when we were nothing. Now he's a baller making millions. He called me into his office tonight before the game, which meant he pulled me from the game. I'd never seen him do that with any player—ever."

I waited for some reaction, but the peanut gallery was behaving.

"They're expanding."

I waited again.

"What does that mean?" Jack asked.

"They've sold out every game for I don't know how many years. The team is cash-rich and debt-free. Boyce wants to expand, open one new team first, then possibly open several more to create a whole league based around Mango baseball."

"Shit," Nate said, pretty much quoting how I'd responded when Boyce told me the news.

"Babe, that's great, but what does it mean for you?" Jack asked.

"Jack, your video exploded. We've laughed about that a hundred times. It's made me the most famous Mango out there.

Boyce wants to ride that wave. He wants me to be part of the first expansion team."

"Seriously?" Jack's excitement was palpable through the phone, but I could tell he still didn't get it.

"Here's the best part. You're gonna die." I was about to explode like a Coke with a freshly dropped Mentos. "Wanna know what the new team's gonna be called?"

"Yes!" Jack almost shouted.

"The Peachtree Pits. The *Atlanta-based* Peachtree Pits."

That's when Jack, Nate, and Cooper completely lost their shit.

Epilogue

Jack

I couldn't remember Steph ever looking more handsome. His hair was brushed back with only a few curls willing their way to the front. His eyes sparkled the deepest blue, brought even more to life by the deep black of his coat. The shy way he looked down, then back up, a boyish grin teasing the corner of his mouth, made my heart flutter faster than a butterfly on crack. He was hot and adorable at the same time, and that was a hard thing to pull off.

I stood before him in my dress blues. He loved my usual uniform even more than I did. Every time I dressed for my weekend of duty, he brushed my shoulders and took note of every pin and patch. He'd never seen me in a dress uniform, and his eyes widened as he took in every detail.

Nate and Coop stood behind him. Coop's smile could've powered the Braves' stadium. And Nate, well, he didn't look pissed. That was something for Steph's stoic best friend.

Eli stood at my side. As flashy as his personality could be ... was ... always was ... he tended toward the conservative side of fashion. His perfectly fitted coat and slacks were elegant in their simplicity, and the bowtie he'd chosen matched his new glasses, an even thicker pair with deep navy rims. Rufus yawled in his arms. Steph had insisted on his participation. Apparently, my furry friend and Steph had bonded more than I'd expected during my year away.

We had walked the aisle, listened attentively, now there were only a few things left to do.

"Steph," the man leading the day intoned. "I understand you've written your own vows."

Steph nodded nervously and unfolded a piece of school lined paper, complete with the ratty edge where he'd torn it out of a notebook. Again, his cuteness knew no bounds.

He looked into my eyes, then down at his paper, and cleared his throat. "Jack, I don't know why the guys invited me on that cruise."

A tittering of curious chuckles drifted through the attendees. These were not vows as they'd expected.

"I guess it doesn't matter now. I'm glad they did. My life changed because of that trip. It changed the moment you handed me champagne and our fingers brushed that first time. I don't know if you felt it, but my heart hammered at that touch. It didn't stop until I left the plane and you were far away. If I'm honest, it never really stopped. It's pounding inside me right now ... because of you.

"I'm just a dumb baseball player—"

A chorus of "hear, hear" rose from the players in the benches before us. Steph smiled and winked in their direction, then turned back to me.

"Okay, maybe I'm a semi-smart baseball player."

The jeers grew louder, and I couldn't help the laugh that escaped.

"Whatever. I'm smart enough to know the best thing that's ever come into my life is you, bar none—you're it. I'm stronger and smarter and better as a man and a person and ... everything ... because you are in my life. I will never be able to thank you for what you give me every day, but I swear, before all things holy and those here who are quite unholy..."

Another round of laughter.

"I swear to love you a little more every day for the rest of our lives. I swear to give every ounce of effort I've got, like my whole life depends on it, to make you happy and safe and secure, no matter what it takes. I belong to you, Jack Sutton, and no other, and that will never change. I promise you that."

The officiant waited, unsure if Steph was done, then turned to me.

"Jack, you wrote your own vows as well?"

I nodded, unfolding only my gaze, pouring myself into Steph's eyes and losing sight of anyone else who might've existed.

"Stephan Breeden, I love you with everything I have and everything I am. You are my best friend, my brother, my partner in crime. You are the man I dream of, and the man I hope to always wake up to. You are the father to my son, and somehow, you've become his pillow."

Steph covered his mouth, biting back a laugh, giving Ruf a quick glance before looking back to me.

"Steph, I promise to love you more each day than the last. I promise to say I'm sorry when I mess up, because I will mess up more times than I can count. I promise to fly you to new heights on every plane I'm allowed to fly, and in ways that might not involve a plane."

Eli and Coop snorted in stereo around us.

"Steph, above all, I promise to be with you, every day, in every way, to help and support and love you, for the rest of our lives. Stephan Breeden, before God and those assembled, I swear I will never, ever leave you, not for one minute, not for one day. You are mine, Steph, mine alone, and I am yours."

Coop had to turn away and wipe his face.

But Steph, he couldn't move. He stared into me, into the very depths of my soul, searching, scouring, desperately hoping my words to be true. I could see it on his face and in his eyes. I could feel it in the bond we shared. His fears were part of him. They always had been and always would be. They might never leave, but I hoped to help them ease.

And then something resolved, and his eyes focused, like a camera lens homing in on its target, and he leaned forward and kissed me so deeply I thought the world might vanish and float away.

Nothing mattered. No one existed.

Only us.

Only that kiss.

Until ...

Yawl!

I HOPE YOU ENJOYED *National Singles Day*. Did you know that readers' reviews are important to an indie author's success?

Your words help others find our work, which helps us grow and create more stories. If you loved *National Singles Day*, please take a moment to leave a review filled with stars at http://www.amazon.com/review/create-review?&asin=B0CVRQ79Z3.

Oh, don't forget your free gift! Visit https://dl.bookfunnel.com/foxhchxb5r to download your free copy of *My Accidental First Date*.

Book by Casey Morales

About Your Author

Casey Morales is an LGBT storyteller and the author of multiple bestselling & award-winning MM romance novels. Born in the Southern United States, Casey is an avid tennis player, aspiring chef, dog lover, and ravenous consumer of gummy bears. Learn more at AuthorCaseyMorales.com.